RESTING
BEACH FACE

A Paradise Bay Romantic Comedy, Book 4

MELANIE SUMMERS

Copyright © 2021 Gretz Corp.
All rights reserved.
Published by Gretz Corp.
First edition
EBOOK ISBN: 978-1-988891-41-5
Paperback Edition ISBN: 978-1-988891-42-2

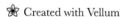 Created with Vellum

"A fun, often humorous, escapist tale that will have readers blushing, laughing and rooting for its characters." ~ *Kirkus Reviews*

A gorgeously funny, romantic and seductive modern fairy tale...

I have never laughed out loud so much in my life. I don't think that I've ever said that about a book before, and yet that doesn't even seem accurate as to just how incredibly funny, witty, romantic, swoony...and other wonderfully charming and deliriously dreamy *The Royal Treatment* was. I was so gutted when this book finished, I still haven't even processed my sadness at having to temporarily say goodbye to my latest favourite Royal couple.

~ MammieBabbie Book Club

The Royal Treatment is a quick and easy read with an in depth, well thought out plot. It's perfect for someone that needs a break from this world and wants to delve into a modern-day fairy tale that will keep them laughing and rooting for the main characters throughout the story. ~ *ChickLit Café*

I have to HIGHLY HIGHLY HIGHLY RECOMMEND *The Royal Treatment* to EVERYONE!
　~ Jennifer, The Power of Three Readers

I was totally gripped to this story. For the first time ever the Kindle came into the bath with me. This book is unput-downable. I absolutely loved it.
　~ Philomena (Two Friends, Read Along with Us)

Very rarely does a book make me literally hold my breath or has me feeling that actual ache in my heart for a charac-ter, but I did both."~ *Three Chicks Review for Netgalley*

Books by Melanie Summers

ROMANTIC COMEDIES

The Crown Jewels Series

The Royal Treatment

The Royal Wedding

The Royal Delivery

Paradise Bay Series

The Honeymooner

Whisked Away

The Suite Life

Resting Beach Face

Crazy Royal Love Series

Royally Crushed

Royally Wild

Royally Tied

WOMEN'S FICTION

The After Wife

The Deep End (Coming Soon)

The Accidentally in Love Stories
WITH WHITNEY DINEEN

For my kiddos...
Who drive me nuts, make me laugh, and keep me humble.
Love you forever, my not-so-little monkeys,
Mom

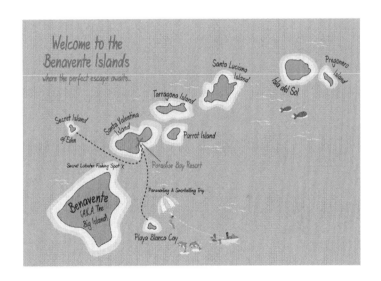

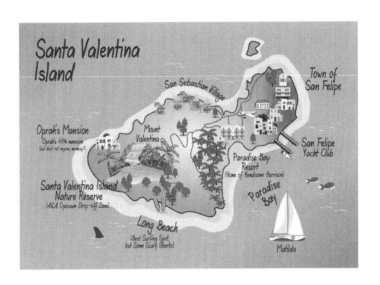

Heath,

Can you believe how lame Mrs. Janz is? Like seriously, who gives four pages of homework on a Friday? A complete psycho, that's who.

Also, I heard you asking Will if Reef can teach you to surf. Are you serious about that because I thought you said surfing is for idiots who have no use for their brains?

Hadley

Hads,

1st, Janz is THE WORST. I'm pretty sure she was Hitler in a former life. In fact, if you look really closely, you can still see the shadow of that stupid mustache. I didn't say that brain thing about surfing. I said it about riding motorcycles. Surfing's cool. What are you doing this weekend? If you're bored, we should grab some crisps and a couple movies. Scott Pilgrim is finally in at the video store.

Heath

Hey you,

Haha - Hitler's moustache. You crack me up. I can't hang out this weekend. I'm babysitting tonight and Chase Williams asked me to go see Grown Ups tomorrow. Sunday is our stupid Jones Family Fake Brunch, and my mum invited the relatives this time so I'll be stuck doing dishes half the day, then I have to write my English essay. Boo. English. I haven't even picked a topic yet. Have you?

H

Hads,

I'm thinking of writing about whether athletes and actors are overpaid. Um...yeah, they are. Obviously. Tough luck about the brunch.

Heathman

P.S. What? Chase Williams?! You're not serious, are you?

I know he comes off as a total jock but he's actually super nice when you get to know him.

Badly

P.S. You're not jealous, are you? Haha!

Eye rolling. Obviously I'm not jealous. I just didn't think muscle-bound jerks, I mean jocks, were your type.

They're every girl's type. Trust me.

Well, I guess that means I'll be alone forever.

Don't say that, my brother from another mother. There's a lid for every pot, dude. And you're one of the good pots so you'll end up with a very good lid.

***

hadley,

i heard Chase Williams asked you out. is that true?
hearts,

tasha

Tash,

YES!!!! We're going to the movies tomorrow. I can't even believe it. He's like the hottest guy in the entire school. Or the hottest guy on the island maybe? I have to figure out what to wear. I'm thinking my grey capri leggings and my A & F hoodie. Thoughts?
Hadley

hadley,

OKAY, Chase is definitely the hottest guy in the entire freaking Caribbean. Your outfit idea is super boring. Wear a tank and a mini skirt. Guys love that because they think you'll be easy access (NOT that you would be). OR you could be, because...Chase!!! NO OFFENSE, but everyone is dying to know how you got him to ask you out!

tasha

Tash,

Umm...nothing. He just came up to me when I was at my locker and asked me what I was doing this weekend. Why? Do people think I tricked him or something? If so, I'm clearly uglier than I thought.
H

hadley,

THAT is NOT what i meant! YOU'RE GORGEOUS! Like seriously, the PRETTIEST girl in our class FOR SURE. Plus you're a dancer and he's the star of the football team so it makes sense. Jock falls for ULTRA-FEMININE dancer type. IT'S SO PERFECT IT'S ALMOST CLICHE.

tasha
P.S. CAN YOU believe MRS. JANZ GAVE US ALL THAT HOMEWORK! LIKE SERIOUSLY! bitchy much! DONOVAN NOTICED THAT she piles ON THE HOMEWORK THE FIRST WEEK OF EVERY MONTH which PRObAbLY MEANS she's ON HER PERIOD OR SOMETHING.
P.P.S. ARE YOU GOING TO WEAR A SKIRT! DRESS! WHAT!!! JUST NOT bORING LEGGINGS!!

Tash,

Not gorgeous. Never was. Never will be. I'm all right, but if I wasn't a dancer, I'd balloon up to the size of a whale in about six months. Yeah, Janz is totally the worst, for sure. I told Heath she's like the Hitler of homework and he said you can still see her leftover mustache! He's the funniest! You should totally go out with him!

Hadley

P.S. I'll see if I can find a skirt at home that looks good. I used up all my babysitting money last weekend buying some cute leggings. Hahaha! #ironic

hadley,

um, i know heath is your friend and all, and he's a nice guy, but ew! he's so skinny!!! and he's like the biggest nerd in the world. the star wars poster in his locker! seriously, does he want to stay a virgin forever? i'll just have to wait for some fab jock with killer abs like chase to come sweep me off my feet...

Tash

Tasha,

The poster is meant to be funny. It's not really Star Wars. It's a spoof of Star Wars. He's skinny but he's got a really good heart and a great sense of humour.

Had

had,

hmmm...if i didn't know better, i'd say you have a crush on heath! maybe you should turn chase down and tell him to ask me out. j.k. girlfriend!

T

Tash,

Heath is like my twin brother. We've been besties since 1st grade so there's no way I could go out with him ever. But he's a catch for the right girl. And um...no about Chase! Back off, BE-OTCH! J.K. (But I definitely want Chase and me to happen so I'm 100% going on the date. And hopefully lots of other dates after that).

H

***

Heath,

Do you want to do the first two pages of Janz's dumb ASSignment and I'll do the last two? Also, four freaking pages? She's insane.

Fidel

P.S. I heard Chase Williams asked out Hadley. Tough break, dude.

Fidel,

As much as I'd love to share homework with you, no way is Janz dumb enough not to notice. Her whole life is trying to catch kids breaking rules.

Heath

P.S. It won't last long. She'll realize he's a total idiot after about ten minutes alone with him, then she'll dump his arse.

Heath,

And that's when you move in...

Fidel

She's cute and fun and stuff, but we're just friends.

Heath

Is that why you've been sketching her in your notebook during health class?

F

I'm not sketching her, it's just a girl. Probably a mix of a bunch of girls I've seen.

Heath

Really? A bunch of girls have the same crazy curly hair and a necklace with ballet slippers on it? Busted.

F

You have to promise NEVER to say a word to anyone.

H

Cross my heart and all that shit. But you should tell her how you feel before Chase has a chance to

get his meat hooks on her. It really seems like she likes you back. She's with you ALL THE TIME,

dude.

Fidel

She just called me her "brother from another mother."
H

Damn, dude. That's harsh.

F

And that's why I'm just going to keep my mouth shut. FOREVER.
H

***

Hads, good buddy,

What'd you put for #10 on the test? I thought it was A, but Fidel said B for sure. You're our tie-breaker (well, until Fuhrer Janz gives us the marks back...)

Heath

P.S. A bunch of us are going down to the beach for a bonfire after the Christmas dance. I can give you a ride if you like.

Heath,

I put C. I bet you got it right. You always do. Urgh. If I don't get at least 70% on this, my parents have threatened to get me a tutor.

Hads

P.S. Chase asked me to go with him to the dance so if we decide to go to the bonfire, he'll give me a ride. Thanks though!

Hads,

A tutor? Hire me. I could use the cash.

Heath

P.S. If WE decide? You two are a 'we' now? Deciding things together?

Heath,

OMG. I didn't realize I wrote that. He officially asked me to be his gf last Friday. Heaven...I'm in Heaven...

H

P.S. If you're serious about the tutoring, I'll definitely see if I can convince my parents to hire you. That would be SO fun. Plus, it'll get them off my back for a while (until my next report card anyway).

***

Heath,

Can you believe we're going to graduate in six weeks?! CRAZY!! We're going to be actual adults. Chase says it's no biggie (of course he would think that since he's already finished two years of college), but to me, this is HUGE. I can finally get away from Doris and Glen!

Hads

P.S. I got a job at the Paradise Bay Resort teaching salsa lessons to guests. Pretty fun summer gig, hey? Have you found a job yet?

Hads,

I know! I cannot wait until the last bell on the last day rings. I'm going to party like it's 1999. (Remember that song? Ha!) Congrats on the job! That sounds super fun. Well, for you. Not for me. But it'll be a pretty cool way to make some cash while you get your dance school off the ground.

Heath

P.S. I'm actually leaving for New York right after graduation. I got a scholarship at NYU in the business undergrad program and they're letting me take summer classes to get a head start.

Heath,

Wow. NYU? Why didn't you tell me?

H

I thought I did. Sorry about that. We've both just been so busy lately I guess. Yeah, I'm going to go take a bite out of the big apple. :)

Heathman

Just make sure you come back, okay? I'm not sure what I'll do without my best bud.

H

***

Heath,

I heard you got the scholarship! Way to go, man! Sucks that you won't be here though...

Fidel

P.S. Last chance to tell Hadley how you feel.

Fiddler,

That ship has sailed. She's been with numb nuts for two years already. They're DEFINITELY going to wind up married with a dozen kids.

Heath

Too bad. He doesn't deserve her.

F

Agreed, but what can you do? Chicks dig jerks. It's the way of the world.

H

***

You Say Obsessive Workaholic, I Say Driven

HEATH ROBINSON

Manhattan

"Are all the corrections loaded?" my boss, Charles Dubanowsky, asks as we hurry to the boardroom for what will be the most important meeting of our lives.

"Loaded them around three this morning. I also found two more errors," I tell him as a not-so-subtle hint that I'm the best man for the upcoming COO position at Dubanowsky Investment Brokerage, and not Tucker (The Wanker) Maloney, who is also up for the promotion.

Charles gives me a knowing look. "Throwing Tucker under the bus, are we?"

"Hey, all's fair in love and the cut-throat world of investment brokers."

"And it's exactly that attitude that tells me you may be the right guy for the job…" he answers. Lowering his voice because we're passing the trainee pool, he says, "But speaking of love, got laid lately?"

"As if I have time for that," I tell him. "I'm here for you and you only, Charles."

Chuckling, he says, "And that's why you're my best whore."

I stiffen slightly at his comment, but keep the easy smile plastered on my face. Charles may be crass and is pretty much a terrible person in general, but he's also incredibly powerful and seventy-eight-years-old which means he's actively looking for his successor. He promised his thirty-nine-year-old wife, Misty, he's going to retire when he turns eighty so they can sail around the world together.

All I have to do is play it right for the next couple of years and that massive corner office he loves so much will be mine (along with the millions in cash bonuses every year that go along with being the top dog). I'm the youngest guy in the running for the position, but over the last six years, I've made sure to become indispensable. Nights, weekends, holidays—I'm here. I keep a change of clothes in the closet of my office and deodorant, soap, and a dental care kit in the top drawer of my desk, just in case I can't make it home to my apartment for a couple of days here and there. It may seem insane to some because I only live three blocks from here, but in this business, the worst thing you can do is let the iron cool down before you strike. And believe me, the temperature can drop in an instant. All it takes is one little comment, one wrong look, one news article to make a client question whether they want to buy out the company they've been salivating over for months. And the deal is dead with no chance of resuscitation.

As we round the corner to the west side of the office, the boardroom comes into view, where in ten minutes (give or take) our client, Ms. Qiao Bao, will be here to go over our prospectus. Ms. Bao (daughter of Gulin Bao, the famed aeronautical engineer) is the heiress to her father's fortune and CEO of Bao Aeronautical. She is looking to take her meager billion-dollar corporation and turn it into something 'worthwhile' as she put it.

Today, she'll bring with her a team of six lawyers, three accountants, her long-suffering assistant, Barry, as well as assistants for each of her minions. It'll be a packed house and even though I only had about forty minutes of sleep last night, my mind is clear, my energy level is high, and I have the confidence of Ferris Bueller himself. It's go time, people—the moment I live for is upon us.

We'll have our own team of twelve staffers in the room, but just for show because all the answers to any possible questions are in my head. I'm the architect for this thing and it's going to be something beautiful. We're setting Bao Aeronautical up with Kurell, a corporation that's sitting on the world's most advanced GPS system. If Bao can pick up Kurell, they'll have the best navigation system ever made installed in all their planes and spaceships. They also won't have to worry about anyone else gaining access to this technology, which will be a huge boon for Bao.

It should be a slam dunk, but if there's anything I've learned after six years of working here around the clock, it's that nothing is guaranteed until the ink dries. So, until that moment, I cannot relax for even a second. I must—and will—be on my game.

The boardroom has been scrubbed until it gleams. Even the enormous Bolivian rosewood table has been refinished for the event. The scent of green tea fills the room (Ms. Bao hates the smell of coffee), and four silver platters of freshly baked, artfully displayed Danishes have been evenly spaced down the centre of the table. I take a deep breath and let myself enjoy the quiet perfection of

3

this moment—one of pure adrenaline and anticipation. *This is it, Heath. You've almost made it.*

Tucker (who was clearly following Charles and me) rushes in after us, still fiddling with his tie. "Charles, good morning," he says, completely ignoring me.

That's fine. I'm going to do the same back.

"Tucker, guess who found two errors you missed?" Charles asks him.

Tucker's face falls and he glances at me, then sighs. "I can assure you, if I'd have been the one who set the deal up in the first place, that wouldn't have happened."

Tucker's pissed that I'm taking the lead on this one. He's been here more than twice as long as I have so he automatically assumes he'll be at the helm of every merger. But I'm the one who thought of putting Bao and Kurell together, so Charles told me to take the ball and run.

"Don't worry about the errors," Charles says, but by the look on his face, he doesn't mean it. "Let's just make sure everything runs like clockwork today and we'll all have reason to celebrate."

The intercom on the table buzzes and Charles hits the button.

"Ms. Bao and her team are on their way up," Candy, the receptionist, says.

"She's early," Charles says. "Have the rest of the team in here immediately."

And now it begins—the flurry of activity that I live for. Within two minutes, the entire room fills with stressed-out, suit-clad executives, all of whom are bending over backwards to please one well-dressed, slight woman in her late fifties. I watch her stride in and sit down, perfectly comfortable with her position in life. Money is the only power worth having, and anyone who tells you different is lying.

When everyone has finally settled themselves around

the table, Charles stands at the front, welcoming our clients with a flourish of flowery words and lofty (but achievable) promises. I stand at the back with an easy smile even though I'm repeatedly telling myself not to screw this up.

"And now, I'd like to welcome the brains behind this incredible opportunity—Heath Robinson," he says. "He's a rising star here at Dubanowski. In fact, he was named one of New York's most impressive thirty under thirty by Forbes earlier this year."

Polite applause fills the room as I make my way to the front. *This is it, Heath. You're about to make history here.* "Welcome, Ms. Bao, and the rest of the team from Bao Aeronautical. We here at Dubanowski were tasked with turning your great corporation into something truly incredible, and we think we've found the perfect jumping off point in Kur—"

"Mr. Robinson," Candy, who has just rushed into the room, whisper-yells.

Ignoring her, I continue. "Kurell Global Positioning—"

"Heath! It's your mom," she says apologetically.

I freeze in place while everyone turns to look at her. "My mother? Is she here?" Dear God, do not let Minerva be here at this moment.

Charles chuckles nervously. "I didn't know you had a mother, Robinson." Turning to Ms. Bao, he winks. "He's such a tiger, you'd think he came into this world as an adult."

I offer Charles a customary smile, then glance back at Candy. "Listen, if my mother is here, could you please have her wait in my office? Or better yet, the staffroom until we're through here."

Shaking her head, Candy says, "She's not here. The San Felipe Hospital is trying to reach you. She's been in an accident."

Never Rely on Luck Because Eventually It'll Run Out or Turn Bad...

HADLEY JONES

"You must be the luckiest woman in the world," Taylor, my newest dance student, tells me.

She's an adorable twenty-one-year-old bride-to-be who wants to surprise her fiancé with a sexy dance performance to "Crazy in Love" by Beyoncé at their wedding reception. Sighing wistfully, she adds, "You get to work here at this gorgeous resort, spending your days teaching happy people how to dance, whereas I scrape their teeth for a living."

I suppose it looks like I have the best job ever, especially to a dental assistant. I'm a dance and yoga instructor at the Paradise Bay Resort, which may sound dreamy, but it actually means I spend most of my time in the blistering heat trying to encourage tipsy tourists to get out of their loungers and learn how to salsa. It was fun at first, but believe me, after ten years of it, a girl gets a little sick of being hit on by old guys in socks and sandals. Not that I'm complaining, because it really is a great place to work. Okay, so the pay isn't exactly amazing, but there are a few perks—free meals when I'm on shift, and when I'm not teaching for the resort, the owners let me use the open-air yoga studio to teach the odd private lesson (like right now). "Well, I do love my job, but honestly, you do something really important for your patients' health and well-being. I'm just giving people a fun diversion on their holiday," I tell her, glancing at the clock. I need to keep an eye on the time because I have a big date tonight and I need to make sure I look my best. "Now, let's take it from the top without the music this time. I'll snap out the beat half-time and you try it extra slow."

She nods her head in time with my snaps and counts out the one, two, three, four under her breath while she mechanically works her way through the first eight bars of the song. That's as far as we've gotten. Eight bars, which is roughly ten seconds out of a two-minute song, and it is *not* going well. With only three months to go until the big day, I'm not feeling all that confident.

We do it again while I think about her assessment of my life. In a way, she's right about me. I really *am* the luckiest girl in the world, but not because of my job. It's because of Chase Williams, boyfriend extraordinaire, love of my life, full-blown hottie. We fell in love in high school and we're living the dream. Well, we will be when things slow down at his work enough for him to actually be here on Santa Valentina Island for more than a few weeks at a time. Then we'll get married and start our family, which is all I've ever really wanted (as pathetic as that may sound to the career-oriented types out there).

Whoops, she turned left instead of right again. That'll mean she'll end up spinning off the dance floor and into the buffet table. Not the effect she's going for. I shut off the music and give her an encouraging smile while she drops her shoulders.

"*Right*, I need to turn right. Why can't I remember that?"

"You'll get it. We just need to practice more."

She struggles through the opening again, then says, "Is there any chance you can stay late to help me tonight? My fiancé has plans and I'm honestly nervous that I'm never going to get this right."

I make a clicking sound, then shake my head. "I'm really sorry, but I can't tonight. I have a date as soon as we're done here." And since Chase has been away for almost six weeks in Chicago, in about one hour and twenty-four minutes, I expect to be on a mind-blowingly fabulous, missed-you-like-crazy date.

"Oh, I didn't know you had a boyfriend," she says, tilting her head.

"Yup, for over a decade already, if you can believe it," I tell her, before immediately regretting adding that bit of info.

She wrinkles up her pert little nose. "Wow, and you're not married yet?"

Shrugging, I say the same thing I say every time someone asks me such a decidedly rude question. "We were practically babies when we got together so we're not in any rush. Besides, we want to make sure we're financially set up before we jump into the full-meal deal."

Yes, I'm so wise. Saving up my pennies so we can have a stress-free wedding, then move straight into buying our forever home and starting a family. None of that is strictly true, but it sounds so much better than 'my boyfriend isn't ready to settle down, but I love him so much I'm patiently waiting for him to grow up.'

"Smart. My fiancé…" (she loves using that word. I've

8

noticed most brides do) "…is from a wealthy family, so we're extremely blessed that we'll have a lot of help. His parents are putting an enormous down-payment on a house for us as a wedding gift."

Huh, maybe *Taylor's* the luckiest woman in the world and I'm just her dance instructor.

"They're just so happy he's marrying me," she says, twisting the cap off her water bottle. "He used to be with this older woman. Well, like his age—twenty-eight—but she really didn't fit in with his family. He needs someone who can handle a lot of hosting duties and such. I guess she's what you'd call 'domestically challenged.' Plus, she was letting herself go already which…hello! If she's doing that before the wedding, what's she going to look like by the time she's forty. Am I right?"

I chuckle, even though I can't help but feel slightly self-conscious. She might as well be describing me. Twenty-eight, can't cook to save my life, and for the last few years, the scale's definitely been moving in the wrong direction (even when I weigh myself naked and/or try to step ever so lightly onto it while holding my breath). I may spend the day moving my body, but my nights are a literal carb fest (mainly on account of my boyfriend being gone all the time). Thank goodness I'm with a guy who loves me for me, unlike her fiancé who sounds like a shallow turd. "We should get back to work. See if we can really nail the next few bars of this song today."

"Right, yeah," she says, putting on a cutesy embarrassed face. "You're just such a good listener, I forget we're not here to hang out."

"I love chatting with you," I tell her. The truth is I don't, but it would feel mean not to say I do. "But I want you to give a performance so amazing, it'll blow the socks off that fiancé of yours."

We manage to add a few more steps before the end of the hour, and by the time I shoo her out and lock up the storage room where we store all the mats and blocks, I practically race along the short-paved path out to the staff parking lot.

The yoga studio was a new addition to the resort a few years ago. It sits on the west side of the property, tucked away in a quiet spot that backs onto the jungle. At first, when the owners told me where it would be situated, I was bummed that it wasn't going to be beachfront, but then, after a while, I've come to love the quiet greenery that surrounds the building. It's also super handy when I'm coming and leaving because instead of having to traverse the entire enormous property, it's just a quick walk.

I strap on my white helmet, in my mind already zipping down the long lane that takes me from the resort to the main freeway. Yes, in fifteen short minutes, I'll be back at my basement suite where a cool shower and a cute dress are waiting. And then…oh! Mama! It'll be on.

Chase and I have been in what one could call a dry spell. The last couple of years, we've been apart more than triple the time we're together, and it's definitely taken a toll on our intimacy level. In fact, it's been over six months since we…you know. And to be really brutally honest, after that long, it can start to get in a girl's head. Like maybe he's not that into me anymore.

But that's crazy talk, right? Every relationship goes through a dry patch.

That's why I ordered a sexy lacy bra and knickers set online, and not only am I going to wear it, I'm going to send him a pic as well. Okay, not of me actually in it (that would just be stupid), but I'll lay them out on my bed and snap a sneak peek for him. That ought to help get things going again.

I'm just about to start the engine when my phone buzzes. I search around in my backpack for it, in case it's Chase. Which it is.

I put on my sexiest voice (which probably sounds more like I'm trying to poo, to be honest). "Hey, babe, I'm just leaving work now. I'll be ready in an hour."

"Yeah, about that..." he says, and the tone of his voice causes my heart to land on the hot pavement with a thud. "I'm really sorry, Hadley, but I got caught up."

"Caught up like your flight is late or like you-haven't-even-gotten-on-a-plane late?"

"The second one," Chase answers with a sigh. "I meant to call you this morning when I knew I wasn't going to make the flight, but the entire day just got away from me. This whole deal has been a nightmare from start to finish. I'm exhausted."

Anger. Disappointment. Slight rage. Deep breath. Reminding myself to focus on the big picture. "Well, hang in there," I tell him, trying to put a smile in my voice. "It'll all be over soon, then we can get back to our normal life."

"You're so supportive, Hadley," he says. "I don't deserve you."

"Aww, sure you do, sweetheart."

"I really don't. Most girls would be furious with me."

"You're right. They probably would have dumped you already," I say, only half-kidding.

"You should. Just tell me it's over. Right now. Break it off and find someone who won't be such a disappointment." His voice is so sincere that if I didn't know better, I'd think he actually wants me to break it off with him.

"Never," I say, meaning it. "You're it for me, Chase Williams, and you always will be. We just have to get through this next little while until your career is off and running," I answer, keeping a chipper tone even though I kind of want to cry. Dry spell (and accompanying insecurities) remains in place. Beautiful red knickers will have no reason to leave the drawer for their inaugural evening out. And instead of us finding our way back to each other like star-crossed lovers in a World War II romance, I'm now faced with another evening alone in the dark hovel I call home. "Do you have any idea when you'll be back?"

"I wish. I hate to even guess because if it doesn't turn out, I'll only end up letting you down again," Chase says. "Listen, I'm sorry, but I have to run."

"Right. Work is waiting," I say, noticing how my thighs are already sticking to the white leatherette seat of my ride. "Okay, well, good luck, sweetie, I love you."

"You too," he says quickly, then he hangs up.

I stare at his picture on my phone, tempted to call him back and yell at him for not letting me know earlier so I could've said yes to Taylor and made a few extra bucks. But I'm not going to do that. This is a temporary problem that requires patience and compassion. Also, I read an article on ForeverinLove.com about how people in long-distance relationships need to forgive the little things (which, according to their list, this definitely is) in order for their relationship to survive. If all you do is fight over the phone, it will never work. What happened today is a temporary problem and there's no use in creating a permanent rift over something temporary.

I consider texting my bestie, Nora, but then decide against it. Nora isn't exactly on Team Chase so having to admit he let me down again will only lead to a conversation I don't want to have. I slide my phone back in my pack, zip it up, secure the chest strap, then start up my moped and begin my sad ride home for another evening of binging on ramen noodles and old *Buffy the Vampire Slayer* episodes.

Good Drugs & Guilt Trips

Heath Robinson

"Oh, hi. You must be Minerva's grandson?"

Standing, I offer my hand to the man in the white lab coat. "I'm her son, Heath."

"Oh, you look..." he glances at my seventy-two-year-old mother, then back at me, "younger than I expected."

"She was forty-five when I was born so she calls me her mid-life crisis," I tell him with the closest thing I can manage to a smile under the circumstances.

He smiles back. "That's very clever."

"She's a clever lady," I tell him, shoving my hands into the pockets of my dress pants.

"I'm Dr. Baker," he says, flipping her chart open and making some notes. Probably something like *'Don't ask if the young man is her grandson!'* "I understand that you don't live here on the island."

"I live in New York."

"And you got here this fast? You must be exhausted."

Shrugging, I don't bother to tell him that twenty hours ago, I was yanked out of the most important meeting of my career, only to be told my mum was in a horrible accident and that I better get home immediately. I neglect to mention that I managed to get from my office to my apartment to pack, then to the airport in under an hour, which included some insanely dangerous driving. Or that the trip included three plane changes and over seventeen hours of bouncing my leg restlessly while simultaneously regretting every holiday I made excuses to skip over the last decade, just so I wouldn't have to come back home. "I'm fine. What can you tell me about her condition? The nurse was...vague."

"The MRI showed a concussion but no brain bleeding or extensive swelling, so that's a relief," he tells me. "She has four broken ribs, her right hip was so badly fractured that we replaced it, and she also broke her femur, tibia, and fibula, so she's got enough pins in her leg to set off a metal detector all the way in Belize from here."

I wince, imagining how much it must have hurt when the bread truck slammed into my mum, pinning her leg between her moped and the road. I glance at her frail body, my stomach flipping that the only proof she's alive is coming from the beeping of the machine next to her bed. Her too-long-for-her-age salt and pepper grey hair is tangled up on her pillow and I can see she's added a few more tattoos on her right arm since I was last here. *Oh, Mum. Why can't you just drive a nice little Corolla like a nice, normal old lady?*

"The paramedics on scene were shocked she was alive, actually. When they got there, they were pretty sure that wasn't the case," he tells me, as if that's supposed to be some comfort.

"She's pretty tough," I say, sitting back down next to her bed and placing my hand on hers.

"Lucky, too," he says, flipping the metal clipboard shut. "You may want to have a talk with her about finding an alternate form of transport. At her age…it's maybe not the best way for her to get around. The driver of the bread truck said she ran a red light."

"That's got nothing to do with her age," I say with a sigh. "I'm actually surprised this is the first time."

"Oh, I see," he says, clicking his pen shut and giving me a long, hard look. "She's going to need a lot of care for several months."

My heart sinks, even though I was already pretty sure this was going to be the case. "I expected as much."

"Do you have other family nearby?"

I shake my head. "I'm it."

"Are you able to stay to look after her?"

I chew on my bottom lip, my mind racing as I try to find a scenario in which I can keep my job *and* be away from my office for 'several months.' "Can I get back to you on that?"

"Of course," he says, opening the door to the hall. "She's not going anywhere for quite a while."

With that he leaves me to become suddenly all too aware of how heavy my eyelids are. I need to sleep, but I also need to email Charles.

I grab out my laptop and open it, forcing myself to stay awake.

Email from: Heath.Robinson@DubanowskyInvestmentBrokers.com
To: Charles.Dubanowsky@DubanowskyInvestmentBrokers.com

· · ·

Subject: Checking In

Hi Charles,

I hope the rest of the meeting went off without a hitch. I'm so sorry to duck out like that, but Ms. Bao seemed to think it was necessary for me to rush home and I thought it best not to disappoint her. I made it to San Felipe about an hour ago and am with my mother in her hospital room now. She hasn't woken up yet from her surgery so I should have several hours right now to work on any changes to the prospectus. Just shoot them over to me and I'll get started immediately.

Heath

One minute later…

Email from: Charles.Dubanowsky@DubanowskyInvestmentBrokers.com

  To: Heath.Robinson@DubanowskyInvestmentBrokers.com

Subject: RE: Checking In

Heath,

Glad your mom survived. I've already got Tucker working on the changes but I'll make sure he sends them to you to triple check everything before we approach Kurell. We're going to have to rush this through as I've heard rumblings that there could be another horse in the race.

  Charles

. . .

P.S. Any idea on how long until you're back? I'm already finding your absence extremely inconvenient.

Thirty Seconds later…

Email from: Heath.Robinson@DubanowskyInvestmentBrokers.com
To: Charles.Dubanowsky@DubanowskyInvestmentBrokers.com

Subject: RE:RE: Checking In

I'll go over the prospectus with a fine-toothed comb. Nothing will be missed. You have my word on that. As to my mother's recovery, it'll likely be extensive. The doctor said several months.

"So this is what I have to do to get you home," my mother says in a croaky voice.

Shutting my laptop, I chuckle, relief flooding my veins. "You didn't have to go to quite *this* extreme."

"Bull shit," she tells me in a sleepy voice, then taps drunkenly on her cheek. "Now come give your old mother a kiss."

Getting up, I do as ordered, noticing how fragile she seems. "I'd ask how you're feeling, but I'm guessing the answer is high as a kite."

"Very. If I'd known how good the drugs would be, I'd have done this a long time ago," she whispers with just the hint of a wry smile.

"Do you want me to get you some water?"

"How about some gin? I feel like I've been hit by a bread truck."

I laugh in spite of myself, then say, "How about water for now?"

"You always were a total disappointment."

"Thanks, Mum, that warms my heart."

"Not mine," she answers, then pats the general direction of her chest. "Wait? Is my heart still in here?"

"Yes, and don't worry, I'm sure it's still two sizes too small." I set my laptop down and start for the door. "I'll be right back with your water."

"Thanks," she croaks. "It's good to see you, kiddo."

"You too, Minerva."

Bacon, Sweet Bread, and Surprises

HADLEY

It's the first Sunday of the month, which means it's family brunch day. It's something my mum started back when my brother, Lucas, and I were teenagers who, let's face it, didn't want to get up before noon and get dressed up, only to eat on my mum's inherited gold-plated China (which cannot go in the dishwasher so don't bother asking). We'd both get up at the very last possible second, brush our teeth, put on our 'Sunday finest' and shuffle downstairs to get scolded for leaning our elbows on the table and mope through whatever culinary creations she set before us that day — usually something with bacon — while our father criticized us. *I'm surprised you only got ninety-two on that essay, Lucas. You're much smarter than that. Hadley, that's enough bacon for you today. You missed ballet on Thursday and you really don't need the extra calories.*

Fifteen years later, the tradition continues, only now my little brother brings his girlfriend, Serena, and I sit next to the empty chair that Chase would sit in were he in town. I'm now old enough to appreciate the luxury of having a fancy, home-cooked meal prepared for me, but I wish it didn't come with a side of 'helpful feedback only a loving mother can give her daughter' and not-so-subtle reminders of the plethora of ways I disappoint my father.

I pull up in front of their tidy white two-story house and park behind my brother's beamer, knowing I'm about to have to see their disappointed faces when Chase (who they adore almost as much as Lucas) is yet again not in attendance. Getting off my moped, I remove my helmet and hang it off the handlebars, then shake out my wild, dark brown hair and start for the back door. Mum doesn't like family using the front door on account of her then needing to clean the welcome mat in case 'real company' shows up unexpectedly. I'm honestly not sure how dirty I'd even get her mat though because I don't make a habit of stomping through thick mud on my way to their door, but whatever. It's her house.

Opening the back gate, I allow myself one long sigh before placing a pleasant expression on my face that will stay there for the next two and a half hours (the proper amount of time for brunch and clean-up, or so I'm told). When I swing open the back door, I hear a loud burst of laughter and I know Lucas has probably just said some-thing my parents found absolutely hilarious. As their golden child, everything that comes out of his mouth is pure…well, gold, I guess.

I take off my sandals and pull on a pair of ankle socks (no bare feet in the house), then walk down the short hall to the kitchen.

"There she is, Twinkle Toes herself," my brother says. He holds up his mimosa while pointing to it. It's his way of asking me if I want one and the answer is always the same.

I nod with a 'Dear God, yes' expression, say hello to everyone, then give my mum a quick peck on her soft cheek. It takes her all of two seconds to start in. "No Chase today?"

"He got delayed in Chicago," I say, then quickly add, "You look lovely," in hopes of segueing into her second favourite topic (right behind giving me feedback and ahead of whatever the fresh gossip is this month).

Ignoring my compliment, she lets out a 'hmph' and tilts her head. "Pants again, Hadley? Really?"

"If I wore a skirt on my moped, I'd flash the entire island," I tell her, then take my drink from Lucas and have a long sip while I wait for my mum to start on her checklist of 'things I must tell Hadley she needs to do to fix herself.'

"Which is exactly why you shouldn't be riding one," Dad says. "Honestly, I can't think of anything less ladylike."

"It saves a lot of money and it's a quick way to get around," I tell him for the thousandth time.

"It's also dangerous," Mum says, then her eyes light up. "Did you hear about Minerva Robinson?"

A pang of nostalgia hits as I hear her name, followed by panic. "No, I didn't."

"She got hit while riding her moped," she says, then shudders. "By a *bread* truck of all things."

"Probably better than a sewage truck," Lucas says.

Ignoring his quip, I say, "Is she all right?"

"She's a seventy-two-year-old woman who got hit by a truck. What do you think?" my mum asks, opening the oven and taking out the freshly-baked sweet bread.

"Did she..." I can't even bring myself to say it. Minerva was like a second mother to me growing up. Her son, Heath, and I were best friends all through school, and I practically lived at their house. Right after we graduated,

Heath left the island, and over the years, I lost touch with both of them.

Serena (who works as a receptionist at the hospital) cuts in to let me off the hook. Serena has absorbed all kinds of medical knowledge during her four years working at the hospital. She also knows all the best gossip, which is why I'm pretty sure my mum prefers her over me. "She's okay. Lots of broken bones, and her hip shattered so they replaced it. She'll be in the hospital for several weeks followed by a long recovery."

Lucas plucks a chunk of sweet bread off the loaf and pops it in his mouth, then avoids the slap to the back of his hand that my mum is about to give him. "I wonder if Heath'll come home to look after her."

I shrug, like it's of no consequence, even though I was wondering the exact same thing.

My mum decides she's got the inside track on that query. "He'll probably pay for a nurse or something. Gloria from the ladies auxiliary club told me he's in the middle of some huge merger so there's no way he can leave The States right now."

My heart sinks and I hurry into the dining room with the bowl of fruit salad to avoid the possibility of anyone reading the disappointment I'm feeling. I rarely let myself think about Heath, on account of getting a huge case of the I-miss-my-friend blues whenever I do. Somehow we totally lost touch with each other, which I honestly would never have believed was possible when we were growing up.

A few minutes later, the five of us are seated around the table, dishing up what really will be a delicious meal.

"So, Serena and I have some news," Lucas says with a wide smile.

Mum drops her fork then tears up. "Please don't tell

me you're pregnant," she whispers in the most dramatic voice ever used at any brunch ever.

"No, Mum," Serena says. (She's been calling my parents mum and dad for a little over a year now, which I find kind of odd, to be honest.) "We're getting married!"

"Oh, thank the good lord," Mum says, doing a quick sign of the cross. We're not Catholic, but she likes the flair of it.

We all get up and do the customary hugs and congratulatory wishes, then when we're seated again, my mum leans toward Serena's left hand and says, "Where's the ring? Lucas, don't tell me you proposed without a ring."

"I didn't."

"Oh, good. Is it being sized or something?" she asks.

Serena shakes her head. "No, actually, Mum, I proposed to Lucas."

Both my parents have the exact same reaction—their chins drop to the table, coupled with loud gasps because that is *not* the way it's supposed to go.

"Are you kidding me, Lucas?" Dad asks. "I told you you were leaving it too long. Ridiculous, making poor Serena here do your job for you. How humiliating for her."

"No, it wasn't—" Serena starts but is swiftly cut off by Mum.

"*Of course* it was. The woman is supposed to feel like *she's* the one being pursued and the man is supposed to do the chasing. That's how it's always been done."

"Times change," Lucas says, clearly irritated that our parents are ruining their big news. "It was really romantic actually."

He gives me a pleading look, so I cut in. "I'm sure it was. So, how'd you do it?" I ask Serena.

"At trivia night at the Turtle's Head. I got the DJ to ask it in the form of a trivia question," she tells me with a grin that says she's already forgotten about my old-fashioned parents' reaction.

"What was the question?" I ask, with an excited double shoulder shrug.

"Okay, so it was the lightning round—"

"—That means they ask a question and the first team to shout out the right answer gets it," Lucas tells us, as if the term lightning round is such a mystery.

Serena grabs Lucas's hand. "Do you want to tell them? You tell them. They're your family, pumpkin."

"They're your family, too," he says.

Err, I hope not or they should definitely not have children.

"Okay, I'll tell them," she says. "The question was: Who wants to marry Serena on Team Rockstars?"

"And I shouted, 'Me!'" Lucas says.

"He did! Right away. No hesitation at all." She gives us an open-mouthed smile. "So, I got down on one knee and said, "Lucas Jones, this is me, Serena Fisher, asking if you will marry me."

"And I told her of course I would, then we…you know, kissed and stuff."

"And everybody cheered," she says.

"They did," Lucas tells us. "Everyone, even those jerks on Team Sexwax."

"It's true. It was perfect."

I glance at my mum to see she's wearing the same expression one would if she and dad were just offered two-for-one enemas in a back alley. "You knelt on a sticky barroom floor?"

"It wasn't sticky," she says, still beaming.

"Well, I'm sure it wasn't exactly clean," my mum says in a pinched tone.

"Anyway, congratulations, you two," I tell them again. "I'm so happy for you. When's the big day?"

"We haven't quite nailed that down yet, but we're hoping for a Christmas wedding."

"Oh, lovely," I say. "Just lovely."

Actually, it's not lovely at all because Christmas is only three months from now and with the way things are going between Chase and me, there's basically no chance we'll even be engaged by then. Also, Lucas is four years younger than me and a wedding is basically my worst nightmare because I'll be surrounded by my awful uncles and aunts who will all take turns asking Chase why he hasn't 'made an honest woman of me' yet. Hardy har har. Fuck off.

The next two hours are considerably worse than a regular Sunday Family Brunch because both my parents are using Lucas and Serena's engagement as rock-solid proof that I really need to get a little more pushy on the marriage front myself. Mum peppers in comments about my biological clock while Lucas does his best to change the subject. But it's no use. They're not going to give up this chance to let me know just how far off track my life has gotten. Just before it's time to wash up, Lucas tells us they have to leave early today so they can go tell Serena's parents the good news.

Lucky me. I get to be alone with Grumpy Glen and Disappointed Doris. We exchange goodbye hugs and more congratulations and my mum waits a full thirty seconds before they start in.

"Can you believe *she* proposed to *him?*" Mum asks. "Honestly, now I'm not so sure he should marry her."

"Why? I think it's sweet," I say. "And more importantly, Lucas loved it and he loves her."

Shaking her head, my mum walks back to the dining room and starts gathering up the plates. "If they start out their marriage backwards, the entire thing is going to go off the rails. There are ways things are done, and that is *not* it."

I help clear the table while my dad seats himself back down and pulls a newspaper off the credenza behind him. Opening it up with a snap, he says, "Your mum is right, Hadley. I know you young people think you know better, but the truth is, a traditional marriage works best. The modern mixed-up stuff where the wife is the husband and the husband is the wife confuses things and ends in divorce." He says divorce like the very word itself might burn his tongue. Raising his voice so we can hear him in the kitchen, he adds what he believes will be the final word on the topic. "And I trust *you* know better than to propose to Chase. He's a man's man and he'd be totally humiliated by a stunt like that."

When my mum and I return to the dining room for more dishes, he continues. "Even if he takes another decade to pop the question, don't you go taking matters into your own hands."

The thought that I might be single for another decade practically gives my mum a heart attack and she starts fanning herself with a napkin. "While I agree with your father about not proposing, I don't think he's suggesting you and Chase wait another decade. Are you, Glen?"

Dad is already lost in the article he's reading, so he has to look up at her from above his glasses. "What's that?"

"I was just saying you're not suggesting Hadley wait another decade to get married, are you dear?"

"God no. Her eggs'll be completely dried up by then."

"Exactly," Mum says, with a satisfied smile in my dad's direction.

Nice. So glad I popped by.

We both load up our arms again and go back into the

kitchen. I glance at the clock and start counting the minutes until I can get the hell out of here. Just twenty-one more until I can excuse myself without reproach, although honestly, I kind of feel like flipping my parents the bird and storming out for once.

My mum must be able to read my mind (sort of, she'd be shocked if she really knew what goes on in here) because she says, "We're just trying to help, you know."

I plug the sink and squirt some lemon-scented dish soap into it, then turn on the water. "I know, but I just wish you could say something nice to me for a change."

"You want nice or do you want honest? Honesty is the foundation of any good relationship—whether work, family, or marriage. Besides, me being nice isn't going to help you get anywhere in this life."

"I'm doing fine, Mum," I say, shutting off the water and grabbing the scrubber from inside the mouth of the ceramic frog Lucas made her in grade eight art class. (Mine mysteriously disappeared a few months after I gave it to her.)

"You're not doing fine. Teaching dance at the resort instead of a proper studio. Living in that awful basement, never seeing your boyfriend. Not to mention the fact that you still have a boyfriend at your age. By the time I was twenty-eight, I already had you and Lucas off to school."

"I know, you mentioned that on my birthday," I mutter.

"Don't get testy, dear. It's very unattractive," she says. "Now, I'm going to tell you something that's just between you and I and the gate post."

I pause what I'm doing and stare at her.

She leans in and whispers, "I think the time has come for you to fake a pregnancy."

"Fake a pregnancy?!" I yell. "What about honesty being the foundation of any successful relationship?"

"There are exceptions," she tells me with a pointed look. "And in this case, it would be the perfect nudge."

"Pretending we're about to become parents isn't a *nudge*. It's an unforgivable lie," I say, shocked that I'm even having this conversation. "And what do I do when no baby comes along? Put Chase through the emotional turmoil of a fake miscarriage?"

Mum makes a hmph sound, then nods. "You could always *try* to get pregnant."

Closing my eyes, I say, "I'm not going to try to get pregnant. Chase is under some massive work stress right now. Once that's over, things'll settle down and we can move on with our lives. I just have to be patient and so do you."

"Do you have any idea how long you've been saying that?" she asks, scraping the bits of bacon fat into the garbage can. "It's been almost six years!"

"And don't you think there's something wrong with that? You started pressuring me to get married when I was twenty-two."

"I was twenty when I got married."

"Well, that's not how women do things these days. We don't rush into things."

"How old do you think I am?" she asks. "Women were off having careers when I was growing up too."

"I know that, which makes your whole 1950's house-wife thing even harder to understand."

"Oh, nice," she quips. "Insult me for trying to make sure you have a good life."

I sigh loudly, glancing at the clock. Dear lord, there's still a whole seventeen minutes left. "Sorry, it's just that I am part of a very different generation than you...seem to be. I love my career and I'm happy to let things unfold in my relationship naturally rather than forcing it."

"You teach dance. And not even to real dancers. You teach it to *tourists*."

She's really hitting all my buttons today. There was a time when I wanted my own dance studio but you can't really have that type of time commitment if you're marrying a man like Chase who's got a huge career himself. Someone has to be able to raise the kids. "I love my job, Mum. It may not be important to you, but I make a difference to the people I meet," I say, vigorously scrubbing the egg off one of the plates.

"Go easy! You'll take the shine off it."

"You should take your own advice," I mutter.

"What is *that* supposed to mean?"

"Nothing."

"No, it means something," she answers, sliding another plate into the sink.

"It's just that your helpful advice sometimes feels like it's…" I trail off, not knowing how to finish that sentence without hurting her feelings.

"Taking your shine off?" she asks.

"Yeah." I shrug. "Sometimes, you know, it can feel like a bit much."

Shaking her head, she says, "I wish you weren't so sensitive. You never could take any criticism from anyone. That's why Madame Le Rose said you weren't going to make the national ballet, you know. Because you'd just close off whenever she'd correct you."

"She used to whack me on the back of my legs with a stick," I say incredulously. Fourteen minutes.

"Tap. She'd tap! You make it sound like I let her abuse you," my mum says, her voice cracking a little.

Oh for…*she's* going to cry? "I didn't make the national ballet because my boobs and hips came in and they take after dad's side of the family instead of yours."

29

Mum offers me a conciliatory nod. "Yes, I suppose that was part of it."

"Look," I say, wanting this conversation to be over already. "I know you're just trying to help. Would I like to be married already? Yes, of course. Not because it's expected, but because I love Chase and I want to start our life together. But I love him enough to know he needs to make his mark on the world before he'll be ready to tie the knot. He's worth waiting for."

"Well, when you put it that way, I agree. He's definitely worth waiting for." That's her way of saying I'm lucky to have him. "Not every girl gets to marry the most popular guy in school who comes from a very good family." Very good means rich.

"And none of that matters to me. I love Chase for who he is. Not his popularity or his parents' money. What we've got together is special, and I'm not going to screw that up because of some artificial timeline other people have set on our relationship. We'll get married when the time is right for us." Ten minutes.

"Of course," she concedes. "Of course you should do that. You and Chase know what's best for you."

"Thank you."

There's a long pause and I know she's not going to leave it at that. She finally opens her mouth and adds, "Just don't wait too long because your father's right about your eggs."

5

Disgusting Vending Machine Coffee & Ill-Conceived Detours

HEATH

"Good morning, Minerva!" A chipper female voice invades the dream I was having. But it's not much of a loss really since I was in the middle of a work stress dream. I sit up in my chair and blink a few times to let my eyes adjust to the bright lights.

"Oh, sorry," the nurse says, noticing me. "I thought she was alone."

"It's fine, thanks," I tell her. "I meant to leave last night but I must have fallen asleep."

She smiles down at me while flipping open the chart. "So sweet of you to stay with your..." she pauses, reading something on the chart, then says, "mum."

Before I can answer, she's already moved on to her patient. "Minerva! Good morning!" she calls again to my mother, who is snoring away. She pats her on the hand. "Wake up! I need to check your vitals."

Without opening her eyes, my mum says, "I'm clearly

still alive, so do you think you could bugger off and let me rest?"

"Mum," I say in that tone that tells her she's being rude. "She's just doing her job."

"Well, she can do it somewhere else," my mum croaks, opening one eye. "I don't like to get up before noon."

The nurse smiles at her. "Well, you can go right back to sleep in a minute. Do you need a bed pan?"

"Gross, no," Mum barks.

"Okay, just ring when you do," she tells her, still smiling in a way that makes me wonder if she pockets a few pills to get her through shifts like this one. Turning to me, she says, "I need to change out her catheter bag so you may want to give us a few minutes, hon."

Shooting out of my chair, I say, "Sure thing. I'll just go make a phone call."

"What? Are you scared?" Mom calls after me. "I used to change your diapers, you know."

"Yup, but I don't think I want to return the favour," I say over my shoulder.

"You better. That's the only reason I didn't terminate the pregnancy."

I hear the nurse gasp as I close the door, leaving her alone with Ms. How to Win Friends and Influence People.

Pulling my phone out of my pocket, I call my office before realizing it's Sunday so Gwen, my assistant, won't be there today. Then I check my emails, wishing I had access to a long hot shower and a bed. I suppose I do, but I'll have to go home to do it. Well, my former home, anyway. Back in the old hood.

Email from: Charles.Dubanowsky@DubanowskyInvestmentBrokers.com

Resting Beach Face

To: Heath.Robinson@DubanowskyInvestmentBrokers.com

Subject: RE:RE:RE: Checking In

Heath,

Where's the prospectus? I thought you'd have it to me hours ago. I hope you're not going to drop the ball on this one. Not when we're about to broker the biggest aeronautical defense merger in history. If you can't get it done, I need to know now.

Also, even though your mother will need months to recover, I'm assuming you'll only need a few days there, yes? Surely they have nurses for this type of thing. Or could she go into a rehab center?

Charles

Shit.

Before I can write back, Nurse Happy comes out of the room (sans the smile) and tells me to go back in. I thank her, then let out a sigh before opening the door and walking in.

"Oh, there you are. I thought maybe you went back to New York already now that you know I'm not dying."

"Nope, I'll probably stick around at least until this afternoon," I tell her with a wry grin (even though inside I have no freaking clue how long I can get away with being here).

"Good boy. Now, I need you to go to Apple Blossoms and pick me up three pairs of knickers," she tells me. "Size medium, high-cut, cotton blend, black." She pauses, then says, "They're closed today so you'll have to go tomorrow. You better write this down."

"Are you sure you're going to need underwear right now?" I ask, glancing at her leg that will likely be in traction for a few weeks.

"The pervy paramedics cut off the ones I was wearing and they sell out fast, so I want you to get them now so I have them when I'm ready."

"You were wearing three pairs at a time?" I ask, then immediately regret the question.

"No, I was already running low on them so you might as well get three," she says. "Do you need a pen?"

I hold up my phone, then open my Notes app and start typing. "Three, size medium..."

"High-cut."

"Right. High-cut," I say, trying not to grimace.

"Cotton blend," she adds.

"Anything else while I'm out?"

"Yes, I'd like some cheezies. Do you remember the ones I like?"

"The orange ones?" I ask, knowing she'll be quite put out that I don't remember. (I do, but teasing is how we show love.)

"The ones in the red bag with the picture of the armadillo on them," Mum says. "Oh, and I want you to bring my bathrobe, the book on my bedside table, my reading glasses, and the stack of unopened mail on the kitchen counter. I might as well go through that while I'm here."

"I hope you don't have any unpaid bills."

Shrugging, she says, "I can't be that far overdue. They haven't shut off the power or anything."

34

"As an accountant, you realize that's like nails on a chalkboard for me."

"That's why I said it," she tells me with a satisfied smile. "Also, because I'm getting you back for pretending you don't remember which cheezies are my favourite."

———

Twenty minutes later, I'm in my rental car on my way back home while I suck back a disgusting vending machine coffee. My mum told me to 'skedaddle' for the afternoon because my general tired aura was 'bringing her down.' I've been ordered to go home, shower, and nap. As good as a nap sounds, I need to sneak in a few hours of work so I can prove to Charles that I'll be just as effective working remotely as I am when I'm there. I turn off the main drag into my old neighbourhood, noticing how everything still looks very much the same since I left. The big house on the corner is still that crazy bright purple colour, although it looks like it's seen a fresh coat of paint. I drive past my elementary school, surprised by how small the building looks.

Instead of turning onto our street, I go the extra three blocks and turn onto the street where Hadley Jones grew up. She was my best friend and first crush, but that was a million years ago. I'm so over her, I can hardly remember the sound of her voice.

Hmm…if I'm so over her, why is my heart pounding a little?

I slow down as I approach their big white house. There's a moped parked out front and I see a woman sitting on it wearing a helmet. Oh shit. That's her! I hit the pedal and take off, hoping she won't notice me.

Once I'm safely around the corner, I let out my first breath of air. That was her. I know it, even though she had a helmet covering her face. Her brown curls were sticking out the bottom of it, and the way she held herself was so familiar.

Dammit. Why am I having this stupid over-reaction to seeing her? I'm completely over her. Like 1100%. At least I should be. After all, it's been over a decade, which is longer than I actually knew her. Well, almost. But here I am—sweaty palms, heart pounding, throat constricting, just at a two-second sighting. My heart is still thumping by the time I pull up in front of my old house. I take the keys out of the ignition and sit back in the seat for a second, hoping that will be the closest I get to having to actually talk to her while I'm in town.

I'll do what I can for my mum, then get the hell off this island as soon as possible. Not only does my job depend on it, apparently so does my foolish heart.

I glance at my childhood home—a tiny two-bedroom off-beige bungalow with a red clay roof. It's definitely seen better days—probably when the previous owners lived here. The front yard is overgrown with knee-high grass and out-of-control shrubs that hide most of the windows. As a teenager, I didn't much care how bad it looked. I'd start up the old mower whenever a warning notice from the city came in the mail. But as a man, the sight of it makes me a bit...sad. I sigh and shake my head. I'm going to have some serious work to do to get this place looking less like an eyesore and more like a proper home. And then I'll have to find someone I can pay to keep it in good repair after I go back to the US.

———

Text Conversation between Heath and Fidel LeCroix (close friend growing up who works at the Paradise Bay Resort):

Resting Beach Face

· · ·

Fidel: Hey man, I heard about your mum. I'm so sorry. Please let me know when the funeral is and what I can do to help.

Me: Hey buddy, she's alive. She'll be in the hospital for a while, then will need months of therapy to recover, but she's most definitely alive.

Fidel: Sorry about that. I clearly got bad intel, but whoohoo! that she's alive. Did she actually get hit by a tour bus?

Me: Bread truck.

Fidel: Ouch.

Me: Yeah. New hip, broken ribs, a bunch of broken bones in her right leg. But she's still the same old Minerva—shocking the staff at every turn.

Fidel: Glad to hear that at least. And super glad she didn't die. I love Minerva. She's who I want to be when I grow up.

Me: You want to be an old white lady?

Fidel: Not really, but I want her attitude. We should catch up while you're in town. Supper at Turtle's Head tomorrow night?

. . .

Me: Sounds great. 7 p.m. okay?

Fidel: Better make it 8 so I can help get the kids to bed before I take off on Winnie.

Me: Smart man. See you then.

I stare at our exchange for a minute wondering what my life would've been like if I'd stayed. Maybe I'd be married like Fidel. He and Winnie have never had much in the way of money but they're really happy together. Oh wow, I must be overtired to be thinking about any of that. Common sense tells me I'm better off alone and flush with cash. Money never breaks your heart.

6

When a Dress Tells You Its Size, Believe It...

HADLEY

Text from Me to Nora Cooper (Best Friend Ever): Is there any way you can take a long lunch and meet me at Apple Blossoms? My mum has decided to throw an engagement party for Lucas and Serena and I need to start looking for a dress so I can look 'respectable for a change.'

Nora: Sorry, Hads, no can do. Libby needs me to do the month-end for her again.

Me: Shudders at the thought of all that math.

Nora: You know you're setting women back a few years every time you speak of your hatred of all things number-related.

Me: You've met my mother. Just be glad I believe it's okay for women to hold down jobs.

Nora: Good point. All right, back to it for me. These accounts won't reconcile themselves.

Me: Good luck, my friend.

Nora: Good luck with your LBD.

Me: My mum would choke if I wore black to an engagement party.

Nora: Exactly.

Me: And that's why we're besties.

Nora: Send me pics so I can vote.

Me: Will do.

Nora: Oh! Any more possible Heath sightings?

Me: No. I'm sure it was my imagination.

Nora: Brought on by thinking about the one who got away?

Me: Brought on by my mum telling me his mum had the accident and that he's probably here to see her.

Nora: Boring!

Me: Dude, I've had a boyfriend for close to twelve years.

Nora: I keep forgetting because it's been almost that long since I've seen him.

Me: Ha ha ha. Get back to work. Those numbers need mathing.

I hate shopping, especially the 'trying on' bit. I'm currently in the tiny stuffy dressing booth at Apple Blossoms, San Felipe's discount women's wear store. They've got it all— petite, tall, plus, old lady styles, young people fashion, business wear, and casual. They also have a nice, big clearance section, which is where I found the four dresses I'm about to try on. I strip down to my bra and knickers, and step into the first one, then attempt to pull it up over my hips. Oh, no. Not this one. Sucking in while I shimmy, I manage to get it off, then breathe a sigh of relief that I didn't rip it.

Huh. I'm usually a size ten so either this dress isn't sized right or my binge eating is starting to show.

The second dress is a flowy tent dress in a floral

pattern, which means it's very forgiving. I stare at myself in the mirror for a second before snapping a picture and sending it to Nora. She writes back immediately: Umm… are you hoping to look like an upside-down bouquet?

Me: I'll put you down for a no.

I get to the last dress in the pile without finding a winner. I stare at it for a second, wondering if I should even bother. It's size eight and to be honest, it looks like a small eight at that. But it's such a great deal. It's regularly four hundred dollars, down to one fifty. It's the top end of my budget, but it's really lovely and I could wear it to … lots of fancy things, if I ever get invited to any. Taking a deep breath, I mutter to myself to just get this over with.

It doesn't have a zipper so I have to pull it over my head. Oh, yeah, that's snug. I manage to wedge both my arms in, hoping that'll help the rest of it to fall into place. Only it doesn't.

I'm stuck.

With my arms straight up in the air.

And a wine-coloured dress over my face.

Well, this is just perfect.

I try a little shimmy and some wiggling, but it doesn't budge. Then I make an attempt at lowering my arms, but a distinct ripping sound stops me mid-lower and the price tag flashes through my mind. I cannot afford to pay one hundred fifty dollars for a ruined dress.

"Oh no," I murmur, feeling slightly panicked. *It's okay, Hadley, just breathe. Stay calm. You won't be stuck in this dress forever.*

I'll just wait. The saleslady will be by soon. Or I can

stay here and survive off my fat stores for a week or so until I get this on. Or off. I'd take either at this point.

Come on, saleslady…

Why do they always play horrible instrumental remakes at these places? Surely it can't be that expensive to pipe in some decent tunes. Is that Nirvana they're playing? Yeah, it is. The elevator-version of *Smells Like Teen Spirit.* I never met Kurt Cobain, but somehow I'm pretty sure he would've hated this version of it.

My phone buzzes and I feel desperation come over me. Why couldn't Nora be here?! She would get me out of this mess.

I hear someone humming to the song, so I decide to take my chance. "Hello?" I call.

"Umm…are you talking to me?"

Perfect. It's a man. And his voice has a vaguely familiar quality to it.

"Yes, I need a salesperson actually. Can you find someone for me? It's a bit of an emergency, to be honest."

"Okay…" he answers. "A clothing emergency in dressing room number three. Got it."

I can't tell if he's making fun of me or not. His tone was somewhat mocking but he also did say 'got it,' which hopefully means he's summoning help.

God, it's hot in here. I'm starting to smell like teen spirit myself. And my hands are definitely falling asleep.

I make fists and alternate with jazz hands, wishing I had not put this stupid dress over my stupid head.

Finally, I hear footsteps and a light knock on the door. "Are you still in there?"

Great, it's that guy again.

"Ummhmm."

"Okay, so there's a rather long line up at the till. When I asked one of the women behind the counter if someone could help you, she said she wanted to know what the emergency is."

"Seriously?"

"Yes, Deena—she's the manager—said that there's a surprisingly large number of women who will claim that they're having an emergency when really it's something like 'I need a different size or does this make my butt look big?' Her words, not mine."

The more this guy talks the more I'm sure I know him.

"This is an actual for-real emergency," I say, then I lower my voice. "I'm stuck in a dress."

There's a pause (he's probably trying not to laugh), then the man says, "Hadley? Hadley Jones?"

Triple shit. We *do* know each other. "Yes?"

"It's me, Heath Robinson," he says, then, as if I don't remember my best friend from age six to seventeen, he adds, "We went to school together."

"Hi, Heath," I answer in a weak voice. I close my eyes. *Now* I have to run into him? Now? At the very last moment I'd want to see anyone? "How are you?"

"Good, yeah," he answers. "New York is amazing."

"Excellent." Well, this seems like the perfect time for small talk, doesn't it? While I'm basically using this dress to mop up sweat from my face and pits. "I heard about your mum. How's she doing?"

He makes a little clicking sound, then says, "Not great. I'm afraid she has a long recovery ahead of her, but according to the first responders, she's lucky to be alive."

"Well, that's something at least."

"Silver lining, right?"

"Yup," I answer, not mentioning that there is literally no silver lining to my current predicament.

"Anyway, I should tell Deena what your emergency is so she can send in a team."

"Thanks," I say, my entire body hot with embarrassment. Yes, get Deena, then get the hell out of here.

I go back to trying to force some blood to circulate to my arms while also staying calm. Not an easy combination. This is actually surprisingly uncomfortable. They should use this as a challenge on *Survivor*. It would take people out in minutes.

More footsteps, then Heath's voice again. "So, here's the thing. Deena said she doesn't consider this an emergency so you'll have to wait until the line clears."

"Are you kidding me?" I ask. "How many people are in line?"

"Let me count." Pause. "Twelve. Apparently, something called a BOGO summer clearance event is happening. Can you wait?"

"I really don't want to," I tell him. "My arms are stuck over my head and I don't know what time it is but I'm due at work at one."

"Well, it's twelve-thirty now. Is work far?"

"The Paradise Bay Resort."

"Oh, wow. You're still there?"

Well, now I just feel like a complete loser. "Yup. Still teaching dance and yoga."

"Good for you," he says, as though we just ran into each other on the street and not during the world's most humiliating shopping trip. "You always loved to dance, so it's nice that you're still working in that field."

"Oh yes, it's…terrific," I say, near tears. "Was Deena's no a firm one or do you think there might be some wiggle room?"

"Firm. In fact, she told me not to cut the line again if I don't want to get kicked out."

I let out a sigh and try to shimmy out of the arms

again. Maybe I've magically lost some weight since I put the dress on.

Nope. I'm going to have to do this, aren't I? But not just yet. "Are you heading back to New York soon?"

"Yes, as soon as my mum is all right on her own," Heath says, sounding slightly confused.

Well, that settles it. I'm going to have to suck it up and get him to help me. He'll be leaving again soon, and by the time I see him again in a decade or so, the embarrassment will have worn off. Maybe. "Listen, you wouldn't be able to help me, would you?"

There's a long pause and for a second I think he may have left, but then he answers. "Sure, no problem. You don't have anything I haven't seen before."

"Yeah, well, things may have changed since we were seven and you talked me into playing doctor."

He lets out a chuckle, then says, "I was a bit of a pervy brat, wasn't I?"

"Definitely."

"Well, I'm not anymore, I promise. I won't even look," he tells me. "Can you unlock the door?"

"Not really."

"No matter. I'll crawl under."

"Perfect."

"Is it?"

"Not a bit."

7

Fantasy vs. Reality

HEATH

So, you know when you're in the shower or on a long drive and your mind starts to wander and you find yourself thinking about that moment when you'll have a chance encounter with the person who tore your heart to shreds? Yeah, of all the ways I imagined this, not one time did I picture myself crawling under the door to a dressing booth, with three pairs of high-cut cotton knickers in my hand, no less.

I imagined I'd be married to a super model who just had my baby (and immediately bounced back into shape, of course) when I'd see Hadley again. I'd be dressed in a suit with just the right haircut and she'd gasp and tell me how awful her life has been since I left and I'd pat her on the shoulder and tell her I hope someday she'll find the kind of happiness I have. Or, I'd be coming home after having accepted the Nobel Prize for Math, and was now about to be honoured by the Prime Minister of the

Benavente Islands. Hadley would be in the crowd waving and trying to get my attention. Then she'd flash her bra and beg me to stay.

Hey, I never said they were realistic fantasies, but then, fantasies rarely are (and probably shouldn't be).

I get down on all fours on the not-so-clean tile floor, then flatten out as though I'm about to do one of those crawl-through-the-mud training exercises the army seems to like so much. A woman with a stroller happens to come out from behind a nearby clothing rack and gasps.

"Oh no! This is not what it looks like. I'm not some perv sneaking a look at women while they change," I say quickly.

She purses her lips and does the one-eyebrow raise while pointing at the undies I'm clutching.

"These are for my mum," I tell her, but I can see in her eyes, this woman has already made up her mind about me. And she's certain I'm a total pervert.

"Wait!" Hadley says. "Is there a woman there? Maybe *she* could help me?"

Yes! Brilliant. I glance back up only to see the woman hightailing it out of here. "She's gone."

"Damn."

"I guess I'm all you've got," I tell her.

Crawling on my elbows, I duck my head as I make my way into the tiny booth, finding my cheek pressed up against her ankle. She's standing as tight to the wall as possible, but there is still basically no room. After much contorting, fumbling, and awkwardness, I'm finally standing face-to-face with the girl of my dreams. Well, my adolescent ones anyway. Since I last saw her, she's been the reminder I need that love doesn't work out so there's no point in bothering. And now that I think about it, technically we're not face-to-face. We're face-to-rolled up dress.

"So, how do you want to do this?" I ask her, trying very hard not to look at her body. Not that I noticed, but wow. She's still smoking hot. She's got a lacy bright-turquoise bra on and soft pink knickers. She's sporting a few more curves than I remember, but personally, I'm a big fan.

"Can you grab the fabric and pull up?" she asks. "But do it carefully because I can't really afford to buy a dress I can't wear."

"Sure thing," I say, then reach up toward her arms. "I'm going to put my hands on the dress now."

"Okay," she says, her voice filled with dread. "Are you looking? Because you promised you wouldn't look."

"I actually am looking," I admit. "But because I realized if I don't use my eyes, I'd have to grope around, and I doubt you want that."

"No, that's a good point," she says.

"Don't worry," I tell her. "I'll scrub this entire incident from my mind as soon as it's over."

"I'd appreciate that."

"Here I go." I take hold of the fabric and give it a tug. Then another. "Wow, you are really wedged in there."

"I know," she hisses, with more than a hint of irritation.

"I'm not sure how possible it's going to be to get this off without ripping it."

"Just try, please."

This time, I decide to focus on one sleeve at a time, using both hands at her left wrist to pull at the sleeve. It moves a little, then I switch over to the other wrist and do the same. "This might work," I mutter. "We just have to go nice and slow."

"Thank you," she says, her voice still muffled from the fabric.

Just for shits and giggles, I start humming that old

stripper song they used to play in movies set in the nine-teen-twenties. Bah-nah-nah-nah…bah-nah-nah-nah…"

"Shut up."

"Sorry. Probably too soon on that one."

"Definitely."

Honestly, I can't wait to see what she looks like. So far, I've seen her with a helmet and now a dress is covering her face. The anticipation is killing me. I swallow hard, ordering my brain to focus on the task at hand without letting my body mistake this for sexy time. But the way she moves each time I tug at the sleeves is…well…bouncy… and impossible to ignore. And this booth is so tiny, we're basically pressed up against each other. And she smells so good—like some sort of lightly-scented expensive soap or a really classy frothy shampoo. Or maybe it's just her.

Oh God. I'm totally failing at not finding this erotic.

Finally, I manage to get the dress over her head and free her from it. Her arms collapse down to her sides and her mouth drops open. We both just stare at each other, breathing heavily from the exertion.

"Wow," she whispers. "You…are a *man*."

Oh, she's attracted to me. I can see it in her eyes.

Giving her a smirk, I say, "Thank you."

"How'd you get so…mannish?"

"Time."

"Right," she says, then she seems to realize her state of undress. "Could you…turn around for me?"

"Oh sure," I tell her, doing as she asked. Only now, I'm pressed up against the metal wall, which is slightly humiliating but also isn't necessarily a bad thing because I do need to…ahem…cool down a little.

There's a rustling of fabric and every few seconds she bumps into me as she gets dressed. "Sorry, my arms are totally asleep so I'm a bit clumsy."

"No trouble really. Would you like me to help you?"

"I'd prefer if you could leave, to be honest," she says, then quickly adds. "The dressing room. Until I'm dressed. It's lovely to see you obviously."

Is she rambling a little? She is, isn't she? How adorable. Oh, she's still going. "But if you did try to leave by the door, I'll end up flashing the entire store."

"Don't be shy. They'd be lucky to be flashed by you," I say without thinking, then immediately regret it. "So, how are your parents?" I ask, hoping the shift in conversation will make her forget I basically just told her she's hot.

"Exactly the same."

"And Lucas?"

"He's good. He's a real estate agent now—he's pretty good at it too," Hadley says. "He's getting married actually."

"Really?"

"Yup, that's why I was shopping for a dress."

"For the wedding?"

"Engagement party."

"Gotcha," I say, wondering if she's almost fully clothed.

"What are you doing here anyway?" she asks.

"Oh, I came back when my mum had her accident," I say.

"No, I meant at this store."

"Picking up a few things my mum needs."

"Like these high-cut knickers?" she asks, dangling them over my shoulder.

I grab them then turn back to her, finding myself dangerously close to her again.

This is a terrible, terrible idea. I was supposed to be avoiding her like a staph infection, not practically ripping her clothes off and pressing myself against her. I stare at her beautiful face a moment too long again. Yup, she's still got those gorgeous full lips and deep brown eyes with tiny flecks of mossy green.

"You're a good son," she tells me.

Shaking my head, I say, "No, I'm not."

"You *did* come here to buy her undies. A lot of sons would refuse."

"Well, those guys don't have Minerva Robinson for mothers."

"Good point," she says, grinning. "I miss your mum."

"Stop by the hospital and have a visit," I say. "She'd like that." So would I.

There's a sharp knock on the door that startles both of us. Hadley reaches out and grabs my biceps and we both wince like we're doing something wrong.

"What's going on in there?" a woman asks.

I mouth 'Deena' to Hadley. "I'm rescuing that customer who got stuck."

"Well, hurry it up, you weirdo, we need this dressing room."

"Righto," I say, offering Hadley a mock-salute.

She covers her mouth with one hand and stifles a laugh.

"I'm serious, you two," Deena says. "I'm going to call the cops if you don't get out of there. We don't tolerate funny business here."

"Believe me, there's nothing funny about what's happening here," I tell her, staring into Hadley's eyes again.

I'm gazing, aren't I? Well, that's just great.

Deena pounds on the door. "Open it. Now."

The two of us have to shuffle in a little half circle before I can reach the lock. I slide it open reluctantly, then we have to snug up together to get the door to open wide enough for us to tumble out. Deena glares at us as we exit the booth, me with my mum's undies, and Hadley with a huge pile of clothes. She hands them to Deena, then says, "I'm afraid none of them were quite right."

"Perfect," Deena deadpans. "And you?"

"These are exactly what I was looking for," I say.

"Bring them to the front counter and someone will ring you up," Deena tells me before giving each of us one last dirty look and walking away.

I turn back to Hadley, trying to remind myself of all the reasons I cannot rekindle our friendship. But at the moment, none of them are coming to mind.

"Well, I should go," she says. "I have to get to work."

"Right, yeah," I answer, nodding.

She gives me a questioning look, then asks, "Did you drive past my parents' place yesterday?"

"Uh…nope. I don't think so."

"You sure? You weren't in a green Mazda rental? Because there was a guy there who looked a lot like you."

Shit. "Oh, wait, yeah, that was me. I was just…touring the old hood." *The old hood? Really, Heath?*

Trying to hide her grin, Hadley says, "Thought so. I don't live with my parents anymore."

"No?" I ask, hope filling my chest a little.

"I live over on Oceanview Drive."

"Oh! Nice."

"Not really. It's on the dodgy end, I don't face the ocean, and I'm in a basement suite," she says, her face falling. "But it's only temporary because at some point soon Chase and I are going to get married, so…"

And there it is.

All that stupid hope just got crushed into dust particles. "Oh, you and Chase are still…"

She nods. "Yeah, since high school, if you can believe it."

"Yup, I can," I lie. "And still dating…"

Rolling her eyes, she says, "We were basically babies when we got together so it's good to give ourselves time to grow up before making that sort of commitment."

That is the most rehearsed line of b.s. I've ever heard. "Okay, well, I better go buy these knickers before the sale ends."

Hadley gives me a sad smile. "Right. Of course. Thanks so much for saving me."

"Don't mention it," I say, and turn toward the till.

"It was really nice to see you, Heath," Hadley says.

Glancing over my shoulder, I say, "Yeah. You too. Good luck with…everything."

8

Downward Facing Girl Talk

HADLEY

"And now it's time for shavasana, or corpse pose. Just let go of everything that happened today or will happen. Let your worries float away into the sky as you close your eyes and feel yourself sink into your mat. Listen to the sound of the gentle breeze rustling in the trees nearby, and let your arms and legs fall out to the sides to release any tension left in your body. We'll stay in this pose for five minutes." I wait until all twelve of the guests are settled on their mats before standing and hurrying over to Nora, who is waiting on the steps that lead to the studio.

I sit next to her and she whispers, "So, Heath?"

I already texted her an overview of my shopping disaster and she promised to come straight to find me when her shift ended. "Crazy, right?" I won't tell Nora this, but I'm more than a little hot and bothered by him, which comes with a side order of significant guilt. My entire body flames. "I've never been so embarrassed in my life."

"Yeah, yeah, I got that," she says impatiently. "But tell me about Heath. You said he had gotten all, and I quote, 'manly.' Explain. Leave no detail unsaid."

I pause, trying to fight the grin that's brewing while the memory of being pressed up against him wiggles its way into the forefront of my mind. "I don't know. He was still basically a lanky teenager when he left. Now he's...not."

Giving me a half grin, Nora knocks my shoulder with hers. "*Now he's not.* Is that your way of trying not to say he's a total hottie?"

Rolling my eyes, I say, "Look, he's um...good looking, objectively speaking. I'm sure he has some underwear model girlfriend back in New York, but if you're interested, I'll see if I can find out if he's single."

"If *I'm* interested?" Nora asks, a little too loud. Waving a hand in my direction, she adds, "Based on the energy coming off you, he's all yours."

I let out a long sigh. "First of all, whatever energy you're sensing is leftover humiliation. Second, I already found the love of my life."

"Right," she says, blinking twice. "Chase. In that case, maybe you *should* set me up with Hot Heath. I'm assuming we're going to call him that, yes?"

My body reacts to that idea with a sharp pang, but I push it aside. "Obviously we are. As to you dating him, he did say he was leaving again as soon as his mum is better so you'd have to be prepared for more of a fling-type situation."

"I'm down with that," Nora says. "All of the hotness, none of the problems of trying to 'make it work.'"

Nope. Nope. Nope. "Great idea," I say brightly.

One of the guests opens her eyes and gives us a glare. I mouth an apology, then give Nora the 'we need to lower our voices' gesture. "But anyway, enough about Heath. Did you get your month-end stuff done?"

She nods. "And even better, Harrison said they're putting out an ad for a temporary accountant. There's no way Libby's going to be able to get back to work anytime soon. Their baby is really colicky. He said she's up literally all night."

"Poor lady," I say, shaking my head.

"Yeah, having kids doesn't sound like a very good idea," Nora says.

Shrugging, I glance at my watch. One minute left. "They aren't colicky forever."

"But I bet it *feels* like forever," she says. "Now, back to you. Did you find a dress in the end?"

"Nope. Nothing. I'm going to have to try again," I answer, my stomach dropping at the thought.

"I wish I could go with you but I'm leaving tomorrow morning to go see my grandparents."

Nora's grandparents live on Benavente Island (a.k.a. The Big Island) and she makes a point of going to stay with them at least twice a year.

"Give them hugs from me."

"Will do, chica," she says. We exchange goodbyes, then I walk over to the group, some of whom are definitely asleep, based on their open mouths and drool. In a gentle voice, I say, "For those of you who want to stay here, you're welcome to do so. Otherwise, it's time to bring your awareness to your body again." I sit on my mat in front of them. "Wiggle your fingers and toes. Take a deep, cleansing inhale, then let it out slowly. Open your eyes and come to a seated position."

All but three of the class sit cross-legged with relaxed smiles on their faces. The others are out cold. "Touch your thumb to your middle finger and let your arms float out to the sides, then rest them on your knees. Let's take one last deep breath as a group, and let it go. Thank you so much for sharing your practice today. Namaste."

We bow to each other, and I wait while the guests get up and leave, thanking me and wandering off in different directions. I stay seated, waiting for the last of the class to wake up so I can clean the mats and put them back in storage. I know from experience that they should all be up within about ten minutes, and I'm happy to sit and contemplate the day for a bit. One-by-one they wake up, looking a little out of it, then offer apologies of varying levels of sincerity.

I stand and start spraying the mats with disinfectant, my mind immediately taking a beeline back to Heath and his lean muscles and his gorgeous smile. And his kindness. He crawled under a door to rescue me and I know him well enough to know that he would have done it for a stranger just as quickly as he did for me. He was always helping someone, whether it was me with math or his mum with looking after their place. He just knew how to make everything better, even when we were kids. And apparently, he still does.

I allow myself to think about him until all the mats have been returned to the closet, then I grab my phone and text Chase.

Me: Hi babe, how's it going in NYC? I miss you so much.

I wait, but there's no answer. He must be in a meeting. I flick through some pictures of the two of us together, smiling at scenes of us goofing around at a campfire on the beach or shots I took of him surfing. Yes, that's my guy. Soon he'll be home more than he's gone and we can start our life together. Heath may be hot, but Chase and I have a long, wonderful history.

Oh, and he's also hot, too, so…

9

Old Lady Gangs and Narcissists
Giving Bad News

HEATH

"What's up with you today?" my mum asks, giving me the Spanish inquisitor look she perfected right around the time I hit puberty.

"Nothing," I tell her in an even tone.

I came straight from Apple Blossoms to the hospital so she could check out her new knickers. I've been here for two hours now, and in that time I've been doing my best not to think about a certain woman in a certain dressing booth with a certain set of curves. Instead, I've been working on my laptop while my mum napped, then, after she woke up, manically keeping the small talk going. Anything to keep myself from reliving my reintroduction to Hadley. To be honest, finding out that she's still with that wanker Chase was a soul-crushing experience. Especially after those few moments of pure...us. Thank God I'm going back to the US in a few weeks because living on that type of emotional roller coaster on a regular basis is the last thing I'd ever want. No thank you. My predictable life in New York is waiting. All I have to do is avoid her until I board that plane.

"Something's up. I know it."

"Just a bunch of work stuff," I tell her.

This isn't necessarily a lie because Charles did leave me a rather terse voicemail a few hours ago about how inconvenient it is that I'm not across the hall when he needs me.

Nurse Happy walks in (although I have to say, she's definitely less chipper than the first time I saw her), saving me from what I know would be the middle (and end) of an irritating conversation. I use the time to start writing a quick email back to Charles, explaining that I'll call him as soon as I leave the hospital, but sadly for me, the nurse leaves before I can finish it *and* before my mum forgets there's something up with me.

She stares at me for an uncomfortably long time before saying, "Nope. There's something else. A mother knows." She leans toward me as much as possible with one leg in traction and broken ribs.

"Well, when you figure it out, tell me because I don't have the first clue what is apparently wrong with me," I say.

The door opens and my mum's crazy—I mean eccentric—friends come in. There are three of them—Bea (a widow with three grown kids and seven grandkids), Harriet (never married, no children), and Nance (a thrice-divorced woman who inherited her ex-husband's shares in Lube Town, the biggest quick oil change chain in the Benaventes). They all start to fuss over me at a volume that one wouldn't say is 'hospital approved,' all talking at once.

"Look at you! I knew you'd grow into those gangly arms and legs," Nance says. "My God, if I were in the market for husband number four, I'd be all over you."

"Thanks?" I say as she pulls me in for a hug I'd rather not have.

"Stop, Nance," Bea says. "You'll get canceled for harassment."

"Oh pish!" Nance tells her. "I'm pretty sure Heath here knows an innocent compliment when he hears one. Don't you, Heath?"

"Yeah, sure," I start, but then get cut off by Harriet, who fixes me with a steely stare while saying, "You're in a lot of trouble, young man. Not coming home to see your poor mother for so long. What kind of son does that?"

"Stop it, you two," Bea says. "You're going to make sure he never comes back."

Thankfully, they turn their attention to Minerva now. Bea reminds me of a hen, clucking while adjusting Mum's pillows and blankets. Nance opens her oversized handbag and starts pulling out Tupperware containers of baking. Next comes a few paperbacks, then some packages of face masks, magazines, and some skin cream. Just when I'm pretty sure she's about to pull a floor lamp out a la Mary Poppins, she closes it up and nods. "There you go, Minerva. That ought to keep you going for a few days."

My phone buzzes again. Charles again, this time via text. *Did you get my email?* "Ladies, it was lovely to see you. I'm going to dash so we won't be over the limit of allowed visitors."

"No way," Harriet says. "Minerva's been waiting years to see you. You stay and we'll go."

"I'll be back later this evening, but I do need to zip home and get a few hours of work done. We're in the middle of a big merger and my boss needs me to stay on top of it."

"If you need to get back to your life, you're free to

leave anytime," Minerva says, even though she doesn't mean a word of it.

"I'm not leaving, Mum. I *want* to be here," I answer, glancing at my phone to see that I'm getting a call from Charles. Nuts. "But I do have to take this. I'll see you in a few hours. Enjoy your visit."

Getting up, I hurry into the busy hallway before answering. "Charles, I was just about to call you back."

"Really? What an amazing coincidence," he says, slathering on the sarcasm milkshake-thick.

"Yes, I got the numbers from Anita but I haven't had a chance to go over them yet. It's been a little busy here today."

"I'm sure it has," he says. "But here's the thing…"

Uh-oh. I don't think 'the thing' is going to work out in my favour.

He pauses, then says, "Your mum's still alive, yes?"

"Yes, she's doing remarkably well considering."

"Good stuff. No chance she's going to pass on or anything?"

"Nope." Where is he going with this?

"Good, that makes this easier."

Makes what easier? I hurry around three doctors flirting with Nurse Happy (oh! So *that's* why she's happy), then make my way down the hallway to the stairwell. By the time the door closes behind me, I've been fired.

"…if it were any other time, I'd be happy to keep you on, but with the Kurell-Bao merger, I need a man on the ground."

If he wants a man on the ground, he's got one because I'm now sitting on a concrete step breaking out in a cold sweat.

"Heath? Are you still there?"

"Yup," I say weakly.

"And you heard all that?"

My mind spins at a furious pace, gathering momentum without my permission. "Yup, I heard it."

"Thank God. That was hard enough the first time. I'd hate like hell to have to fire you twice."

"That would be awful for you, I'm sure," I answer with sarcasm I know he'll interpret as genuine concern for his welfare. Nope. I cannot let this happen. Not after all those years of intense effort. Not after giving up any sort of life other than my job. "Listen, Charles. Let's not be too hasty, okay? Granted, the first couple of days here were a little hectic, but I promise I'm on top of everything. In fact, I was just leaving the hospital for the rest of the day to dedicate myself entirely to the file. I'll get everything polished until it's perfect. Every line. Every decimal will be checked thoroughly. I've more than proved myself to be a loyal, dedicated employee. Just give me until tomorrow morning to show you I can do everything you need from here. Then I'll—"

"—Heath, don't beg, okay?" he says, sounding bored. "I don't want to lose respect for you."

"I'm not begging," I say, utterly offended at the accusation. "I'm fighting for my job. A job I've done incredibly well for over six years, I might add. I'm your go-to guy. Evenings, weekends, Christmas Day, I'm there and you know it. Who do you think is going to replace me? Tucker? Anita?" I ask, raising my voice. "Where were they on New Year's Eve when you needed them?"

"You're begging, Heath. And to be honest, you're also getting a little pushy now."

Shit. Shit. Shit. "Charles, don't do this. For your own sake. *I'm* the guy that catches everyone else's mistakes. Remember the TechBox deal? Who noticed that Denton inflated their Q1 numbers? It was me, Charles. Everyone else let that slip through but I caught it."

"I've got to tell you, bragging is *not* a good look for you. I'm going to hang up now so you don't humiliate yourself any more than you already have," Charles says. "You'll get paid till the end of the month."

"I'd better be. I'm using my vacation days to be here and I've got like six weeks banked."

"Oh, well, that works out better for you than I thought it would. Anyway, someone from HR will contact you to wrap everything up," he says, adding, "I have to run. Good luck to your mother...and you."

And then he's gone.

And so is my job.

And let's face it, my life.

Four years of busting my arse at university, then six years of weekends, all-nighters, giving up holidays, saying no to literally everything and everyone other than Charles.

One massive bonus and a huge promotion that I should be getting as soon as the deal goes through.

Poof.

Swept away like so much dust.

I sit staring at a jagged crack in the floor, part of me wishing it would open up and suck me into it so I wouldn't have to face the shitshow my life has just become. The career I've been killing myself for is over. And I'm too far away to fix it.

10

Getting Hit by a Bread Truck...
Relationship Version

HADLEY

"Great work, Taylor! You really nailed that intro," I say. "Now, let's see if we can get all the way to the chorus. After that, it'll be basically repeating the routine from the beginning."

"Perfect, because to be honest, I've been a little nervous that I won't be able to learn it in time. I'm just so busy with all the pre-wedding stuff," she says with a dramatic sigh. "You have *no idea* how much goes into being a bride. It's exhausting."

"I bet," I tell her, irritation clawing at my chest at the whole 'you have no idea' comment. "Where are you getting married anyway?"

She grins. "The ceremony will be at the cathedral at two in the afternoon. We wanted to give our out-of-town guests the morning to relax and enjoy the island. And we have to go with the cathedral because we need a space that can hold eight hundred people since my fiancé's family has so many business connections all over the Caribbean. It's going to be so elegant—all-white flowers absolutely filling the inside of the church. And we're having an arbor installed in the garden behind the building for photos. It's going to be so dreamy. Then my fiancé and I are going to leave by horse-drawn carriage for a private photo session at Moonstone Cove—just the two of us at sunset. Then to the Sapphire for the reception."

"Wow…that's so weird," I say. "That's literally exactly what I want to do for my wedding."

"Really?" Taylor asks, tilting her head.

"Yeah. I swear to God, that's precisely what I've had planned for…like years," I say with a smile. "You're like my wedding plan doppelgänger. If there were such a thing, I mean."

"Well, to be honest, all those ideas are from my fiancé," she tells me. "We started talking about it right after he proposed and I was just so touched that he'd put any thought into it at all, I agreed to everything he suggested. Not that I don't love all his ideas, because I totally do."

"Who wouldn't?" I joke, then I add, "That is just so crazy that his ideas and mine are so similar—like exactly the same. Right down to the colour of the flowers."

She gives me a skeptical look, like maybe she doesn't believe a word I'm saying. I guess it does sound unlikely. My cheeks heat up when it occurs to me she thinks I'm lying. "Anyway, it is so refreshing to hear about a super-involved groom. Most of them just show up."

Her smile returns. "I'm so lucky. Is your boyfriend not really into the whole wedding idea?" she asks, her face morphing to pity.

"He will be when the time is right. He's just so busy with work that he doesn't even have time to think about it."

Or so he told me when I launched into a diatribe of my perfect wedding.

"Totes," Taylor says.

"Okay, so let's work on the next few bars."

The hour zips by, and when we're finished, we've added another minute to her routine. I get her to video me doing the dance so she can play it back for herself while she practices. The entire time we're working, I have a nagging feeling that something is wrong, but I can't for the life of me put my finger on it. My mind keeps slipping back to Taylor's wedding plans and somehow, even though it's really silly, I feel like I'm losing something very special. But that's just silly because who will care if we have the same plan for our big days? It's not like it'll take anything away from mine. We don't even know the same people.

I pull out my phone and open my calendar. "Now, I know your life is nuts right now, but is there any way you can make it twice next week? Or even three times? If we condense our sessions, you'll actually have an easier time remembering the moves."

"Definitely," Taylor says, digging around in her bag for her phone. "I was actually planning to ask if you might be able to meet more often."

When she lifts her phone up, my stomach immediately flips and all the breath leaves my body in one huge *whoosh*. Her screen saver is a picture of Chase. I swallow hard, then stare at his gorgeous face, suddenly putting everything together. Chase is her fiancé. *I'm* the older woman who's letting myself go. A wave of nausea comes over me and I feel like my legs are going to give way. It's all I can do to not sink to the floor. "Is that…your fiancé?" I ask, my voice barely audible.

She nods and aims the screen at me. "Yup. Chase. Isn't

he gorgeous? Like seriously, he could be a model. In fact, he was asked to model by—"

"—A woman from Ford who met him at Long Beach?" I finish for her.

Her head snaps back and she says, "How did you know that?"

"Because he's my boyfriend."

———

I ring the doorbell several times then wait impatiently for the enormous wooden door to the Williams family home to open. Finally, I see Julia, the maid, whose mouth drops when she sees me. "Miss Hadley, it's been such a long time since I've seen you. Are you okay? You look upset."

"I am upset, Julia. Is Chase home by any chance?"

She shakes her head. "He's still in Chicago."

I walk past her into the house. I need answers and I'm not leaving until I have them. "Are his parents home? I need to see them."

She hurries to catch up with me. "Mr. Williams is at the office and Mrs. Williams is hosting a fundraiser meeting in the library."

I stalk down the hall with Julia in tow.

"She won't appreciate being interrupted. Why don't you come back later?"

"This can't wait," I say, bursting into the room, only to see half a dozen well-dressed women with plates of fresh fruit and pastries balanced on their laps.

"Hadley, what are you doing here?" Betty Williams asks, her face going through all the emotions in under a second—irritation, pity, discomfort, then returning to her usual icy calm.

"I need to see Chase," I tell her, wiping tears off my cheeks and doing my best not to sniffle.

She stands and glances nervously around at her guests. "I'll be right back, ladies."

Linking arms with me, she leads me in the direction of the front door. "Chase isn't here, but I'll make sure he knows you stopped by. Can I tell him what this is about?"

I stop walking and she turns to me. "It's about me finding out that he has a fiancée."

"Oh," she says as she pats me stiffly on the arm. "I'm sure it must be hard for you to find out he's moved on, but really, Hadley, it's for the best. You two were never a good match."

"Well, he should have told *me* that."

She freezes. "It's hardly any of your business. Quite frankly, it's a little odd for you to expect him to fill you in on every detail of his life."

"No, it's not. *We're* supposed to be getting married—Chase and me, not Chase and…and…someone else."

"I know it probably feels that way," she says in a placating tone. "It's hard to let go of a dream, but you really must. This isn't good for you."

"No…what are you…" I sputter for the right words, my pulse pounding in my ears so hard her words are muffled. Finally, I manage to yell, "We never broke up!" Lowering my voice, I add, "Well, not since that one time in high school, but that was only for a couple of weeks and we were practically still kids."

"Hadley, stop. You're embarrassing yourself. You know very well you two broke up last year." Her entire demeanor is a lesson in condescension.

"No, we didn't." Fresh tears spring to my eyes and I don't even bother to wipe them away as they fall down my cheeks.

"Yes, you did," she says forcefully. "He broke it off with you just after my birthday dinner," she tells me.

"No, he really, *really* didn't. We're still together, only now I find out he's getting married to someone else."

Opening the front door, Betty says, "You must be having some type of breakdown because there is simply *no way* my son would be cheating on Taylor. She's the love of his life. He adores her. Now, I'm sure that hurts to hear, but you'll find some…nice man eventually. For your own sake, let him go, Hadley. This is very awkward."

Putting one hand on my upper arm, she gently pushes me outside onto the steps.

"That's not true! He didn't break up with me!" I shout, spinning on my heel to face her. "We've been making plans for the future! *Wedding* plans!"

Her shoulders drop. "Oh, you poor thing. You know what? I'll have Julia send you the name of my sister's shrink. She's a miracle worker. She can help you out with this delusional episode you're having."

With that, she shuts the door in my face. My mouth drops to my chin and my heart pounds wildly in my chest. I'm so furious I feel like I could kick the door down. I consider ringing the bell again but instead, I sink onto the red brick steps and start to cry. After a few minutes, I grab my phone out of my bag and call Chase.

When he doesn't pick up, I leave him a sniff-filled message. "Hey Chase, guess who's been coming to me for dance lessons so she can surprise you at your wedding with a subpar rendition of "Crazy in Love?" Yeah, Taylor! Your fiancée, I guess? Call me now, you coward."

Next, I text him: *I know about Taylor and she knows about me. Call me immediately.*

A voice comes on over the intercom. It's Julia. "Mrs. Williams says you need to leave now. Her guests will be exiting the house soon and she can't have you there sobbing on the porch."

"He's been cheating on me, Julia," I say.

There's a long pause, then Julia says, "You have to go, okay, Hadley?"

"I can't believe Betty doesn't believe me. We're still a couple. I promise." My voice cracks.

Julia lowers her voice and says, "You're better off without him."

———

I try calling Nora, but when I don't get an answer, I remember she's gone to Benavente to visit her grandparents for a few days. That fact alone makes me want to curl up in a ball. I need my bestie right now. For some stupid reason, I drive straight to my parents' house, shaking and crying the entire way. I definitely shouldn't be driving. My turns are all wobbly, I cut off a minivan by accident, and my vision keeps going blurry from tears.

I'm in shock. Like actual shock. I catch sight of my reflection in my side mirror and my skin has gone pale. I park and get off my moped, not even bothering to take off my helmet as I walk around to the back door.

Chase is cheating on me.

He's a cheater.

A lowdown dirty lying sack of shit cheating mother fucker.

And he's been lying to his entire family about our relationship status.

He's getting married.

And not to me.

Well, maybe. Taylor was every bit as upset as I was when I told her. First, she denied that it could be the same guy until I showed her pictures of us together on my phone. Then she immediately launched into a very insulting line of questions and comments that sounded a lot like what Betty just accused me of—being insane. She was so positive he had broken up with me months ago and that I wasn't accepting it. So I showed her our latest texts. That shut her up.

I walk into the house without knocking, startling my mom who's busy cutting up veggies. "Oh, Hadley! You scared me out of my wits!"

Bursting into tears, I sink down onto the nearest chair while she rushes over. "What happened? Did you get in an accident?" She yells for my father. "Glen! Glen! Hadley's hurt!" She leans down toward me. "Should I call an ambulance? Should I immobilize your neck? Is your helmet stuck on your head?"

I shake my head and she takes it off while I try to stop my chest from heaving out huge sobs. But it's no use. I'm so heartbroken, I may never stop sobbing.

My dad comes around the corner, panic on his face. "What happened? I knew we should never have let you get that moped."

"The big mistake was letting her spend so much time at that awful Minerva Robinson's place," Mum tells him. "If she hadn't done that, she'd be driving a car like a normal person."

"I wasn't in a collision," I manage. "It's Chase." More loud sobs accompanied by a wailing sound that resembles a freshly-harpooned whale (or so I imagine).

My mum hurries over to the counter for a box of tissues. When she returns, she plucks a couple out, holds them to my nose, and tells me to blow. I do as ordered, glad I came home. My parents will know what to do. They'll take care of me. Maybe I can stay here in my old room for a few days until I feel stronger. It's a home gym now, but maybe we could squeeze an air mattress in or something.

"What happened to Chase?" my dad says.

"Oh, Lord, did his plane crash? Is he *dead?*" my mum whispers.

I shake my head and yell, "Worse! He's in love with someone else!"

My parents freeze in place, then my dad says, "That's hardly worse, dear."

"Yes, it is. I'd rather he was dead." Sniffle, hiccup, sniffle, blow. "He's getting married to a dental assistant named Taylor…and she can't even dance!"

"Are you serious?" my mum asks, her face blanching.

"Very. She can barely even point her toes."

"No, about Chase getting married," Mum says impatiently.

I nod, then cry some more while she straightens up and folds her arms across her chest. My dad shifts awkwardly from one foot to the other, then nods at me and says, "Uh, I think this is a situation your mother should handle. Girl talk and all that. I'm sorry that happened to you, Hadley."

With that, he disappears into his den, probably to watch cricket.

My mum pours me a tall glass of water, then sits down perpendicular to me at the table. "Okay, so tell me everything, right from the start."

I launch into an incoherent version of the day's events, skipping around in such a way that I'm certain none of it make sense. I talk about how he stole my perfect wedding and how Taylor is no Beyoncé and how he must have told her I'm fat and old. Finally, when I'm done, she sits back and stares at me, doing something she would totally tell me not to—chewing her bottom lip. "You know what? It's fine. It'll be fine."

"Haven't you been listening?" I bark. "He's in love with someone else. They're getting married in three months!"

"Not necessarily. It's not too late to get him back."

"Oh my God, are you serious right now?"

Pointing a finger at me, Mum says, "You've given him the best years of your life. You can't just give up now. This...this...*other woman* is just a blip. You just need to remind him of what you two have together. First, you go on the three-day military diet and lose a quick ten. I'll book you at my spa for a full facial and some light Botox—"

"Botox? I'm not even thirty!"

"—Well, that frown line says otherwise. Then, you go to New York, seduce him, tell him you forgive him, and hopefully by the time you fly back, he'll be with you and you'll be pregnant."

My mouth hangs open and I stare at my insane mother.

"It'll work. I know it will. You are *not* going to lose to some dental assistant," my mum says, setting her jaw.

"I can't believe you want me to try to get him back," I say in a quiet tone.

"Of course I want you to. I never expected you to land a fish that big to begin with. Now that you're about to reel him in, you can't cut the line!"

My head swims in circles and I have to shake it to make it stop. "So, you'd rather I spend my life with a cheating asshole than be alone?"

"Language, Hadley."

I glare and she seems to realize now's not the time for comportment lessons. "Listen, if it were just some random guy, of course not. But this is *Chase Williams* we're talking about. Men like him are one in a million."

"Mum, he asked another woman to marry him. They set the date, the deposits have been paid. He clearly doesn't love me," I say, my voice cracking.

Throwing her hands up, she says, "What is love? I mean, really? Some ridiculous romantic notion that isn't worth a hill of beans in the long run. What's more important is to have a good partnership where both the husband and wife have clearly defined roles and work together to create the perfect life."

"How could it possibly be the perfect life if he doesn't want to be with me?"

"Of course he wants to be with you. This is just...I don't know, pre-engagement jitters," she says with a wild look in her eye. "You know your father had a fling before we got married."

Gasping, I wish she came with a mute button because I can't hear anymore of her insane denial.

"It's true. Her name was Rita. She worked with him at the gas station over on Third Street the summer after high school. A real piece of work. She was after him from day one and after a few weeks, he couldn't resist her advances. They..." She lowers her voice here to a whisper. "Slept together even. Twice during one shift. Right there in the gas station back room. When I found out, I was devastated. Not quite as theatrical about it as you, but still, upset."

Why did I think coming here was in any way a good idea?

"This is hardly some gas station one-night stand," I say, numbness setting in.

"Well, no, but it's not fatal, I promise you. You just have to get right back on that horse. Show him what he'll miss out on, and make it work."

"It's over, Mum. And even if he did want to give it another try, I wouldn't. I could never trust him again. Besides, I want to be with a man who loves me."

"That's a huge mistake. Honestly, Chase is your best chance at a perfect life. Stick with him. Someday the two of you will laugh about this."

I give her a deadpan expression until she says, "Okay, maybe not laugh. But it'll be a distant memory, tucked away behind all the wonderful ones of the family you'll build together."

Plucking my helmet off the table, I slide out of my chair and walk toward the door on wobbly legs.

"Where are you going?" my mum asks.

"I don't know. Not here," I mumble.

"Why don't you stay for supper? I'm making a big salad. That would be the perfect start to your diet."

I turn and look at her, pain radiating through me as the reality sets in. My mum really doesn't care if I'm with someone who loves me. Her need to have me keep up appearances is the only thing that matters to her. "No thanks. I'm in the mood for a giant burger."

She purses her lips together. "You know, that defiant streak you've got may just be why Chase has decided to move on."

"Wow. How to blame the victim," I tell her, then I turn and pull the door open and step outside. I have no idea where I'm going, but as long as it's away from her, it'll be much better than here.

11

When One Door Closes...

HEATH

I'm sitting at the busy rooftop bar at The Turtle's Head Pub and Grill wishing I'd postponed my plans with Fidel. Even though weather-wise, it's perfect for a long visit (a warm evening with just enough of a breeze to keep the mosquitoes away), I'm not exactly in the mood to catch up with an old friend. I got here twenty minutes early and have been slowly working my way through a pint of ale while I try to figure out my future. The shock still hasn't quite worn off.

I was fired. Me.

I was fired.

I was *fired*.

A sense of shame comes over me again and I have a big swig of my drink to douse the heat rising from my neck. I shouldn't be ashamed. I should be pissed. Which I am. But also, there's just something so humiliating about being fired. Dismissed. Let go.

Especially after doing everything right for so long. How is this even possible? And how the hell do I bounce back from this?

My apartment is sitting empty (and costing me a small fortune), and the truth is, I don't know that it'll be easy to find another job. It certainly won't happen while I'm here. But even when I can get back to New York, the thought of starting over somewhere and working my way up all over again makes my head ache. Unfortunately, I have no choice but to do exactly that. I've already been locked out of the company's server, email, and cloud. Just for fun, I tried emailing myself from my gmail account to see what reply I'd get.

Heath Robinson is no longer an employee of Dubanowsky Investment Brokers. Please forward all inquiries to Tucker Hanson.

As to my work mates, I haven't heard from anyone yet, and I doubt I will. Out of sight, out of mind and all that. Or, more likely, they won't want to put themselves through that type of awkward conversation filled with long pauses and a fear that my voice will crack, or even worse, allow a sob to escape.

"Hey Heath!" Fidel says from across the rooftop.

I stand and grin, glad to see a friendly face. He walks over, we give each other quick man hugs, then settle ourselves at the table. "You made it out," I say to him.

"Just barely. Our oldest, Harrison, found a gecko tail and decided it would make sense to hide it in his bed in hopes that the gecko will 'grow back.'"

I let out a laugh. "Seriously?"

"Yeah, it wasn't exactly a fresh tail either so we had to strip his bed and put his back-up sheets on. And also get the tail away from him, which upset him greatly," Fidel says, shaking his head. "It was a whole thing."

Thank God I don't have kids. "I can't even imagine."

Our server comes by to take Fidel's drink order, then hurries off.

"So, how's your mum today?" he asks.

"Back to being a complete terror, so I guess that's a good sign," I tell him. "How's Winnie?"

"She's great. Busy, happy, runs off her feet with the kids all day, but she's having fun with it too for the most part," he says with a genuine smile that tells me how he really feels about her. "What about you? You found 'the one' yet?"

Shaking my head, I say, "Not going to happen. The single life is too great. No offense."

"None taken, but only because I don't believe you," Fidel says with a wide grin.

I roll my eyes and am about to launch into a monologue on how wonderful it is to be totally free when the server drops off Fidel's drink.

"What can I get you fellows to eat?" she asks.

"A loaded cheeseburger with the sweet potato fries," Fidel tells her.

"That sounds good," I tell her. "I'll have the same. And another beer, please."

She nods and disappears, leaving us with a lot of time for Fidel to fill me in on who's married, who's divorced already, who went to jail (surprisingly, Tasha Young for identity theft). By the time we're eating, I've managed to enjoy myself enough to forget that I'm jobless. That is, until Fidel says, "How's work going? You still taking over the US one merger at a time?"

My gut churns and I set down the fry I was about to pop into my mouth. "Actually, I got fired today."

He freezes with his glass halfway to his mouth. "Seriously?"

Nodding, I say, "Yup. My company was in the middle

of what will be the largest aeronautical security merger in history when my mum got hurt. My boss decided I'd been away too long—apparently four days isn't acceptable even though I've been working from here. But he called earlier and let me go. Just like that. After six years of nights, weekends, holidays…giving up having a personal life. Over in one phone call."

"Shit, man," he says. "That totally blows."

"Doesn't it?" I ask. "Now I've got to see if I can find something else, but it's not like I can do any job hunting from here." I have a sip of my beer, letting the cool liquid slide down my throat.

"Are you strapped for cash?" he asks.

"I'm good, thanks," I tell him. "I just don't know how long I'll have to be here. Probably a few months, actually. I'll put out some feelers soon—let people in the industry know I'm looking."

"Maybe this is your chance to make a change. Maybe somewhere tropical?" he asks with a hopeful grin.

"San Felipe isn't exactly a hot zone for investment brokers."

Fidel shrugs. "But what about some other type of accounting? We actually need someone at the resort. Temporary to start but it could turn into something. Harrison and his wife Libby had another baby so they need someone to take over her duties for a while."

Bookkeeping at the hotel Hadley works for? No thank you. "It's really nice of you to let me know. I appreciate it, but it doesn't sound like my thing."

I don't know if he can read my mind or is just really good at guessing, but he says, "Ah, I get it. It would be too hard for you to work at the same place as Hadley."

"Who? Hadley Jones?" I give him an expression that I hope says I couldn't care less, but I may actually look like

I'm holding in a fart. "I've been over her for a lot of years, trust me."

"Really? Because as I remember it, you were a guy with a one-track mind and that track always led to that girl."

"Oh, come on," I tell him. "I was a kid. To be honest, I haven't thought about her in years. She means nothing to me. In fact, I ran into her a couple of days ago. Nothing. No spark whatsoever. She might as well have been Mrs. Janz for all I care."

"Our old English teacher? I forgot about her," he says with a shudder.

"Yeah, or...anyone, really." I pop a fry into my mouth.

"You're sure going out of your way to let me know you have no feelings for her," he says with an irritating smirk.

I have a sip of my beer, then say, "You see? This is why I left. Small towns mean everyone knows everyone else's business and they're so bored, they have nothing better to do than make stuff up."

He gives me a conciliatory shrug, but then says, "If you don't care at all about her, it shouldn't bother you to see her at work, should it?"

"It wouldn't. But I really don't want the job. It's not the kind of accounting I do."

"That's a shame, really, because Harrison could really use your help. He's absolutely drowning dealing with the books. He's got an assistant but she's more of an event planner."

"I'm sure he'll find someone."

"Yeah, probably," he says, picking up a fry and dipping it into the garlic aioli sauce. "Say, didn't Harrison teach you how to surf? And fish? And didn't his Uncle Oscar give you a summer job every year when he was running the resort?"

He's going to guilt me into this, isn't he? Bastard. I stare at Fidel for a long moment before answering. "I don't remember you playing this dirty, Fidel."

Grinning, he says, "I've learned a few tricks from my wife. So? What do you say? Come help out an old friend? You know, since seeing Hadley has absolutely no impact on you and all…"

12

Disappointed or Disappointment?

HADLEY

Text from Luke: Mum told us about Chase. What a shithead. Serena and I are just sick about it. Want her to kick his ass for you?

Me: If she can find him, tell her to have at it.

Luke: Why don't you come to trivia night with us tomorrow? Dustin and his latest girlfriend broke up and we could use a fourth.

Me: Are you seriously trying to set me up with Lustin' Dustin?

Luke: NEVER. We just thought it might take your mind off things for an evening.

Me: I'm pretty content here on my couch binge-watching the entire Buffy the Vampire Slayer series, but thanks for the offer.

I stare at our exchange for a second, trying to figure out why it irks me so badly. It's the 'we,' isn't it? How can 'we' have a thought—like one thought between the two of them? Sickening. I'm so glad I'm never going to be part of an obnoxious couple again.

Yuck.

———

Voicemail from Mum: Hadley, it's your mother. I haven't heard from you for a few days. Did you get my email with the military diet instructions? You could be down ten pounds by now. I've also been thinking about this whole Chase situation. My guess is that the other woman has probably ended things, so there's a good chance he'll come running back to you with his tail between his legs. If that does happen, you need to be ready to negotiate the new terms of your relationship. Insist on a quick wedding and no more dating other women, obviously. But you'll have to be willing to give a little too. There's clearly some reason he felt the need to seek comfort elsewhere, so find out what it was and make sure you don't put him in that predicament again. Also, have you found a suitable dress for Luke's engagement party? It's this weekend.

———

Nora: Hey sweetie, are you still on the couch?
Me: Yes.

The phone rings and I stare at Nora's name for a couple of rings before deciding to answer. "I'm fine."

"No, you are not. You've been on that couch for three days straight—hang on, what about work?"

"First two were my regular days off. Today I called in sick. I know, I'm an awful person."

"You're not an awful person," Nora says. "And if you ask me, being heartbroken is a form of illness."

"Right?" I ask, glad that she gets it.

"But listen, you need to promise to get out of there *today* or I'm going to change my flight so I can be there in

84

time to drag you out for an evening of dancing and debauchery."

"I appreciate the offer, Nora. I really do, but I feel like this is the place I need to be right now." I glance down at the delicious spread in front of me (inspired by my mother's message). "On my couch, dipping plain crisps into vanilla ice cream."

"Oh, that sounds…well, so gross it might just be amazing," Nora says.

"It's both, especially before I ran out of caramel sauce," I tell her, staring at Sarah Michelle Gellar's frozen face. Even with her eyes half shut, she's gorgeous. Life really isn't fair. "Anyway, how's your visit going?"

"The usual. Grandma keeps trying to sneak random gifts into my luggage without me noticing. Today, it was a pickle jar with half a pickle left."

"That won't make a mess at all if it breaks in your suitcase."

Nora chuckles. "Yesterday it was some tins of tuna circa 1999 and a vintage Scooby Doo Mystery Machine lunch box," Nora says. "I actually kind of love the lunch box."

I offer a customary laugh-type sound even though I'm not feeling it, then my heart aches for Nora to be here with me watching Buffy. "Oh, God, Nora. I'm in this awful limbo where we haven't officially broken up yet, but I know it's over and I want to smash his face with a pickle jar."

"I take it you haven't heard from dingle nuts?"

"No. Can you believe him? Like, seriously, he doesn't even have the decency to phone me back and just tell me the truth. What kind of man did I fall in love with?"

"The wrong kind—handsome, rich, and narcissistic."

I sink my face into a nearby throw pillow while she starts the pep talk I knew was coming.

"Hads, you can't sit there anymore. You need to go have a shower and wash all that grief stank off—"

"What makes you think I haven't showered?"

"Have you?"

"No, but still, I don't appreciate the assumption."

"My apologies. Now, go shower, and get out for a couple of hours."

"I don't want to see people. People suck," I say, then add, "Obviously you're not included in that category."

"Thanks, but you have to get out. Even if it's just to ride on your moped and let the wind blow through your hair, then...I don't know, get a milkshake, or go to the pub, have a couple of shots, then kiss the first man who talks to you."

"No one is going to talk to me. Also, eww. What if he's, like, old and gross?"

"Doesn't matter. Just do something. I don't want to come back and find you welded to your couch by your own filth."

"Thanks for that delightful image."

"Oh, damn, I have to go. Grandma just started toward my room with a potato plant she just pulled out of the garden. Dirt and all. I do not want that in my suitcase."

"Go. Save your suitcase. I'll see you soon."

"Yes, you will," Nora says. "Now, promise me you're going to leave your place today or I'm calling your parents and telling them you're suicidal."

"You wouldn't."

"Would and will."

"Bitch."

"Yup, and proud of it," she says. "Text me a picture of wherever you go. If I don't receive something in three hours, I'm calling Doris."

She's gone before I can protest, so I flip the show back on and resume my mid-morning snack.

A little while later, I get a text from her. *Saved the suitcase but will now be bringing home the potato plant in a massive Ziploc bag. T minus 2 hours.*

"Oh fine," I mutter, shutting off the TV.

This is a horrible idea. I've been riding around aimlessly for twenty minutes now, looking for a stupid photo op for my stupid friend who's stupid blackmailing me. Like really, Nora, do I need that shit right now? I think not.

Then it pops into my head.

Minerva.

She hates men too. I should go see her. Heath did say she'd love to have a visit. I do a quick u-turn and start toward the hospital, stopping at a liquor store on the way where I pick up a box of boozy chocolates and a mickey of vodka. I snap a quick pic of myself in the whiskey aisle with a crazed grin on my face and send it to Nora with the caption: *Does this count?*

Nora: No.

Me: Fine.

A few minutes later, I'm standing in the hallway outside Minerva Robinson's hospital room, second-guessing the whole plan. *What if she doesn't want to see me? Or what if Heath is here and he thinks I'm stalking him?*

Nope, this is too weird. I'm going to just leave the chocolates at the front desk and go home. I haven't seen her in years and she probably doesn't remember me anyway.

I'm just about to pivot and take off when the door swings open and a doctor comes out, allowing Minerva to see me and me to see her seeing me. He steps aside to let me in, leaving me no choice in the matter. Putting a bright smile on my face, I walk in. No Heath. First, relief, then, oddly, a pang of disappointment hits.

"Hi Minerva," I say, my heart beating with nerves.

"Well, if it isn't Miss Hadley Jones," she answers, stretching her arms out for a hug. "Look at the rack on you! You've gone and gotten yourself some huge knockers. Are they real or were they expensive?"

Yup, same old Minerva. "Real. How are you?" I ask, crossing the room. I give her a careful hug, then straighten up and smile down at her, trying not to act shocked at how frail she looks.

"Not worth a damn," she says. "Just look at me. I'm telling you, Hadley, getting old is for the birds."

"I think most people would end up in the hospital if they got hit by a truck, regardless of age."

"Nope. There was a day when I would have gotten hit by a truck that size and just dusted myself off and walked away. Now that I'm in my seventies, it's a new hip and traction and 'you shouldn't be riding anymore for your own sake and the safety of everyone else on the island.' Wankers. Have a seat."

I hand her the chocolates and then sit on the chair next to the bed. "I'm sorry about your accident."

Shrugging, she says, "Got the prodigal son home for once, so it's not all bad." She pulls the plastic wrapper off the box. "The liquor sampler. Nice."

"As soon as I saw it, I thought of you."

Minerva gets that mischievous look I remember. "If I were smarter, I'd be offended. Thanks, kiddo." Then she looks around the flower-filled room and rolls her eyes. "Unlike all the other people who thought flowers were a good idea. 'Here, have something you can watch slowly die while you're trapped in a bed for weeks on end.'"

I chuckle. "In that case, I'm glad I didn't choose poorly."

"Speaking of terrible choices, please tell me you're not still with that awful jock, what's his name? Chad? Chet?"

"Chase," I manage before tears cloud my vision and I find myself struggling for words.

Minerva makes a clucking sound, then says, "Sorry, that was offside. Let me guess, you married him and you're absolutely miserable. You've come to me to see if I know people who can take care of him for you." She gestures for me to move toward her and when I do, she nods. "It can be done, but it's not cheap."

"Tempting, but probably not worth the risk," I say, swiping at my wet cheeks. "We just broke up. At least, we will break up when he bothers to return my calls. I found out he's getting married to someone who isn't me."

Shaking her head, she mutters, "Snake."

"Pretty much." A leftover sob from this afternoon's crying jag escapes my throat, and I apologize.

"Now don't tell me this upsets you. You dodged a bullet there, girly. He always was a total dickhead." She offers me a bottle-shaped chocolate, which I happily accept. "When'd you get the good news?"

Glancing at my watch while I sink my front teeth into the bottle neck, I bite the top off, then say, "Three days, twenty hours, forty-six minutes and a few odd seconds ago."

"But who's keeping track?"

"Certainly not me." I lift the tiny bottle in a cheers gesture, then suck back a quarter ounce of mystery liquor. "The best part is I found out from his bride-to-be who I've been teaching dance lessons to for several weeks. She hired me to help her come up with a routine to do at her reception to surprise her fiancé, only it turned out her fiancé has been my boyfriend for over a decade."

"A dance routine? What the hell are you talking about?"

"You know, at the reception. Sometimes brides get their grooms to sit on a chair just off the dance floor and they do a big dance number for them."

She stares at me for a second, then says, "So today's brides need *more* attention than being the centre of attention all day? Now they need to shake their money makers in front of their grandparents?"

I can't help but laugh. "I think it's nice. And it's not like they're stripping or something. It's just something fun to do."

She sucks back the contents of another tiny bottle. "You're only saying that because you get paid to help them make all their guests feel horribly awkward. Now, back to Chase, the bastardly son of a bitch," Minerva says. "Did Dancey Pants know?"

I shake my head. "It was as much of a shock to her as it was for me."

"What a coward," she says, biting the top off the last bottle in the box. "I think we're going to need more booze."

Grinning at her, I lower my voice. "I have a bottle of vodka in my bag."

"Crack it quickly before Nurse Ratched comes to check on me again."

"Oh God, is there really one that mean here?"

"Meh, that's what I call them all," she says with a shrug. "Surprisingly, they don't love that joke."

"You don't say?" I find myself laughing, a real one this time.

———

I am drunk. Like, really, fabulously (but also horribly) drunk. I've been matching Minerva shot-for-shot but that woman can put away *a lot* more alcohol than I can. I've gone from giving her a basic overview of the last decade of my life to sobbing about the fact that Chase is getting married (and so is Lucas, while I'm totally alone) to complaining about my parents. We've just had a case of the giggles that got so loud one of the nurses just walked in to shush us.

"Are you two…drinking?" she asks, pointing at the open bottle of vodka on Minerva's food tray.

"Yes, you want some?" Minerva asks with a proud grin.

"No, I can't have any…I'm on duty. And you shouldn't be drinking either, Mrs. Robinson. You're on pain killers!" She crosses the room and grabs the bottle and the cap. "How much have you had?"

"One," Minerva says.

The nurse purses her lips at her until Minerva says, "It's true. One at a time."

She makes a loud *tsk*ing sound, then turns to me. "Did you bring her this?"

I nod, trying to look gravely serious but failing miserably and snorting out a laugh instead. "Sorry. I know I shouldn't have, but I just found out my boyfriend was cheating on me. I didn't mean to…"

"Didn't mean to what?" she demands.

"I have no idea. What were we talking about?"

Minerva bursts out laughing, which is quickly halted when she winces in pain. The nurse glares at me. "You're going to have to leave. And if you ever want to come back to this hospital, you'll leave your booze stash at home!"

I attempt a salute but end up poking myself in the eye instead. "Shit, that hurt."

"Can you be a dear and take a look at her eye?" Minerva asks her.

Scowling, she spins on her squeaky rubber heel and walks out, letting the door slam against the wall on her way out. The good girl in me would be horrified at myself if her sense of decorum weren't deliciously paralyzed by booze.

"What's up her butt?" Minerva asks.

"A giant stick, obviously." I snort.

"Seriously, who takes someone's booze away?"

"Especially someone who is a cuckold…Wait. Can women be cuckolds?" I ask.

"I think you need a cuck for that."

I snort laugh, then say, "Screw it. I'm a cuckold." My mind wanders back to my current predicament and I let out a long sigh. "Why do men cheat?"

"Lots of reasons—poor impulse control, fear of death, wanting out of a bad relationship but being too chicken to be direct about it…"

"Hmmm…Chase doesn't have poor impulse control, and he's too young to fear death…" I say, realizing that leaves the 'bad relationship' as a possibility. "Any other reasons you can think of that would save my already-battered ego?"

"No, sorry, but I am on some pretty good pain meds," she says.

"And you've been drinking," I tell her.

"That too," Minerva answers. "Listen, just because you were in a bad relationship doesn't mean you're a bad person. Sometimes people just aren't right for each other, but for whatever stupid reason, they try to make it work anyway. In your case, I'd blame your mother."

I bust out laughing, then say, "You may be right about that. Do you know what she said when I told her what happened?"

"That you should make it work?"

"How did you know that?"

"I've known your mum for a lot of years. Appearances are her top priority."

"Tell me something I don't know," I say, letting out a puff of air.

"Yeah, you really lost the parent lotto, didn't you, kiddo? Just think of who you'd be if you had a mother who believed in the real Hadley, and not the version she so badly wanted you to be."

Her words would sting if I weren't numb to my feelings at the moment. "Meh, it's not all her fault. I mean, she can take a share of the blame for teaching me to ignore my instincts and overvalue anyone with a penis, but at the end of the day, it was me in that bad relationship. I just wish I knew why it was bad for him. All I did was dote on him, do whatever he wanted to do, and wait around patiently for him to have time for me. I tried to be the perfect girlfriend —never too demanding, always letting the little things slide..."

"In that case, you weren't a girlfriend, you were a door-mat. And, Hadley, my dear, no man wants to fuck a doormat."

I stare at her for a moment, considering her words with my fuzzy brain. "Oh my God, you're right. Can I ask you something?"

"Sure."

"How is it you know so much about men when as long as I've known you, you've been single?"

"Oh, that's easy, I had a lot of life before you met me.

Forty-some years of trying on men for size and finding they didn't fit," she says.

"Right, that makes sense," I answer. "Who finally caused you to give up?"

"Heath's father. A real turd. We'd been together for four years when I found out I was going to have Heath. He told me he was thrilled and couldn't wait to be a father, that he thought he'd never have the opportunity (he was in his fifties already). So, we started planning a life together, bought a house, he asked me to marry him before the baby came. I said no, of course, because I have my limits," she says. "Then, as soon as I went into labour, he drove me to the hospital and said, 'Yeah, turns out I can't do this.' Left me there on the sidewalk and when I got home the next day, he had cleared out. All his stuff and half of mine was gone. The bastard even took my record player. I still miss that thing. Amazing sound."

I stare at her, trying to digest this awful story. "I'm really sorry that happened to you, Minerva."

"I'm not," she says with a shrug. "If he'd stuck around, Heath would have learned to be a total turd too."

"Definitely for the best then."

"Yup. Just like you not ending up saddled with that Chase moron. It's for the best."

"You know what? You're right. I'm better off without him."

"Obviously."

"In fact, I'm better off without a man, period. Men suck big hairy balls."

"Well, some do, but more of them want us to."

It takes me a few seconds to understand her meaning, then I burst out laughing so hard, I end up on the floor.

When I'm done, Minerva tilts her head over the side of the bed. "Feel better?"

I nod. "Surprisingly, yes. Thank you. I really needed this. I didn't realize how much I've missed you."

"Well, just don't forget about me again," she tells me. "I'm literally the only person in your life who can teach you to stop caring so damn much about what everyone else thinks."

"It's true, you really are," I say, slurring a little. I crawl to get back in my chair but quickly give up and sprawl out on the floor. My mother would have a stroke if she saw me like this. "I forgot I wanted to be you when I grew up. Brave, bold, wild, and free." Pointing in the air, I say, "I do ride a moped like you, but otherwise...I'm a total disappointment to independent women of the world. I hung all my hopes and dreams on a *man*. And now they've been ripped out from under me. Serves me right for being so stupid."

"Oh, now, don't be so hard on yourself," Minerva says. "That's my job."

Shaking my head sloppily, I say, "All the signs were there that he didn't love me. He's been ghosting me for... well, over a year, probably."

"Ghosting? What is that? Like some weird sex thing?"

"No," I say, laughing until tears spring to my eyes. "It means avoiding me."

"So, in a way, your life won't be that different without him."

"Other than believing that soon I'll have a family with the man I thought loved me..."

"Meh, dreams change. And they shouldn't depend on someone else to begin with. People are unreliable wankers."

"Not some people," I say. "Like Heath. He's reliable."

"He is when he bothers to show up," she says. "Which isn't very damn often."

I let out a long sigh. "That settles it then. There are no good men left on the planet. It's you and me 'til the end, Minerva."

"Sounds good, kiddo," she tells me. "We can go out Thelma and Louise-style."

I grin at the memory of watching it with her back when I was in senior year. "Remember when they shoot up that truck and it explodes?"

"Best scene in a movie ever."

I stare up at the ceiling tiles but in my mind I'm imagining myself as Susan Sarandon holding a gun up to that disgusting trucker. I put on a Texas accent and say, "You better apologize."

"For what?" Heath asks, looking down at me.

I scramble to sit up, wobble a little, then claw at the chair in an attempt to stand. "Hey, Heath. I didn't hear you come in."

"I got a call that my mother and her friend were creating a disturbance and that I was to come pick her up immediately," he says, crossing his arms. "I didn't think *you'd* be the friend, however."

"She's just been dumped," Minerva tells him. "By a total coward."

"Istrruue," I slur, giving up on standing in favour of sitting on the chair again. Lifting one finger in the air, I add, "I've decided to swear off men forever so I can be xactly like Minerva here." Leaning toward her, I pet her forehead and nose lazily. "She's my official role model for happiness."

"Okay, well, that's great, but I have to get you out of here before they call security. The nurse called me as a courtesy but she was very clear that we're under a strict deadline." Heath takes my hand, helping me out of the chair, looking thoroughly put out.

He gives his mum a nod. "Good night, Minerva. I'll see you in the morning."

"Good night, Binkie Boo," she says. "And good night to you, my sweet Hadley. Stay strong, girl!"

"Yeah!" I say, raising my fist in the air. "Pirl gower!"

"You mean girl power," Heath says.

"That too."

"Come on. Let's get you home."

13

Not Really a Man...

HEATH

"Twelve years. Can you believe it?" Hadley over-pronounces her words so as not to seem drunk, although I'd say the wobbling is a dead giveaway to the young woman she's been talking to for five minutes now.

We're out in the hospital parking lot which took twenty minutes to get to since Hadley has stopped to tell every person we've come across about her awful ex-boyfriend. It's super awkward for me because they all assume I'm the terrible, spineless 'waste of skin' until Hadley corrects them by telling them I'm 'just an old friend she barely knows anymore.'

"Men are dogs," the woman says.

"Amen, sister!" Hadley goes in for a high five, but the woman doesn't return the gesture so she winds up spinning in a circle due to the momentum. She makes eye contact with me, then stops and points at me. "Except him. We don't hate him..."

Oh, well, that's nice at least.

"...'Cause he's not really a man."

Huh. Not so nice.

I shift impatiently while they finish their conversation and the stranger pumps up Hadley's fragile ego. Finally, I manage to get her to the car. Once we're both buckled in, I pause for a second before starting the engine. "Listen, you need to tell me if you're going to throw up, okay? The rental place charges an extra two hundred for vomit."

"I'm not going to vomit," she says, her head lolling against the seatback. "I'm fine."

"All right, but if you do wind up feeling like you might, say something. Now what's your exact address?"

"Here," she says, digging around in her purse and handing me her license. "Don't laugh at my picture."

An involuntary snort comes out of me at the sight of her surprised face. "Did a scary clown jump out at you when they took the picture?"

"Ha ha. Shut it."

As soon as we're on the road, I open the windows to get some fresh air in the car. Hadley's eyes are closed and the last thing I want is for her to pass out. Well, I suppose that's the second-to-last thing. We ride in silence for a few blocks before I finally decide to say something. "I'm sorry about you and Chase."

Her eyes fly open and her face crumples. Damn. I should not have brought it up. "Thanks," she whispers. "My whole life is over, Heath. Every dream I had was with him. The house, the kids, a dog..."

"You could get a dog without him. And, well, even children, really. Lots of women do it."

She shakes her head. "Nope. I can't afford anything. I live in a yucky basement suite and they won't let me have a pet. Not even a goldfish. I axed them once."

"Maybe that's why they won't let you have a pet," I say with a wry smile.

My comment goes completely over her head and she sighs loudly, then mutters, "Twelve years. Fuuuccckkk. Now what do I do, Heathy?"

Heathy. I forgot she used to call me that sometimes. From anyone else, I'd find it awful, but from her... "I guess you give yourself some time to grieve, then you'll get on with things. Find a new dream."

She shakes her head. "I don't want a new dream. Dreams are scary." Almost immediately, she's asleep, mouth hanging open, light snoring and all.

By the time I pull up in front of her house, she's got drool sliding down her chin. Still cute, though. How is that possible?

I think of the lies I told Fidel earlier this evening about how she has no effect whatsoever on me, but the truth is, I'm drawn to her in a way you only read about in epic romance sagas. The kind that make me want to gag.

I park and pat her on the knee to wake her up. "Hadley, we're here. Wake up, okay?"

She makes a little grunting noise and snuggles into the seat. Sighing, I get out, slamming the driver's side door in hopes of waking her, then walk around to open hers. She's out cold. Perfect.

A few minutes later, I manage to carry her fireman-style into her suite. I flick on the light and see a cozy set up, complete with some plants and lots of wicker for a natural vibe. It's all one space with a tiny kitchenette, an area for her couch and TV, and, off to the left, a bed with too many pillows. What is it with women wanting a hundred pillows on their beds? Why would anyone want to spend that much time arranging them every morning?

I gently put her down on the bed, then remove her

sandals and cover her with a blanket. Hurrying to the bathroom, I get a wastebasket, trying not to notice the bras hanging to dry over the shower curtain rod. When I get back, she's sprawled out on the bed, snoring loudly like a muscle car with no muffler.

How did I end up here looking after someone I used to know? I should be at home sorting out my future (or at least sulking a little). Besides, I'm just someone she 'barely knows anymore.' Only we do know each other. We were best friends for our entire childhood and right through the teenage years. I know she cries when she watches *Miracle on 34th Street* even though she's seen it dozens of times. I know she hates green peppers with everything in her and that she makes a little squealing sound every time she sees a puppy, even if it's a picture in a textbook. I know she lost her virginity to stupid Chase in the back of a limo after the stupid Starry Night Prom. I know she probably still wishes fairies were real and spiders weren't. I also know she'll never see me as anything more than a friend so I should make my exit from her life again right frigging now.

I flick on the light above the stove in case she needs to get up later, then open the door, already looking forward to crawling into my own bed. Yup. I'm out of here. I got her home safely. That's all I needed to do. I'm going to leave her to take it from here. I start work at the resort bright and early tomorrow morning. A good night's sleep is in order so I can bring my A game.

Sigh.

No, I'm not.

Because I'm only going to wind up worrying that she'll get sick and choke to death like Jesse's girlfriend on *Breaking Bad*. I wonder if Hadley watched that series. And if so, did she love it as much as I did? Suddenly, I can picture us cuddled up on her couch repeating, "I'm the one who knocks," then laughing at our lame impressions.

"Shit," I whisper, shutting the door. Taking off my shoes, I walk over to the couch and sit down, putting one of her girly throws over myself. Only, as soon as I close my eyes, my mind starts spinning. The last thing I wanted to do was get sucked into island life again, and yet...here I am, looking after Hadley, taking a job at the resort again, and doing what I tried to do the entire time I was in high school—purge myself of feelings for the woman who is currently murmuring something about someone named Taylor.

If I had to come up with a less-appealing situation, I'd be stumped. Maybe janitor at a men's prison? Yeah, that would be worse I suppose. So at least there's that...

14

Know-It-All Men and the Hungover Women Who Hate Them...

HADLEY

"Hadley, wake up."

Who is that? And how dare he speak to me when I'm about to vanquish this dragon with my bowl of oatmeal?

"Hadley. I have to go," he says again.

"'Kay, great," I answer without opening my eyes. "See you there."

"You need to wake up." Now he's poking me on the shoulder.

I make a little grunting noise and turn over onto my side to get away from the mystery irritation. "No thanks."

"Will you need a ride back to the hospital to get your moped?" he asks loudly. "Because I start my new job today so I have to run."

Okay, I should really find out who the hell is in my home. I open one eye and turn my head just enough to see Heath standing next to my bed. Wait. What is Heath doing here? Am I having a dream within a dream? "Heath? Is that you?"

"Yup."

"And are you really here or are you in my imagination?"

"Unfortunately, I'm really here."

I blink several times while I yank the blanket up around my neck. "Did we...?"

Shaking his head, he says, "I'll give you the recap. You and Minerva got wasted in her hospital room so a nurse called me to pick you up. You passed out pretty much when we got here and I slept on your tiny couch in case you started to asphyxiate on your own vomit."

"Did I?" I ask, my mouth as fuzzy as an econo-bag of cotton balls.

"Thankfully, no," he says. "Look, I really need to get back to my place to shower and change. Do you need a ride to the hospital or not?"

I quickly do the math on how much it would take to Uber it there to get my moped. The answer is way too freaking much to not take him up on his offer. "Can you give me five minutes to get ready?"

"Yup. But no more, okay, so don't get all caught up putting on your face."

I scowl at him. "I don't put my face on. It's right here all the time, you dummy."

"It's an expression," I tell her.

"Yeah, I know. Now, can you please go over to the kitchen and avert your gaze so I can get up?"

"Sure," he says, taking the four steps required to be in the 'other room.' He stands facing the window while I force myself out of bed and quickly start opening and closing drawers in search of a cute outfit.

"No peeking, right?" I tell him, feeling slightly

panicked at the thought of him seeing me in my…wait, I'm still in my clothes from yesterday.

"Why is it we keep ending up in these situations? With you changing while accusing me of wanting to watch you…"

"Don't take it personally. I'd say it to any guy."

"Is that because you've sworn off men for life and are going all 'ride or die' with my septuagenarian mother from now on?" he asks.

I pause for a moment, a memory of that conversation coming back to me. "Yup," I answer in a firm tone. "I'm done with men forever."

He snorts out a laugh, and not a particularly friendly one at that.

"What?" I ask, finally selecting a grey tee to go with my jean shorts.

"It's just that you've never been alone in your life," he answers.

Never been alone? Well, that's rude. "How do you know? You've been gone for a zillion years."

"It's just over ten and I know because last night you told everyone with a pulse at the hospital that you've been with what's-his-face since you were sixteen."

I scowl at his back even though he's right about both things.

"Well, that was the *old* me," I say, hurrying toward the bathroom to get dressed. "The new me is fiercely independent."

Just before I close the door, I add, "But, I really do need a ride so please don't leave without me."

By the time we're in Heath's car, I'm in a foul mood. I'm hungover, badly in need of more sleep, and am frankly more than a little perturbed by Heath finding it laughable that I plan to be alone. I risk a glance at him, still finding it a bit of a shock at how handsome he is. He was always a cute boy with eyelashes so thick they were the envy of every girl in school, but he was a boy. Even when he boarded that plane right after high school. We were all kids, but Heath, more than others.

Now...now he's gone and got all good-looking and gets to have a front row seat to my worst nightmare. I'm suddenly irritated by the fact that he's turned into a hottie. How dare he do that while I've been busy 'letting myself go?'

Chase's face pops into my mind to torture me, and my stomach lurches at the fact that I've been replaced. And that the love of my life couldn't be bothered to tell me. Nothing has ever hurt this much and I suddenly feel like I have to gasp to get enough air. Unrolling the window, I let the warm ocean breeze fill my lungs while we zip past a long stretch of beach toward the hospital. Neither of us says anything for the longest time, then finally, Heath speaks up. "I am sorry about you and Chase. Not that he ever deserved you, but I'm sure it must hurt. Especially, the way he handled things."

"Or didn't handle them," I say, my head pounding and my stomach churning. Is it from the vodka or my new reality? Probably both, I suppose.

"That too," he says, as we pull into the parking lot.

"I'm sure you must feel a sense of redemption," I tell him, even though I know I shouldn't.

"Why exactly?" he asks, parking next to my moped.

"You were never exactly a Chase fan."

"Is it any wonder why?" he asks, giving me a pointed look.

I always hated when he looked at me that way—with a cross between pity and disgust. "Must be nice to know everything."

"It is," he says without a trace of irony.

"How's *your* love life been?" I ask, suddenly remembering something Minerva said last night about him never having had a serious girlfriend.

"What?" His face turns slightly red.

"Must be amazing since you do know everything about everything." Now, I'm being a bit nasty, but I don't really care. I'm being judged as too stupid to live for loving the wrong guy.

"My life is exactly how I want it, thanks."

I stare at him for a moment, unable to tell what he's thinking. There's hurt in his eyes but he's doing his damnedest to bury it deep.

Gathering my backpack, I say, "Okay, well, thanks for the ride and for looking after me last night. I'm sorry I made you do that."

"You're welcome," Heath says with a little nod.

"Have a great life, if I don't see you before you skip town again."

"Don't tell me you're joining Minerva's guilt campaign," he says dryly.

"You really should spend more time with her. You're all she's got." There. Two can play the advice game.

"She's got you now too, Thelma. Or are you Louise?" he asks with an amused smile.

Opening the car door, I say, "Who I am is none of your business since I probably won't see you again until Minerva's funeral."

"She's going to outlive us all," he says. "And there's a good chance I'll see you sooner than you think."

"Doubt it."

"I don't."

"Were you always this much of a know-it-all?" I ask him, stepping out of the car.

"Pretty much. Enjoy your day."

"You too, and thanks for the ride!" I bark, slamming his car door, then spinning in my Keds.

I stalk over to my moped, furious at Heath. And Chase. And men in general. They can all suck it.

15

Angry Salsa Dancing

HEATH

Exactly an hour later, I'm driving down the long palm-lined road that leads to the Paradise Bay Resort. I should be in a good mood because I'm going to see Harrison Banks, an old friend. Plus, working will provide a welcome distraction from thinking about Ms. Hadley 'I Hate Men' Jones. Talk about ungrateful. I take her home, sleep on her couch in case she needs me, and give her a lift this morning, and all I get is crap. I'm honestly confused about how we were ever so close.

I pull into the employee parking stall, then take a moment to collect myself before getting out of the rental. I'm in a dress shirt and slacks, no tie because this isn't that type of resort. The walk to the open-air lobby that also houses a set of offices is a pleasant one—only the sounds of the palm trees swaying and the calls of the birds in the jungle nearby. I can't help but compare it to the cold crowded sidewalks of Manhattan where you better not stop moving or someone will knock into you, likely spilling their coffee on you. It's probably drizzling there today with that awful wet cold that goes right through to your bones. I never have gotten used to it, to be honest. It's something I just put up with, not something I'll ever enjoy.

When I get to the steps of the lobby, I see Emma Banks hurrying along in front of the building. She's wearing a chef's uniform, but other than that looks exactly the same as she did in high school, complete with a low ponytail swinging behind her as she strides along. She does a double take when she sees me, then yells, "Heath? Heath Robinson?"

Grinning, I say, "Hi Emma," as we both hurry over to each other. I went to school with her brother, Will, who is now a raving success as a nature documentarian/survivor man (and incidentally just married a member of the Avonian royal family). Emma's a year older than us and is now married to a wildly successful author, Pierce Davenport (of *Clash of Crowns* fame).

"You're still working?" I ask her. "I thought you'd be happily laying poolside while your husband creates his next horrifying masterpiece."

"Are you kidding? I'm never going to retire. Not when I can boss dozens of people around every day," Emma says with a grin. "I heard about Minerva. How is she?"

"She's giving the nurses a run for their money," I tell her.

"She would. Now, where are you heading? I'll walk you."

"Just to the back offices," I tell her. "Fidel roped me into a temporary position in the accounts department."

Looping her arm through mine, she says, "Thank God, because Harrison and Libby are in way over their heads with the new baby. I'll take you to him right now."

"Are you sure?" I ask. "You looked like you were in a hurry."

"There's always time for an old friend. Plus, I'm the boss so if I'm a few minutes late, I'm the only one who will yell at me, and I'm not scared of me so it's all good."

When we get to Harrison's office, she knocks, then opens the door without waiting for an answer.

Harrison, who is sitting at his desk and talking on the phone, gives her a dirty look, then sees me and smiles, waving us in. "No, I know. It's very painful." Pause. "No, obviously I don't *know* what it's like to have cracked nipples, sweetie. That's not what I meant." Long pause with him wincing. "Okay. I'll be there as soon as I can. In fact, our new accountant just walked in the door and he's a real ace so I should be able to spend a lot more time at home starting this afternoon." Pause. "Yup. I haven't forgotten. Okay. See you in a bit."

He hangs up and stands to greet me, letting out a long sigh. "Am I ever glad to see you."

———

So as far as boring accounting jobs go, a guy could do a lot worse. Employees eat free, and the work uses just enough of my brain to keep it from atrophying without having enough stress to increase my blood pressure. My office overlooks a lovely garden, which I have to admit is a vast improvement over my old view of the office building adjacent to ours (and the middle-aged couple who were carrying on a not-so-discreet affair without ever closing the blinds. It took Harrison three hours to explain my duties to me and show me their accounting system, then another hour for me to get all the login codes from the surly IT guy.

At one o'clock, I decide to walk over to the poolside burger bar for some lunch. On my way, I catch sight of Hadley who is dressed in a tank top and a sarong. She's mic'd up and is leading a small group of guests through the salsa. There's one young couple and the rest are all seniors, and even though the music is happy, she clearly is not.

As I wait for my burger to be prepared, I can't help but witness her spectacularly bad conduct.

"I'm supposed to ask if you're here celebrating anything special," she says, her tone devoid of emotion.

"We're on our honeymoon," the young man says.

Giving him a dirty look, she says, "Oh, are you? Congratulations."

Oh shit. That was some heavy sarcasm.

"I was supposed to be engaged too, but it turns out my jackass boyfriend was busy proposing to someone else. And one, two, three, four!" She calls out the beat while moving her hips to the music. Shakira was wrong. The hips *can* lie.

"How about the rest of you?" she barks. "Anyone else here having an anniversary? How about you two?" She points to the oldest looking couple. They nod and must say something about celebrating an anniversary because she says, "Happy fortieth! How many infidelities did you have to overlook in your years together?"

They stop moving their feet in protest, and I'm pretty sure they're both denying there's been any cheating at all. But clearly, Hadley's not having it because she says, "Soul mates?! Pffft! Come on. Pick up your feet, grandpa! Nobody ever learned the salsa by standing still."

The old man starts to move again, but this time with much, *much* less enthusiasm.

A bell at the counter dings and I turn to see that my burger is ready. Grabbing a couple of napkins, I take my plate and Coke and go find a table in the shade where I can keep an eye on Hadley. I'm just into my third juicy bite when I hear Hadley shout, "Okay, everyone, let's try it again, only this time pretend you're dancing with someone you like and respect, instead of the person you're married to!" Then she laughs like a crazy person, which, at this moment, she just may be.

It's at this point that the class disperses, and Hadley's left alone on the pool deck with the music still blaring. Shrugging, she does the salsa on her own, her body moving like it's a baggie of Jell-O in a hurricane. Her eyes are closed and she's giving it everything she's got. I'm not sure if I should be happy for her because she clearly doesn't care what anyone thinks, or worry for her mental wellbeing. Maybe both? I continue to eat, my eyes trained on her, my entire body starting to react to watching her move like that. It's an all-too-familiar feeling for me, which makes me realize I'd be better off walking to the far side of the resort to get lunch from now on. When the song ends, she shuts off the music, removes her mic, and starts to gather her things. Her eyes land on me and immediately, her shoulders drop. "Seriously?"

Giving her a small wave, I swallow the last bite as she walks over to me.

"Told you I'd see you again soon."

"What are you doing here?" she asks, folding her arms across her chest.

"Having lunch."

"Yeah, I see that. But what are you doing at the resort?"

"I work here now," I tell her.

She blinks a few times, then says, "Really?"

"Uh-huh."

"You work here."

"Yes, I'm helping out in the accounts office for a while.

Harrison needs a hand and there's not much I can do for my mum until she's out of the hospital."

"Well, that's just perfect," Hadley says, mouth curling like she just ate some rotten prawns.

"Yeah, it kind of is. I can help some old friends, make a little cash, and keep busy. Why? Are you not happy to see me here?" I ask, playing dumb.

"Obviously not. Not after this morning."

"You mean when you were super ungrateful about me getting you home safely, staying the night to look after you, and taking you to pick up your moped?"

"That is how you'd see it."

I stand and pick up my paper plate and empty can, then walk over to the garbage. Hadley follows me. "You don't know everything, you know."

"I'm confused. How could I not know everything I know?" Okay, so I knew what she meant, but she's being rude so I've decided to return the favour.

"That's not what I meant. I meant you don't know everything."

"*That* I do know," I say, stuffing my hands in my front pockets and starting back toward the lobby. "I better get back to work. Lots to do. Enjoy your afternoon."

"Look, there's another burger bar on the other side of the resort. Would you mind going to eat your lunches there from now on?" she asks.

Even though I'm already planning to do that, I'm not going to let her in on that fact. "Why? You don't want me to see you yelling at people for being happily married?"

Her entire face turns red and she blinks back tears.

Great. Now I feel like shit. "I'm sorry," I tell her. "That was offside."

"No, I deserved it. I was awful to those poor people,"

she says with a sigh. "I should go home. I don't think I'm capable of being fun today."

Just then, Rosy Brown, one of the head administrators at the resort for the last million years, walks up. In a low voice, she says, "Hadley, hon, can I talk to you for a few minutes?"

Hadley nods and follows her to the lobby, while I slow my pace so as not to seem like I'm trying to eavesdrop. I do, however, manage to hear Hadley say, "Did someone complain about me?"

"Yeah, an older couple said you accused the husband of cheating..."

Their voices fade as they continue on, and I can't help but feel sorry for Hadley. She shouldn't have said what she did, but she also shouldn't have had a lying scumbag for a boyfriend. And I shouldn't have been acting like a judgmental prick today, either. If I were to be really honest, I'd say I was trying not to care that she's going through a rough time. Because caring for Hadley has never worked out well for me in the past...

16

Deep Fried Reinforcements

HADLEY

"I brought a family-sized container of fries and gravy along with two large bags of fresh mini-donuts sprinkled with cinnamon in case you're still in the binge-eating phase of your break-up. Or we can forget about those because I also picked up terrible kale smoothies in case you're in the 'Getting in Revenge Shape' phase already." Nora holds up a large brown bag in one hand and a cardboard drink tray with two huge cups of green sludge in the other.

"You're a good friend," I tell her, taking the brown bag.

She follows me inside and we start to dish up. "What'd you end up bringing home from the big island?" I ask, not wanting to talk about Chase at the moment.

"The tuna, the lunch box, a block of some sort of unidentified cheese, and a necklace she picked up at a market with a 'lovely leaf because you love nature so much' on it," she says, putting on a grandma voice.

"It is a marijuana leaf?"

"Yeah, and she insisted I wear it home too, so airport security was extra thorough with me," Nora says, free-pouring gravy onto both our plates.

"Your grandma is the best," I tell her.

"She really is. But speaking of humans who are at the opposite end of the quality spectrum, have you heard anything from Chases Women yet?"

"Not a word," I say, popping a hot, salty fry in my mouth.

"Cowardly bastard."

"Right? How was I ever in love with him?" I ask, my words muffled by food.

"Honestly," Nora says, glancing up at the ceiling, "I think it had a lot to do with his abs. They had you under some sort of wicked spell because I've always thought he was a total shitbag. On the flight home, I was thinking about the whole thing, and I realized he's been trying to get you to break up with him."

I freeze, all the pieces falling into place at once. "Oh my God, you're right."

"He even *told* you to dump him."

The truth makes me feel like my entire body is going to be sucked into the linoleum under my feet. "Shit. How did I miss all the signs? How?! I must be the stupidest person on the planet."

"You're not stupid. You're just...very trusting," she says, dipping a fry into the gravy.

"Same damn thing." I pop a donut into my mouth and let it melt on my tongue a little before I add, "That's it. From now on I trust no one—present company excluded."

"No way! *You* don't have to change anything. *He* should be the one reflecting on how he lives his life. Not you."

"Uh-uh, I *do* have to change, Nora. I can't just blindly trust a man ever again. Not after...this." I shovel two more donuts in this time and chew them as quickly as possible given how full my mouth is. "Twelve years."

Shaking her head, Nora says, "Twelve freaking years. And this is how it ends. He steals your perfect wedding plans and passes them off as his own. That bit makes me extra furious."

"Same here. It's like cheating on your marriage exam or something. And he's tainted the entire plan for me now because even if I did find a man who isn't total scum, and somehow I decided to give relationships another try, in like thirty years or so, I could never enjoy it because he stole it."

"I *suppose*, but it's not like he's going to use it, right?" she asks, grabbing a donut. "I mean, surely this Taylor person isn't going to go through with it."

"I don't know," I say, shaking my head. "She was pretty determined to believe he and I broke up a long time ago."

"Wow. Just wow."

"Yeah, and I haven't even told you about what happened at work today…" I let out a long sigh.

"What?"

I close my eyes for a second, then tell her about how I chewed out some of the guests for being happy, and how Rosy had to come down on me in front of two of them because they threatened to write a terrible review on Trip-Advisor. "She totally didn't want to do it, and in fact, she told me as much before we got back to her office where they were waiting, but then, she really did it."

"Oh, so the work version of 'this'll hurt me more than it hurts you.'"

"So humiliating." I close my eyes in an attempt to shut out the memory. "I started to cry, then I ended up telling them what happened and then they felt bad and started apologizing to me—they're Canadian—then they offered for me to come stay with them in Newfoundland for a while until I get my feet under me again. Apparently, they have a very nice grandson who would be perfect for me. Urgh, it was a whole thing." Flopping my head down, I rest my forehead on the painted wood. "Shit."

Nora rubs my back and says, "I know, Hads. I know. It feels awful right now, but I promise it'll get better."

"I doubt it, but thanks anyway." I groan, then add, "And the stupid engagement party is tomorrow and my mom still thinks I can salvage things with Chase and I know she's going to push me *hard* every chance she gets to go 'patch things up with my man.'"

"Maybe don't go to the party," she suggests. "You could tell Lucas the truth, he'll understand."

Sitting up, I sigh. "I can't do that to him. Besides, it'll make me look like a bitter old spinster if I don't go. Which is essentially what I am."

"You are not. You're young and beautiful and...and carefree. And on the plus side, now you can join me in the fabulous world of dating," Nora says enthusiastically. "I can't wait to help you—when you're ready, of course. No rush. Things have changed a lot out there since you were on the market. There are hookup apps and apps for real relationships. Well, those are really just women who want relationships finding men who pretend *they* want relationships so they can hook up so forget I said anything about the apps."

Giving her a deadpan expression, I say, "And that's why I'm done with men forever."

"Are you switching teams?"

"Sure, if there's a team for people who want to sit on the bench for the rest of their lives, I'll join that one."

A knock at the door startles both of us, and I get up to answer it.

"I hope that's Chase," Nora says, "Because if it is, I'm giving him some vanilla nut taps."

"Vanilla nut taps?" I ask.

"Two hard taps to his nuts."

I burst out laughing and shake my head as I pull the door open. The sight of Heath causes my smile to fade. Before I get a chance to say anything, he says, "I wanted to apologize for being so hard on you earlier. I would have called but I don't have your number."

"You don't have to. Besides, I wasn't exactly Polly Sunshine today."

"Who would expect you to be? Of course you're upset and I shouldn't have piled on like that. It was unfair of me." He glances down at his Vans then back up at me. "You okay?"

God, he's cute. Too bad I hate men now. I nod, then say, "Nora's here and she brought deep-fried reinforcements."

"Oh, brilliant," he says, even though he looks slightly disappointed. "You're in good hands then. I'll leave you to it."

"No, come on in," I tell him, stepping aside.

He walks in and he and Nora exchange quick hugs while I grab a stool from the closet so he can sit with us at the table.

"Wow, that *is* a lot of fried food. Not that I'm judging," Heath says, settling himself on the stool. "I've just never attended a post-breakup...what is this called? Event? Session?"

"Post break-up revenge plotting," Nora offers.

He nods. "Come up with anything yet?"

"No," I tell him. "Anything come to mind?"

"Well, that all depends," Heath says, helping himself to a fry. "If he ends up going through with the wedding, there's the old Visine in his drink trick. That'd ruin the wedding night."

I groan at the thought of him having a wedding night, and immediately, Heath says, "Sorry. I shouldn't have brought that up."

"It's okay, you're new at this," Nora tells him. "You'll get better." Then she snaps her fingers. "I know. We find out where they're registered, tell them we're wedding planners, and change up everything on their list. We could order them like fifty sets of really ugly towels and no dishes."

Heath and I just stare at her for a second, then she says, "That sounded more evil in my head."

Heath swallows and says, "Now this might be totally crazy, but hear me out. Have you thought of going 'the life well-lived' route?"

"If you're not going to try, you might as well leave," I tell him.

"So, no high road. Got it."

We spend the next half hour coming up with ways to get revenge on Heath, all of them terrible, but we wind up laughing so hard, I'm in tears by the end of it (good ones for once) and at least I know fun and friends will be part of my life again.

"I should go see my mum," Heath says. "I didn't really mean to stay. I just wanted to check on you."

"Thanks," I tell him. "I appreciate it."

"Let me know if there's anything I can do, okay?" he says, standing up.

I'm about to say I will when Nora cuts in with, "She needs a date tomorrow for her brother's engagement party. Otherwise her mum is going to make her life hell trying to convince her to find Chase and beg him to take her back."

My face flames with what? Embarrassment? Hope? I

can't tell. "Oh, no…I couldn't…you do *not* want to come to that. All my awful relatives suggesting we're an item and comparing you to Chase, because you know that's going to happen. The awkwardness, the speeches…it'll basically be your worst nightmare."

He opens his mouth and I'm suddenly terrified he's going to say no. Why I care, I have no idea, since I've taken the oath of celibacy and all. I quickly add, "Also, I'm not dating again, ever and you're a man, ergo the enemy—no offense, it's guilt by association on account of the Y-chromosome and not personal in any way."

"I'll go," he says with a smile.

Did he just say that? "Really?"

"Definitely. It's the least I can do after being such a shit earlier. Besides, we're friends, right?"

"Yeah." I nod. "We are, which is why I can't let you go with me. It's going to be just terrible."

Shrugging, he says, "I'll be fine. I already know your entire family."

"For God's sake, Hads, let him go," Nora says. "It's the perfect plan. Everyone will be so focused on Heath, they'll forget all about Dumpster Fire."

"Is that what we're calling Chase, or Hadley's love life?" Heath asks Nora.

"I meant Chase, but…" she says, tilting her head from side-to-side as if she's considering.

"Oh nice," I say, picking up three fries and jamming them into my mouth.

"Too soon?" Heath asks.

"Uh, yeah," I answer with a full mouth.

"Okay, well, I should go, but what time should I pick you up tomorrow?" he asks.

"It starts at eight," I tell him.

"How about I swing by at six thirty and we grab a bite

first? Surprisingly enough, I can't get a good conch salad anywhere in New York," he says, then quickly adds, "Not a date, but a bite of dinner as two old friends who understand that you are never dating a man again so long as you live."

"In that case, sure."

"Perfect. I'm looking forward to it, especially if you're wearing that dress from Apple Blossoms," he answers with a small grin.

I close my eyes, trying to rid myself of the memory of me stuck in that dress. "I shall not be wearing that."

"Too bad. It would make quite the statement with your arms flailing above your head while you flash all your mum's stuffy friends," he says.

I chuckle, then smack him on the arm. "Jerk."

Then we exchange a long smile and suddenly, we're back to being who we were when we were kids. He's so familiar to me, like the comfort of an old sweatshirt, and I know deep in my bones it's exactly what I need right now.

When he leaves and I turn back to Nora, she's giving me a meaningful look.

"What?" I ask, rolling my eyes.

"Oh nothing," she says. "Except I have a pretty good feeling you're not going to stay on the bench too long because that exchange totally said you're ready to get back in the game soon."

"Pffft, no." I tell her. "No way. Heath is like a brother to me."

"Umhm. You've got a real brother, and if I'm not mistaken, I've never heard you go on and on about how hot Lucas is."

"Ewww! Gross!"

"Exactly."

———

Text from Me to Nora: How about this dress?

I'm standing in the change room at Magnolia Boutique. (Definitely not in my budget, but hey, I need a massive ego-lift so going for a designer dress is just the thing. Also, for some reason, having a 'date' for the party makes me want to put in that extra effort.) I stare at myself in the mirror while I wait for a reply, but I already know this is the one. It's a turquoise halter dress with a flowy skirt that comes down just below my knees. The colour gives my skin a deep glow and brightens my dark eyes. I twirl around, then I look up at my face in the mirror. I'm smiling. A real smile. Who knew that was buried in there?

Nora: Yas Queen.

17

This is Not a Date

HEATH

"They aren't going to take the cast off just because you threaten to die of boredom," I tell my mum, who has been trying to convince me to sweet talk the head nurse into springing her a month early.

"But I'm sure I'm fine by now. I have those fast-healing bones. It's a genetic thing."

"That's not a thing."

She glares at me. "You're only saying that because you didn't inherit my superpower."

Letting out a long sigh, I say, "Fine, I'll tell them you'd like an x-ray because you're positive you're all healed up."

"No! No x-rays!" Minerva shouts.

"Why ever not, Mum?"

"Because they'll just fake that I'm still injured so they can keep bilking the taxpayers for my medical expenses."

"I feel very confident that the hospital has no need to drum up business. Besides, you've been such a pain in the arse to everyone here, they'll happily spring you the second you're able to leave."

"Okay, you may have a point there," Minerva says with a little nod.

"I know I do. Now, is there anything else I can do for you before I leave? I'm going out tonight so I need to shower and get ready."

"You got a hot date?" she asks with a grin.

"Nope. Just going for dinner and to a party with an old friend," I tell her, doing my best not to let out a smile.

"Hadley Jones, right?"

"How did you know that?"

"You always get that goofy look when you talk about her."

"I do *not* get a look," I say, feeling a bit irked that she knows me so well.

"Sure you do. You always have, in fact. It's like the mention of her name makes you want to smile but you're forcing yourself not to because you don't want anyone to know you *like* like her. The end result is you look like you did when you were a toddler and you needed to make a poo."

"Oh my God. I *like* like her? What is this? Middle school?" I ask.

"No, it's worse because you're a grown ass man who's too afraid to admit you have feelings for someone," Minerva says, shaking her head. "Honestly Heath, it's getting a bit pathetic. You're nearly thirty."

"Thanks. So glad I stopped by," I tell her, leaning over and giving her a kiss. "I'll see you tomorrow. Try not to piss anyone off this evening."

"What would be the fun in that?" she asks, and I'm reasonably sure that for her, it's an honest question.

"See you, Mum."

"Tell your date hello from me."

"She's not—okay, fine. Bye."

———

"Wow, you look…amazing," I tell Hadley. And she really does. She's got her wild hair pinned up into some sort of messy-yet-formal sort of do, she's in a dress that's the colour of the Caribbean on a calm day, and her makeup is light but somehow highlights her best features (which is pretty much her entire face, to be honest).

"Thanks. You look good too," she says, tucking her handbag under her arm and stepping outside. "Thanks so much for doing this. I'm not sure I would have gone if I didn't have you going with me."

"I'm happy to help," I say.

I walk behind her down the sidewalk to my car and can't help but inhale the scent of her. That is some lovely perfume she's wearing. It's filled with the promise of a summer morning. Hurrying around her, I open the passenger door and hold it while she gets in. Then I close it like I would if this were a real date, which it definitely isn't. I remind myself of that fact while I walk around to the driver's side. This is not a date. We are not now, nor ever will be dating. We are just friends and that has to be good enough. Period.

I start up the engine, then smile at her. "Ready to go?"

"Uh-huh."

"Have I mentioned how pretty you look?"

"You have."

"Well, it's true. Chase is a moron to let you get away."

Dammit. I shouldn't have brought him up. Now she's staring out the window. "The funny thing is, he hasn't let me get away. Technically, we still haven't broken up yet."

"Are you kidding me?"

She shakes her head. "Nope. He hasn't returned my calls or texts so I guess it's sort of like the equivalent of when someone disappears but they never find the body. After a few years, we can declare the relationship dead but..."

"A few years? No way. We need to fix that immediately," I say, pulling out onto the road.

"How exactly? Should I fly to New York, hunt him down, and dump him?"

"I'd bet a thousand dollars he's back on the island," I say, turning off her street onto the main road.

She pauses for a second, then says, "To fix things with Taylor."

"Yup," I answer. "What do you say? Should we swing by his place so you can officially dump his sorry arse?"

She swallows hard, then lets out a tiny smile. "I do look pretty great."

"You do. Highly..." I let my voice trail off before I use the word fuckable, because a) crass, and b) not what you tell a buddy.

"Highly what?" she asks, knowing exactly what I was going to say.

"Highly dressed."

Hadley bursts out laughing. "That doesn't even make sense. You were going to say fuckable, weren't you?"

"Nope," I tell her, keeping my eyes on the road. "I've never heard that term before. Is that something people say?"

She swats my arm. "Liar."

"So, are we going or what?" I ask her, glancing over at her. "It's your chance to find the corpse."

"Or create one..." she mutters.

"Not worth it."

Five minutes later, we pull up in front of the Williams' residence. I stop and take the key out of the ignition, then turn to her. "You ready to do this?"

"No," she whispers. Then finding her voice, she says, "What if I cry?"

"Then you cry. He deserves to see what he's done."

"I'd prefer if he sees what he's missing out on."

"Then don't cry."

"Okay," she says, opening the door and getting out. "You know what?" she asks, leaning back into the car. "I might just give him some vanilla nut taps."

"What?"

"Nothing," she says with a devious grin.

I wait until she's halfway up the sidewalk to unroll the window and say, "Give him hell, Hadley. I'll be right here waiting for you."

She lets a fist pump go without turning back, and I watch, my heart in my throat as she strides purposefully up the steps to their massive house.

18

You Can Lead a Horse to Water...

HADLEY

I force myself to ring the bell without hesitation. Hesitation will kill you in a situation like this. But also deadly? Going in completely unrehearsed.

Shit. I have no idea what—

The door swings open and Mr. Williams stands before me in his polo shirt and khakis which means he just got back from golfing. He narrows his eyes in confusion then says, "Can I help you?"

Nice. He doesn't remember me. "I'm Hadley, I dated your son for twelve years."

He snaps his fingers, his face showing no signs of the embarrassment he should feel. "Right. Of course you are. Come in, Hadley." Stepping aside, he adds, "Sorry I didn't recognize you at first. I don't think I've ever seen you with your hair up."

He has. Dozens of times. "Is Chase here?"

"Yup, he's out back by the pool," he says. "I'd take you

but I just got home from golfing and I need to shower before dinner."

"I know the way." I start in that direction, my heels clacking away on their marble floors.

My heart pounds so hard in my chest, I feel like it might just make a break for it, and by the time I open the French doors leading to the backyard, I'm sure my throat is going to close up completely and I'll die before I can say anything.

Totally let herself go.

Old.

Nope. Young. Strong and relatively good-looking, especially in this dress.

There he is, sitting at one of the many round tables on the far side of the pool. Taylor's with him and they look like they're deep into a conversation that I know he'd rather not be having. Neither of them notices me as I make my way over to them. That's what it's like for the rich— they're so used to having servants, they don't have to bother to acknowledge real humans who are approaching them.

"But, babe, for real, *you're* the only one I've ever loved," he whines.

His words are like sand in your butt crack, but then I decide to take a brief second to enjoy the sight of him groveling before I find my voice.

"I disagree," I say. "The only one he's ever loved is himself."

Chase glances at me, does a double take, then settles on an appropriate amount of terror as he stares at me. Mouth open, eyes wide. That's right, Chase. Go ahead and poo your pants because I'm here now and I'm not going to make this easy for you.

"Hadley, what are you doing here?" he asks.

"You wouldn't return my calls so I thought the right thing to do would be to come and dump your sorry arse in person," I say, stealing Heath's line. Glancing at Taylor, I say, "Hi, Taylor. You doing okay?"

She shakes her head, tears filling her eyes. "Not really."

"It's hard when the man you thought loved you turns out to be a narcissistic coward."

"Okay, that may feel fair to you so I'm going to let you have that one, but to be honest, now's not really a good time," Chase tells me, narrowing his eyes at me.

"Oh really? I'm sorry," I say putting on a sweet smile. "Should I come back later? Would that make you more comfortable?"

Tilting his head, he says, "I feel like you don't really mean that."

"What would make you think that?" I ask, letting my face spread into a crazy-eyed Joker grin.

Chase sighs and says, "Look, Hadley, you had to know it was over for a long time. If you didn't, you were just fooling yourself. We haven't seen each other in months."

"That's because you've been in Chicago the entire time, working so very hard for our future, remember?" I ask. "At least that's what you told me before we had phone sex last month."

"You had phone sex with her?!" Taylor demands.

"He sure did," I say, then I wait for her to slap him across the face, link arms with me, and we'll both walk out of here together, heads held high. Two independent women ready to start our lives. Oh, this is going to be delicious.

"Babe, come on. It meant nothing. I felt sorry for her," he tells Taylor.

"You *felt sorry* for me?" I ask, leaning in toward him.

"So sorry you had phone sex with me instead of telling me you were getting married?!"

"This is all a big misunderstanding," he says smoothly. "Who's to say who was with who when? Time isn't some linear thing. The important thing, Tay, is that I'm totally in love with you and I'm ready to start our life together. I'd marry you right this minute if you'd have me."

Oh, daggers! Straight to my chest. I let fury force them to bounce off me.

"Well, too damn bad, because you're caught, jackass," I say, pointing at him. "And there's no way she's going to marry you now!"

I hold my hand out to Taylor. "Come on. Let's get out of here. He doesn't deserve either of us."

She glances at me, then back at Chase. Seriously? This is a hard choice for her?

"Don't leave me, Taylor," he says, suddenly launching himself from his chair and onto his knees in front of her. "I can't live without you. I know I should have broken it off with her sooner, but I'm just too kindhearted to do it. I've been trying to get her to dump me instead, but she just wouldn't."

"You have?" she asks.

Oh for...

He nods, looking like he's going to break into sobs. Or song. Or maybe both. "I stand her up with no notice, like, *all the time*. And I even told her to break up with me the last time we spoke."

Turning to me, Taylor asks, "Is that true?"

"Yes, but does that really make it better? He treated me like garbage. Just tossed me aside and left me waiting for him to come back and start a life with me. Who does that to another human being?" I ask her. Then, turning to him, I add, "An awful, cowardly, horrible person, that's who.

Someone who doesn't deserve to have love because he abuses it without reservation." I look back at her again. "He's been cheating on both of us. And once a cheater, always a CHEATER!" I shout the last word, right into his stupid face.

He winces, then turns back to Taylor. "I'd never cheat on you, babe. I'd rather have the gardener yank my toenails out with dirty pliers."

"EWW!" (That's coming from both Taylor and me.)

He ignores us and continues begging. "You're it for me. I made a huge mistake but let's not let it ruin our future. I'm in love with you and I'll never stop."

Are you kidding me? I came here—looking this fabulous—only to be a side character in their fight? "You're not going to fall for this, are you?" I ask her. "Please tell me you're smarter than this. Don't end up like me, Taylor."

She doesn't look at me but just keeps staring at him. "I love you too, but I don't think I can trust you ever again."

"You're exactly right," I tell her. "Because he is not someone you can trust. No way. Nuh uh. Never. NEVER."

"Tay, you're my sweetness, you're my sun and moon. You're all that matters. I'll do anything. I'll walk the earth if that would change your mind. Even the desert parts with no water. I'll walk until I drop dead from dehydration if that's what it takes."

Ha! That was pure idiocy. There's no way anyone would fall for that. Except now, her face morphs into a doe-eyed lovey-dovey expression. Leaning down, I block him from her view. "Say no, Taylor. Kick him to the curb and find a man who deserves you. He's not worth another minute of your time."

She gives me a sad look and nods. "I can't. I just love him too much."

"What?! How can you—?"

"Because the pain of this is so...painful, it must be real love," she says, gazing back at him.

"Love's not supposed to hurt, you dingus," I tell her. Somehow my entire goal has shifted from telling Chase off to making Taylor come to her senses. I don't even care about hurting him anymore. I just want to save her. "He's a cheater and a chronic liar. And...and just look at how he's treating me right now? After twelve years, I'm not even an afterthought. He moved on and didn't have the courtesy to tell me. He stole all my wedding plans and passed them off as his own. Who does that? An asshole, that's who!" I yell.

His shoulders drop and he says, "She's right. I don't deserve you, Tay. You should just dump me too. Find a better man."

"Yes, Taylor. I'm sure it's the only thing I'll ever agree with him on. You should definitely end it," I say.

She tilts her head and tears spring to her eyes. "Oh babe, don't say that. You can be my better man."

Seriously?

She launches herself into his arms and now the two of them are kissing passionately, while I look on.

"No, no, no!" I say, prying them apart with my hands on their foreheads.

There is no dignity in what I'm doing but I don't even care. This cannot happen. He does *not* get his happily ever after after making me swear off men for life. He has to be miserable too. I push him onto the stone patio and her back into her chair. "That's enough. Do not kiss him!" I tell her, leaning toward her. "He's a total asshat. You can do better."

"But I don't want to," she says to me.

I let out a disgusted sigh, knowing there's no use. "Fine. Have him then. I'll go." Turning to Chase, I say, "But I want to say a few words to you before I go."

He rises to his feet and looks at me. "What is it, Hadley?"

"This," I say, then reach down and give him a double rap on his nuts like I'm knocking on a heavy door.

He crumples to the ground, rolling around and moaning in pain while I wipe my hands together, spin on my fancy heels, and stride back to the house. "Vanilla nut taps," I say, grinning to myself. "Delicious."

19

The Part Where the Old Friends
Go for a Non-romantic Dinner...

HEATH

I watch as Hadley hurries down the front sidewalk, looking like an angry runway model. I don't think I've ever seen her look so confident. Good for her. She yanks open the passenger door and gets in.

"So? What happened?" I ask.

"Let's just say he was on the ground writhing in pain when I left," she says, putting on her seatbelt. She lets out a shaky breath, then adds. "I worked up quite the appetite. Let's go eat."

I start up the car. "Okay, let's do this." I hit play on my phone, then say, "I found the perfect song for the occasion."

Rhianna's "Take a Bow" comes on, and Hadley manages a smile at me. "You remembered."

"How could I not? You wore out the speakers on my old Corolla with this song."

She turns it up to max and I roll down the windows so

we can feel the breeze while we zip through traffic. If I missed anything about island life, it would be this—the open road running along the ocean, the freedom of it all. And I can tell, freedom is what Hadley's feeling right now too, and something about it makes me perfectly happy.

When it ends, she grabs my phone and puts on M.I.A.'s "Paper Planes" and Hadley belts out the whole thing (with both of us doing the finger guns at the gunshot sounds, obviously). By the time we pull into the restaurant parking lot, it feels like it's only been a few minutes instead of a decade since I left. All the stuff that happened between grade twelve and now disappeared and it's just the two of us, best friends, back together again. We grin at each other while the song winds down, and Hadley grabs my hand, causing that familiar rush of blood. "Thank you, Heath."

"You're welcome."

"No, seriously. I'm so glad you talked me into doing that. It's exactly what I needed."

"Closure?"

She nods and inhales a deep breath, then straightens her shoulders. "I'm better off."

"You really are."

"Still hurts like hell."

My heart squeezes at the thought that she's in pain and I tell myself it's because I care about her as a friend. Friends don't want to see their friends hurting. "It'll get better."

Nodding, Hadley says, "Yeah, it will. Today was step one. A thousand more to go."

"I'll be here for as many as I can."

———

When we step inside Fish Tales (the best seafood place on the island), we're greeted by a teenage boy behind the podium whose name tag reads "I'm Kai, Ask Me For my Best Fish Tale." I don't. Instead, I ask for a table on the patio out back which overlooks Paradise Bay. He walks us through the crowded restaurant and outside, then seats us in the corner. "Are you two celebrating anything this evening?"

"Yes," Hadley says. "My emancipation from the clutches of evil."

Kai gives her a confused look, then says, "Uh…great. In that case, do you want some champagne?"

"Sure," she says.

"I'll let your server know."

We seat ourselves and I stare at Hadley while she watches the tide pull in and out for a few seconds. I forgot how beautiful she is. Or maybe, I spent the last decade lying to myself about her.

"You okay?" I ask her. "It's all right if you're not."

Nodding, she gives me a small smile. "I'm sort of in shock, maybe. I mean, that's it. It's done. Never to be resurrected. I mean…I knew it was over the moment I found out, but now it's officially official. He knows I know and we're through. Somehow it's more final."

"Makes sense," I tell her.

Our server appears with a bottle of champagne in a bucket of ice and two flutes. "I'm Callie. I hear we're celebrating. Did you quit your job?"

"Better," she tells him. "I quit a bad man."

She glances at me, and I say, "Not me."

"Rebound guy?"

We both start shaking our heads and saying 'no' and 'just friends.'

Shrugging, she says, "Too bad, you'd make a cute couple."

"No, I'm his worst nightmare," she says.

"Well, I wouldn't go *that* far," I tell her. "I'd say being dropped into a pool of barracudas would be slightly worse."

Laughing, Hadley says, "Slightly worse? Are you sure?"

I put on a face like I'm trying to decide, then say, "Pretty sure, yeah."

Callie chuckles at our exchange, then pops the cork on the bottle and pours each of us a glass. "Do you already know what you want?"

"Yup, I'd like a conch salad, and I believe she'd like the mac and cheese with crab and a side of biscuits," I say, then I look at Hadley. "Still your favourites?"

She nods and grins at me while Callie tells us she'll be back in a bit with our dinner.

After she walks away, I hold up my flute. "To old friends."

Hadley clinks her glass to mine. "To *good* old friends who show up at exactly the right moment."

I wait until she has a sip to say, "You mean, when you're stuck in an improperly-sized article of clothing?"

She chokes on her drink, then says, "Hey, that tag was wrong."

I have a drink, enjoying the promise of the cold bubbles. Setting my glass down, I stare out at the water and watch as the sun disappears in the distance. "This is the most relaxed I've been in years."

"Really?"

Nodding, I say, "My job was what you'd call high-stress."

"*Was?*"

Sighing, I nod. "I got fired earlier this week."

"For what?" Hadley asks, her face filling with concern.

"For being here when I'm supposed to be there," I tell her. "We were in the middle of the biggest aeronautical merger in history when Minerva ran that light. My boss needs someone twenty-four seven and I can't exactly do that at the moment."

"So that's it? Your mum gets in a serious accident and you get fired for doing the right thing?!"

"According to my boss, the right thing would have been to send flowers."

"Wow, I'm sorry, Heath," she says. "I've been so caught up in my own shit, I never bothered to ask how you're doing."

I shrug off her comment. "How could you possibly have known?"

"I should have at least asked. What kind of friend am I?"

"One who's in the middle of her own crisis. And one that I'm happy to have in my life again." And that's as far as it's going to go. Seriously. Just friends. Forever.

I find myself telling her about my life in New York—my apartment that overlooks a lovely view of a dumpster, the impossibly cold, wet air in the dead of winter, the stifling heat bouncing off the pavement in the summer, the fact that all I've done is work for the last few years, and how I should be making partner in a few weeks instead of starting over. She listens carefully, fully connected to me in the way a good friend is. Except with more eye contact and the odd glance at my lips (or is that wishful thinking?)

"Will you go back?" Hadley asks, just as Callie returns with our meals.

We thank her, then we start to dig in while I answer Hadley's question. "Yeah, I'll go back. I shouldn't have trouble finding another position there. But I'll wait until

Minerva is all right on her own. And then I'll have to start over again from the bottom and work my way back up."

Hadley forks a piece of crab and a couple of macaroni noodles dripping with cheese. "Are you sure you want to do that? You don't sound excited about it."

"I'm not excited about having to start over, but I love what I do and I make a lot of money."

"You've also sacrificed any type of personal life through most of your twenties for a job you just called 'high stress.'"

"But at the end, I'll have won because I'll have the most toys," I say with a wry grin.

"That's bull and you know it."

"I like New York and I do love the excitement of my job, most days. It's stressful, but when the deal comes together and you count all those zeros, it's a total rush."

Not quite the rush of sitting here with you, but a close second.

"What about you?" I ask, spearing a piece of conch meat with my fork. "Any thoughts on what your future holds?"

"A deep collection of high-quality vibrators," she tells me, popping another bite in her mouth.

I give her a conciliatory nod. "Other than that?"

"Wait. I get no reaction on that one?"

"What did you want me to do? Choke on my drink?" I ask, feeling rather amused.

"I was hoping to shock you," she says, pouting ever-so-slightly.

"That would be much easier to do were I not raised by Minerva the Menace," I tell her.

"Right," she says. "I forgot."

"Now, back to the matter at hand. Since love isn't in the cards for you ever again—"

"—I'm serious about that," Hadley says, pointing her fork at me.

I hold up both hands in surrender. "I believe you. No need to threaten me. But, since you're going to go the spinster route forever, where are you going to put your energies?"

"Spinster?" she asks, wrinkling up her nose. "So, you get to be a bachelor and I have to be a spinster?"

"I don't make the rules, Hads," I tell her. "I just live by them. Now, fess up. How will you spend your life?"

"You really are a brat," she says.

"Answer the question." I say, having a gulp of champagne.

"I don't know. I haven't really had time to think about it, to be honest. Up until very recently, my only goal was to get married and have children. It's going to take me a while to come up with a new dream."

I stare at her long enough for her to look up at me, then say, "What?"

"I'm wondering how such a smart, talented person has forgotten what she wanted so badly out of life."

An uncomfortable look crosses her face, and I'm pretty sure it's because no one has called her smart or talented in quite some time. Her family really is full of total shitbirds.

"Well?" I ask, arching one eyebrow.

"Are you talking about the dance school thing?"

"Yes."

Shaking her head, she says, "That was just a dumb idea I had when I was a kid. Do you know how much work it is to set up your own dance school?"

"No, do you?"

"You have to lease a space and renovate it, then do a ton of advertising to attract students—none of which are in my budget, by the way—then you have to hire teachers and learn about scheduling and tax stuff, budgeting… insurance. No, forget it. It's impossible."

"Nelson Mandela said everything seems impossible until it's done," I tell her. (That was on a motivational poster in the lunch room at work, but I'm not going to tell her that.)

"Well, Nelson Mandela never had to deal with dance mums," Hadley says with a small grin. "Terrifying."

"Joke all you want but I'm serious. You'd make a wonderful dance teacher. You're great with kids, you'd be a wonderful employer, and despite what you may think, you really are quite intelligent. There's no reason you couldn't make it happen."

She tilts her head a little as though considering it. "It would be fun to put Madame Le Rose out of business."

"Is that awful woman still in business?" I ask, remembering all the times Hadley would leave the studio crying because she had yelled/sworn at her for not being perfect.

"Can you believe it?" Hadley asks. "She's still the only dance school on the island so she's got a captive clientèle."

"In that case, I imagine there'd be a huge market for people who want to send their daughters to a kinder, gentler dance school…" I tell her. "There could be some real money in it."

"As nice of an idea as that is, I wouldn't even know where to start. Besides, I'm broke, remember? I can't actually afford to start my own studio."

"I'll let you in on a little secret. Almost no one has start-up money. They have to go out and get it."

Taking a biscuit off the plate, she rips off a bit. "No one's going to give me that kind of cash."

"Don't be so sure," I tell her. "With a solid business plan, you may find a backer quicker than you imagine."

"I don't know how to write up a business plan."

"But I do." I pick up my glass and have a sip, then add, "I don't want to push you. Just think about it, okay? I'd be more than happy to help you while I'm in town."

"Thanks," she tells me, her eyes locked on mine. "You know, you're going to have to stop rescuing me like this."

"Why?"

"Because I'll get too used to it and when you leave, I won't know what to do."

———

"So, how do you want to play this?" I ask her as we walk up the sidewalk to her parents' place. There are so many cars parked her for the party that we had to find a spot nearly a block away. A couple of wispy clouds lazily pass in front of the moon and a soft tropical breeze blows while we walk side-by-side.

Hadley's a little tipsy, having had to handle most of the champagne since I'm driving. She puts her arms out to the sides as if she's surfing and does a little twirl that I'm sure has some French name I don't know. "Let's pretend we're engaged too."

I stop walking and stare at her. She stops too. "Just kidding, obviously." Then she groans. "Heaaaattthhh, I don't want to do this."

"I know."

"They're all going to be asking a million questions I don't want to answer. Then I'm going to get the pity face from like…twenty of my relatives."

"Just keep your chin up and act like the whole thing was your idea," I tell her.

"Right, yeah," Hadley says, starting to walk again, slowly this time.

"In a way, it was your idea, you know," I say. "As soon

as you found out he was marrying someone else, you ended things."

"True," she says. "When you put it that way, I sound a lot less pathetic."

I stop walking again and touch her arm. When she turns to me, I say, "You're a lot of things, Hadley Jones, but pathetic was never one of them."

Pulling away, she says, "Oh sure, I'm an almost thirty-year-old woman who just got out of what I thought was a forever relationship that turned out to be a total lie, I live in a basement suite and teach incredibly basic dance moves to drunk people on their holidays. I might as well just start adopting cats and get it over with."

"Well, in that case, I should start adopting cats too because I'm an almost thirty-year-old man who's never even had a serious girlfriend and who just lost his job."

She chuckles, then says, "You can be a crazy cat man."

"I'll get a sweatshirt that says 'cats are my people.'"

"No, no! Get one with a pouch for carrying your cat around in!" she says.

I laugh at the thought. "We can get matching ones."

"Purrrrfect."

We turn up the sidewalk to her parents' house and she stops. "Nope. Not doing this. I can't."

I put my hand on the small of her back and give her a gentle push. "You have to do this. For Lucas. But I promise it won't be that bad because I'll be right by your side the entire time."

"Fine."

"It will be."

"How do you know?"

"Because I have a plan."

20

There's Nothing Like a Great Dress and a Lot of Champagne to Strengthen Your Backbone...

HADLEY

The house is packed with guests when we walk in the front door (you know, like regular people). Light jazz is playing over my parents' stereo, competing with the hum of chatter that fills the air. Taking a deep breath, I glance up at Heath, hoping like hell that whatever his plan is, it's going to be amazing. He gives me a confident nod and we make our way into the living room to mingle.

Lucas spots us first, hurrying over to greet us. He gives me a long hug, then pulls back and lowers his voice, "How are you? Still devastated about numb nuts?"

Shrugging, I say, "I'm hanging in there. You remember Heath?" I point over my shoulder with my thumb and Lucas's eyes light up.

"Of course," he says, offering his hand to Heath. "Great to see you, man! How've you been?"

"Can't complain. Congratulations on your upcoming nuptials," Heath says, shaking his head.

"Thanks," Lucas says. "I'm so happy. Serena's the best." He seems to suddenly remember my beloved wasn't 'the best' and his face falls. "Sorry."

"All right, none of that," I tell him. "We're here to celebrate you and Serena. I'm happy for you, so don't spend a second feeling guilty about numb nuts and his stupid numb nuts which are probably either numb or really sore at the moment." I let out an evil grin.

"What did you do?" Lucas asks.

"I may have knocked on them earlier this evening…"

Heath and Lucas both wince and laugh at the same time, then Heath says, "I thought you were just joking."

"Newp."

Serena walks up and loops her arm through Lucas's, then smiles at Heath. "I'm his soon-to-be better half, Serena."

"Heath. Congratulations."

My mother descends upon us with my Aunt Velma in tow. Velma's the one who taught mum everything she needed to know about being a Stepford wife.

"Hadley," Aunt Velma calls. "You poor, poor thing! Your mother told me everything."

She pulls me in for a hug, then lets go and takes me by both shoulders. "Don't worry because she and I already have a plan for getting Chase back."

"Like a revenge plan?" Heath asks.

Velma gives him a dirty look. "Who's this?"

"This is Heath Robinson. We grew up together," I tell her.

My mother gives Heath a nod and a phony smile. "Good to see you, Heath. My, you've turned into quite the handsome young man. How's Minerva?"

"She's healing fast," he tells her.

"Good. Have you two renewed your little friendship?"

she asks, tilting her head while she points back and forth between us.

I'm about to say yes, when Heath slings one arm over my shoulder and pulls me in to his side. Wow, does he ever smell good. Yum. I wouldn't mind taking a bath in that aftershave. "We have, Doris, but I'm hoping it turns into more."

My eyes pop open and I grin up at him, still a little tipsy from the champagne. Or is it from being so near to him? It better not be, because I seem to recall swearing off men forever...

"Really?" Aunt Velma asks, putting on a skeptical face.

"Really," he says. "I haven't been able to stop thinking about Hadley here since I left for the states. Even after years of brokering some of the biggest deals in history, after having super models throw themselves at me, I can't get this one out of my mind."

Velma blinks at him like a confused poodle and he continues smoothly, "I know the timing's not right, but if she ever decided to give this a try, believe me, I'll be right here waiting for her."

Dear lord, did that actually work? Velma's face morphs into a teenage girl who's just been gifted a kitten. "Just like that Richard Marx song..." she says.

"Well, I don't think that's likely to happen," my mum says, her sour face making it clear what she thinks of the idea of her baby with a man raised by Minerva Robinson. "This whole situation with Chase is just a blip. He'll be back to Hadley before we know it, and they'll live happily ever after."

I shake my head at her. "Not happening, so just drop it, Doris."

With that, I tug on Heath's hand and start to walk away. "Let's go find us some drinks."

When we get over to the bar area, I whisper to Heath. "So that's your plan? You're pretending you're in love with me?"

He nods, then says, "Yup. You cool with that?"

"Sure," I say, trying not to notice how his eyes seem to shine. "I don't know if anyone will buy it, but I appreciate the effort, buddy."

An hour later, we've done the same routine at least a dozen times, with Heath pretending he's mad for me while I try not to enjoy the ruse too much. He does little things like the old, 'you've got something on your cheek, let me get that while I gaze into your eyes,' or the tucking a lock of hair behind my ear, or the gaze, glance down at my lips, and grin. So, a lot of gazing, really...Meanwhile, I've sucked back another two glasses of champagne, trying to prevent the flames he's starting from burning me up from the inside. I'm talking some serious smolder here. Hmm, the champagne may have been a bad idea, because I've completely forgotten about a) proper decorum at an engagement party, b) that I totally hate men, and c) that Heath's taut buttocks are not mine for the massaging.

I don't even know if my relatives are buying what we're selling (well, other than Velma), but my lady bits sure as hell are. We're currently in the kitchen and I've got him pinned up against the counter while we talk about our favourite show, *Clash of Crowns* (so much to catch up on after over a decade apart, not the least of which is the fact that we're both total Crownies—i.e., huge fans of *Clash of Crowns*). I'm absent-mindedly running my fingers along the ridges of his abs (yeah, real ridges—Chase's abs have nothing on Heath's). "I disagree, the hottest scene was definitely when Oona and Lucamore are finally reunited after she's been running through the maze of death."

Heath swallows hard, then says, "That was a pretty

good one, I'll give you that. But *come on*, when they were stranded on the Isle of Hynabeatha and they first...you know...on that beach with the waves crashing all around them."

Oh dear. I *do* remember that scene. That one had me feeling flush for days. In fact, I'm feeling rather flushed right now. "Oh yeah, that one."

"Hadley, can I see you for a moment please?" my mother asks in a terse tone.

I pull away from Heath and try for a casual 'whatever' look even though I'm suddenly tense (or I would be if I weren't not-so-suddenly drunk). I follow her down the hall to her bedroom and wait while she shuts the door. Folding her arms across her chest, she says, "Listen, I know you're hurt by what Chase did, but having some public affair with...Heath...isn't going to help matters."

"Oh, I don't know about that, Mum," I say with a lopsided grin. "It might just help a lot."

She rolls her eyes. "Look, if you play your cards right, you and Chase could still end up together. Fine if you want word to get out that you've got another man after you. That could prove useful, but don't do anything that will cause Chase to think twice about taking you back. Men like their brides to be *their* brides, if you catch my drift."

She means they don't like chicks who sleep around but she's too polite to say it. So, I think I'll play dumb because that sounds like more fun than dutifully understanding her cryptic meaning. "I don't get it, actually. You mean Chase won't want to marry me if I'm already married to Heath?"

"No! Not the wedding part. The wedding *night* part."

"Umm...but that comes after the wedding so..." This is fun. I wish Heath were in here right now. He'd get such a kick out of this.

Sighing, she whisper-yells, "Sex! I'm talking about sex.

They don't like women who have slept around."

"Oh, Mum, first off, we're in the twenty-first century. Nobody waits for marriage anymore."

She starts to protest, but I shake my head. "*Nobody*. Second, I don't want Chase back. For real. I don't. He's a cheater and a liar and I'm better off on my own."

"No, that's crazy talk," she says. "What are you going to do, Hadley? Live in that dingy basement suite forever? Why don't you get a bunch of cats while you're at it!"

"I think I will. Because it has just finally occurred to me that I'm an adult who doesn't have to do everything her mother tells her. I can make my own choices."

She purses her lips, then says, "I'd let you make your own choices if you wouldn't screw them up. Chase was the only good thing you had going for you. You cannot let him go without a fight."

"I'm leaving, Mum. With Heath. I may have sex with him. I may have sex with an entire fleet of naval officers if a ship happens to dock here. Chase and I are done. Forever. Don't ever mention his name to me again."

I spin around and pull open the door, only to find Aunt Velma has been listening. She gives me a deer in the headlights look, then chuckles awkwardly, then looks at my mum. "There you are Doris. We're almost out of sweet and sour meatballs."

I walk back into the kitchen, grab Heath by the hand and say, "We're out of here."

We make our way to the front door, then I turn back to the crowded living room. "Lucas, Serena, congratulations you two crazy kids. I'm off to celebrate being newly single and my plan is to sleep with anything that moves, starting with this hottie here."

I mime a mic drop then spin on my heel, open the door, and walk out into the wild night air.

21

Moonlit Races and Blurred Lines

HEATH

"I hope you don't mind that I implied that were going to sleep together," she says as soon as we're safely in the car. "I didn't really mean it. I just...sort of got caught up in the moment and went with it, you know?"

"Why would I mind? You were just going with the plan." I say, brushing aside disappointment. "Where to? Are you tired? Should I drop you at home?"

"No way. I'm just getting started," she says with a grin. "Let's go to the beach."

"The beach it is," I say, starting up the engine. Hadley opens the window and sticks her arms and head out. "Whoohoo! I'm free! I'm totally free," she shouts into the wind.

After a few seconds, she tucks her arms back in the car. "When I really think about it, I suppose I've always been totally free. Well, I guess, at least for the last year. I just didn't realize it. But I mean like tonight I feel really free. Like, for the first time, I'm not afraid to upset my parents. It's like I've finally realized that this life isn't *their* life. It's mine and I can do what I want with it."

"Yup. It's true."

"I'm an adult now," she says. "Which is a shockingly late revelation for me. And you know what? I'm thinking I may not even show up for brunch next Sunday. I think I'm gonna call and tell them I don't feel like it."

"Good for you," I say with a firm nod.

"Yeah," she says. "Good for me." She tilts her head to the side, staring at me while I drive. "This is just like old times. Except, instead of driving a car full of drunks, there's just one drunk tonight."

"Yes, history definitely repeats itself," I say, thinking of how I'm exactly where I was back when I was seventeen— wanting the same girl who doesn't want me back.

We pull into the parking lot at Hidden Beach — a well-hidden gem that the locals have kept to ourselves. It's late, and there are no other cars in the parking lot.

"This brings back memories," I say.

"I actually haven't been here since we were in high school," Hadley says as we get out of the car and I pocket the keys.

"Seriously? This is the best beach on the island."

"I know, but somehow it just didn't feel right coming here without you."

We hurry along the sandy path through the trees, for no other reason than how good it feels to run toward something. The only light is from the moon, but the path is well-worn and I know it so well, my feet remember when to lift a little higher to avoid the odd root sticking up here and there. When we reach the clearing, the world becomes the shimmering reflection of the moon on the water that is nothing short of magic and a thought pops into my head without my consent. *There's no other place on this planet that I want to be.*

Hadley stretches her arms out as though she's trying to touch all of the air at once. She kicks off her sandals and dances along to some tune I can't hear, every once in a while doing a little jump in the air and shouting that she's free. Then suddenly, she stops and turns to me. "Let's go for a swim."

"Maybe another time. We don't have any swimsuits."

"What happened to 'it's nothing you haven't seen before?'" she asks as she tugs her dress over her head and stands before me in her bra and knickers.

My brain completely disengages from my tongue for a minute. As I gawk at her, I say, "Right. Yeah. True."

She giggles, then tugs my arm. "Come on, very serious accountant Heath. Let yourself have some fun for once."

With that, she lets go of me and takes off, racing down toward the water. I kick off my Keds and strip down to my boxer briefs, calling, "Okay, but I'm only coming in to keep you from drowning."

"Ha! I'm a better swimmer than you, remember?"

I hurry after her, and, by the time I reach the water's edge, she's already in up to her hips. As soon as the waves roll over my feet, they bring back a flood of memories and emotions. The warmth of the Caribbean Sea, being here at this beach under the stars, with this girl. It all rushes to the surface as though the truth is hidden deep in my bones —this is home.

"I'll race you to Smugglers Cove," Hadley says, pointing to a tiny island nearby.

"Get ready to lose," I say with a wide grin.

We swim side-by-side and it feels like we're the only two people left on the entire planet and I don't even mind.

"I'm so happy!" she says suddenly, then she lets out a laugh.

"And you're a little bit drunk."

She stops swimming and treads water next to me. "I don't feel drunk. I just feel good."

When we reach our destination, we both drop onto the shore, panting from the exertion. Then we lay back, staring up at the stars.

"Are you thinking what I'm thinking?" Hadley asks.

"I doubt it," I say, because I'm thinking about that sexy beach sex scene from *Clash of Crowns* we were talking about earlier.

Turning to face me, she says, "I was thinking we should reenact that scene with Oona and Lucamor..."

Dear God, yes, please. "Ha! Good one," I say, much to my entire body's chagrin.

She keeps a grin on her face, even though I think I may spot disappointment in her eyes (although it is pretty dark out here, and I may just be seeing what I want to see).

"Of course, I'm just kidding," she says. "You're my best friend, Heath. Nora's amazing and I totally love her, but I don't think there's anybody that knows me as well as you do. Not even my mother...especially not my mother."

"Yeah, I think that happens when you grow up together. We've seen each other through a lot." Oh, the disappointment, it's like actual physical pain.

"What happened to us?" she asks me, turning onto her side and propping her head up on her elbow.

You broke my heart. "Oh, you know, I moved away, you moved on with your life. It happens."

"Well, it shouldn't." She stares at me for a long moment before adding, "I don't want to lose you again."

"Well, since I'm out of a job, I may have to stick around for a while."

Rolling onto her back, she lets out a sigh. "I know it sounds silly because you only just got back here, but somehow the thought of you leaving again feels like it would be harder than what I've been going through."

"I'm pretty sure you feel that way because of what you're going through," I tell her, shifting onto my side and propping myself up on my elbow.

She shakes her head and her gaze hardens. "No, that's not it." Lifting herself up, she brings her mouth in line with mine. "That's not it at all."

Swallowing hard, I tell myself not to kiss her—that it's a terrible idea, that it can't go anywhere, that she is going to break my heart if I let her. I tell myself that the timing could not be worse. When that doesn't work, I mentally yell at myself to learn from the mistakes of my past.

Then I forget about all those things and press my lips to hers.

We kiss softly at first, tentatively, testing each other, then things become more heated as she opens her mouth to let me in. Our tongues move together, time stops, and all logic disappears, and for a brief moment in my life, I forget that people will always disappoint you, and that love slowly fades or burns out fast, and I let myself show her exactly how I feel. The truth comes out—that she's it for me and always has been. And the way she responds tells me she feels it, too. After far too long, I pull myself away from her, leaving us both in shock.

"Wow. I don't think I've ever been kissed like that," she says.

"I don't think I've ever kissed anyone that way before."

Suddenly, it's all too intense for me, and I realize that if I let things go any further, my heart will be smashed to smithereens. "We should stop," I say, tucking a lock of her hair behind her ear. "You've been drinking. Besides, I'm a man and you've already promised yourself you're giving up on us Y-chromosome-carrying scum."

"Right. I almost forgot," she agrees, not moving even an inch away from me. "We shouldn't have done that just now."

Disappointment crawls its way into my chest and settles there. "Agreed. Horrible timing. You're literally only a few hours out of your thing with what's-his-nuts, and I'm leaving as soon as humanly possible. I say we chalk it up to…curiosity and too much champagne, and never talk about it again."

"Deal," she tells me with a wink. "Although…you only had one glass of champagne, so, I guess it was just curiosity on your part."

"Well, and all that talk about *Clash of Crowns'* best sex scenes…"

"That too."

There's an awkward silence, then I say, "Glad that's settled."

"Me too. Now we can get back to normal," Hadley says with a firm nod.

"Yup, back to being old school chums."

"Perfect."

"Definitely for the best."

"Absolutely. It's the logical decision," I say, glancing at her lips.

"Totally," she says, leaning toward me just the smallest bit.

Nope! Do not start kissing her again for all of the aforementioned reasons. "Should we swim back and make sure our clothes are still there, old pal?" I ask in a chipper tone.

"Definitely, buddy."

I stand, help her up, then wade back into the water and dive in to douse the flames of pent-up want.

And that, folks, was the single hardest thing I've ever had to do...

22

From the Mouths of Babes...

HADLEY

"Okay ladies, let's really use those hips!" I yell, leading a group of four women through a mambo. It's mid-afternoon, we're in the shade near one of the pools, and I'm pulling out my best moves in hopes of Heath popping by to say hi. We haven't contacted each other since last night, so each hour that passes by, I'm increasingly worried that things are going to be weird when we do see each other. I promised myself I won't text him, or worse, stop by his office today, because it might look like I'm desperate or I was just using him to boost my ego—which I would never do. But what if by *not* reaching out, I'm treating him like a rebound?

Dear lord, how do people survive in the single world? I honestly don't know what I'm doing here, but I do know I don't want to mess this up.

Urgh. I should just forget all about Hot Heath and the fabulously erotic beach fooling around from last night.

Even though it was the single most passionate moment of my entire life. Which is insane since I was with someone for so long, but honestly, not once did it feel like it did with Heath. It was *that* incredible. Like, mind-blowingly wonderful. The way he looked at me was like…I'm the only woman who's ever walked the earth. And the way he touched me—it went straight through me to my soul.

Or was that all my imagination? Probably, right?

The truth is, I've been desperately lonely for so long that maybe *any* human touch would feel like the most amazing thing ever. Yes, that's got to be it. I need to find a way to file away last night as a one-off, fun time and nothing more.

Oh! There he is! In a dress shirt and slacks. Wow. Just look at him. My entire body floods with all the feels.

He grins at me, then joins in the class, making all the ladies laugh with his ridiculous attempts to mambo. "Don't mind me!" he tells them. "I'm just the accountant here."

Dancing his way over to me, he says, "How are you feeling today?"

"Great," I tell him.

"Good stuff. I wanted to make sure you weren't hungover or anything."

"I'm not."

"Brilliant," he says. "Okay, I ordered a burger to take back to my office. I need to duck out early for a meeting with my mum's doctor."

"Everything okay?"

He nods. "Her body is healing fine, but this is about her behavior. A bored Minerva is a bad Minerva. She's driving the nurses absolutely nuts."

"Maybe I should stop by after work and keep her company," I suggest as he takes my hand and spins me.

"Oh! Yes!" he answers. "Please do. She won't misbehave if you're there." He grabs me and dips me, and I close my eyes, hoping he's going to lay one on me, but he doesn't. Lifting me back up, he says, "Gotta run. My food's ready. See you later."

I keep right on dancing while the entire class, including me, watches him walk away. One of the women asks me if he's my boyfriend.

"No, we're just old friends."

"You should make a move," she says. "You know, lock that shit down as my granddaughter says."

I let out a slightly shocked laugh, then say, "He's only back in town for a few weeks."

"So what?" she shouts over the music. The song ends just as she yells, "A few weeks shagging a man like that would be totally worth the heartbreak."

Her husband, who has been sitting at a table nearby reading, looks up. "Maybe you should go find him. Sounds like you'd enjoy it."

Yikes. I back away from the impending fight, only to bump into someone. When I turn around, I see a beyond-exhausted Libby with a baby strapped to her chest in some sort of snuggy thing that looks like it would be both really heavy and uncomfortably hot. We both apologize to each other and I'm about to ask her how she is when four-year-old Clara starts jumping up and down, tugging on her mum's hand. "Mummy, I want to go swwwwwiiiimmmm-minnnggg," she whines.

"I know baby, soon, okay?" she says. "I just have to go to the office for five minutes to talk to Daddy, okay?"

Dropping her shoulders, Clara says, "Five minutes? It's never five minutes. It'll be a bamillron."

"Million," Libby says. "It'll take mummy a *million* minutes in Daddy's office."

Clara gives her a glare one would expect from a

teenager, not a four-year-old, and Libby looks up at me with desperation all over her face.

"You know," I say, "Clara could hang out with me for a bit if you like. I could teach her to mambo." Looking down at Clara, I ask, "Would you like that?"

She grins broadly and nods her head so hard I'm concerned about whiplash.

"Would you do that?" Libby asks. "Really?"

"Of course. It'll be fun."

"You're a lifesaver, Hadley. Literally. I can't put little Will down, not even for a second or he starts screaming. I've pretty much been holding him for three months straight, even in the shower and on the toilet. He won't even go to Harrison. Just cries his eyes out. I sleep in an armchair with him in my arms."

She looks at Clara and smiles reassuringly. "Okay, sweetie, now stay with Miss Hadley until I get back, okay?"

Clara lets go of her mum's hand and latches onto mine as Libby starts to go the wrong way.

"Oh, Libby," I tell her. "The office is that way."

"Right. The office. I'm going to the office..." she mutters, spinning around. "Oh God, Clara, why am I going there?"

"To talk to Dad about the schedule problem."

"Right, right," she says. "Thanks, sweetie."

Clara and I watch her for a few seconds, then we look at each other with matching concerned expressions. Then she shakes her head and sighs. "That poor woman is losing it."

My attempt to stifle my reaction fails miserably, and I wind up laughing while Clara looks on with a proud grin. Finally, I rein it in and say, "Mambo or salsa?"

"Mambo. I don't like anything spicy."

This time I just smile, then say, "Makes sense. Let's get started."

The next half hour is so fun, I'm actually disappointed when Libby comes back. "She's a natural," I tell Libby. "Have you thought of putting her in dance lessons?"

"It's on my to-do list," she tells me, bouncing up and down to keep a now-fussy Will calm.

"Do you want to leave her with me for the afternoon? I'll be doing a class at the east pool and Clara here could be my assistant."

"Are you serious?" Libby asks, her eyes lighting up with hope.

"Definitely. She's already got all the moves down and the guests will love it."

"Can I stay, Mom? Please, please, please!" Clara yells, jumping up and down.

"You sure?" Libby asks me quietly. "She's a lot of energy."

"It would be my pleasure," I tell her. "I love kids and Clara's hilarious. She's had me laughing the entire time."

"Perfect," Libby says. "I might even be able to nap. If it doesn't work out, can you take her over to the lobby and leave her with Rosy?"

"Sure," I answer.

"Or Harrison," she adds, seeming to remember Clara's father is also on site.

"You got it, but we'll be just fine. Don't worry."

"Go, Mum!" Clara says, clearly having had enough of the grown-ups talking. "You need the rest."

Libby does as her daughter says, bounce-walking away. As soon as she's out of earshot, Clara looks up at me. "What do you say to an ice cream? It's on me."

23

Bad Influences, Bad Liars, and Bad News...

HEATH

"How was your non-date?" Minerva asks me as soon as I walk into her room.

"It was fine. How are you feeling today?" I ask, plucking a vase of wilted flowers off one of the night tables and taking it to the adjoining bathroom to refill the water.

"Bored to death, which is why I want details on your big night out," she calls to me.

"We ate, we went to her brother's engagement party, then to the beach, then I took her home."

"That sounds exactly like a date."

"Dates don't typically start with you driving over to her boyfriend's place so she can dump him," I tell her, setting the vase down.

Her eyes light up and she claps her hands. "Ooh! Did she let him have it?"

"I think so. She even did something to his guy parts. I didn't ask. I don't want to know."

A wide grin spreads across Minerva's face as she leans forward. "Vanilla nut taps?"

"I have no idea but she did say he was on the ground clutching his manhood when she left."

Nodding, my mum says, "She nut tapped him. That's my girl. So are you two going on another non-date again soon?"

I shake my head, trying to shove down the torrent of emotions that come with the idea of us going out again. "It wouldn't be fair to her because I'm not staying. Besides, she's not exactly in the right frame of mind to start a new relationship." I quickly follow that with, "Not that we would be starting a relationship because we don't have those feelings for each other."

"Really?"

"Yup," I tell her, doing my best to look like I have no opinion on the matter whatsoever.

"Then how'd you get that hickey on your neck?"

Freezing in place, I say, "What are you talking about? I don't...I don't have a hickey."

Leveling me with a glare over the top of her glasses, Minerva points to the left side of my neck. "Heath, I've been around the block more than once. I know what a love bite looks like."

I clamp my hand over the area. "It's a mosquito bite. I couldn't stop scratching it. Super itchy. Anyway, what'd they serve for lunch today?"

"A steaming bowl of who cares with a side of don't change the subject. Now, quit being so dull. I don't want details—"

"I should hope not—"

"But what else happened?"

"Nothing, which is exactly as it should be. Hadley and I are old friends. All that's happening is we're spending some time together while I'm in town. After that, we'll probably text each other from time to time," I say, trying to convince myself that what I'm saying is what I want.

"Maybe you won't go back," Minerva says. "You already found a job here."

"Yeah, but it's not a job I want. It's temporary, the pay is an insult, and it's just a favour for the Banks family."

"It's accounting. You're an accountant. How could you not want a job in your field in a place that is literally paradise?"

"Because it's basically bookkeeping, it's boring as hell, and I like New York. They don't call it the Centre of the Universe for nothing—there's always something going on there, unlike here. Plus, that's where my real life is, remember?"

Shrugging, she says, "Your real life. *Pffft!* You do nothing but make other people rich and try to keep your jungle berries from freezing and falling off."

"Can we not talk about my berries?"

"Why? Does it make you uncomfortable?"

"Frankly, yes. And as far as my work goes, it's exciting, and I'm really good at it. Someday I could run my own firm."

Wrinkling up her nose, she says, "How did I raise someone so horribly dull?"

"I'm not dull. I'm busy."

"You're *dull*. You've been an old man since you were a toddler. You didn't want to go skydiving when I got you those passes for your eighteenth birthday, you don't have a bunch of girlfriends, you don't do any extreme sports, you refused to meet me in Spain to run with the bulls last year..."

"First of all, I was in the middle of a huge deal when you called. Second, I've actually met some of the Chicago

Bulls when they were in town, which was pretty thrilling…"

"Did they chase you?"

"Not that kind of bull," I say, frustration starting to build. "Anyway, doesn't matter. I love my life there and I'm going back to it as soon as I can. I didn't spend four years in university and work my arse off for the last six years just to give up and wind up back where I started."

"Fine, but I doubt you'll be getting any 'mosquito bites' in New York."

Dr. Baker walks in, saving me from the rest of the conversation. "Good evening, Minerva, how are we feeling today?"

"I don't know how you are, but I'm fully healed so you can let me go already."

He gives her a placating smile, then says, "What has it been? Three weeks?"

"No, I'm pretty sure it's more like three months since the incident," she tells him.

He flips her chart open, prompting her to speak up. "You don't have to look at that. It's all a bunch of lies."

"Hmph, yup, three weeks tomorrow since you moved into the Hotel De FixYouUp."

"Well, I'm fixed so it's time for me to check out."

"Mum," I say. "How about we let Dr. Baker do his job? He probably wants to go home soon."

"You know who else wants to go home soon? *Me.*"

"And I promise you, Minerva, the second we can spring you, we will," he says, walking over and holding a pen light up to my mum's eyes. "Until then, I need you to stop inviting friends over for small parties, okay? It's extremely disruptive to the other patients and your consumption of alcohol is quite dangerous. We'll have to stop giving you anything for pain management if you do it again."

"Well, what else am I supposed to do? Just lay here?" she asks.

"That's the idea, yes," he says, jotting something down in the chart. "Some patients take up knitting or Sudoku while they're here. One woman managed to get caught up on her photo albums—fifteen years' worth. You could read, watch TV, play some games on a tablet…I promise you there are lots of things you can do other than hosting parties."

"Everything you just listed is for old ladies."

"That's not true," I say. "Old men like some of those things too."

Dr. Baker gives me a look, then says, "Listen, my job isn't to keep you entertained. It's to get you healthy so you can go back to your life with as few restrictions as possible. But I need you to cooperate."

"Fine," my mum says, rolling her eyes. "But how much longer am I going to be here? Because I'm ready to jump out the window."

"Another three weeks minimum, but only if you've got help at home and can get rides to therapy three times a week. Otherwise, we'll have to send you to a rehab clinic for a few months until you're able to care for yourself."

Minerva sighs and looks at me. "Well?"

Shit, shit, shit. "I'll be here."

Dr. Baker looks at me. "Brilliant. I suspect the soonest Minerva will be completely independent will be sometime in mid-December."

She smiles hopefully at me. "In that case, you might as well just stay through Christmas."

"We'll see," I tell her, my heart sinking at the thought of being here for another three months.

The good doctor closes the chart, clicks his pen closed, and says, "So for the next few weeks, no parties. Oh, and stop calling the nurses Ratched. They're just trying to look after you."

"Fine," Mum says with a heavy sigh. "When did people get so sensitive?"

———

I pull up in front of the house and sit with my head against the seatback for a second. Three more months. Dammit. That's way too long to be out of the game. It might as well be three years because in this line of work, you're only as good as your last deal, and since I was working on the Bao merger for close to eight months, that'll put me at over a year ago by the time I'm back.

I drag myself out of the car and stand, staring at the dilapidated house. It looks like how I feel. I think about my mum laying in that bed in pain (and being a pain) for another three weeks, then starting a long road to recovery, and facing an uncertain future after. Definitely her future won't include flying around on her moped with the wind in her hair. It could very well include walkers, or even worse, wheelchairs. And here I am feeling sorry for myself. Pathetic. As I start up the cracked sidewalk, I decide to do something nice for her for once in my life. I'm going to fix up her house so at least she'll have a home she can enjoy, since she'll be spending a lot more time here than she's used to.

24

Uninvited, Unwanted, and Surprisingly Insightful Guests...

HADLEY

It's early evening and I just got out of the shower and did what I've been doing all freaking afternoon and evening—checking my phone in case Heath tried to reach me. Not because I have a thing for him, because I totally don't (even though that snogging was absolutely, unforgettably incredibly incredible. Is unforgettably a word? If not, I think it should be). Anyway, I only want to talk to him so I can tell him about teaching Clara today and how fun it was and how maybe, *just maybe*, he was right about the whole dance studio idea.

Nope. Still nothing. Cool your jets, girl. He's probably still busy with his mum.

I take my time changing into my pajamas, my thoughts floating to last night, then to him surprising me by showing up and joining in my class. Chase would never have done anything like that. He hated silliness of any kind. In fact, he hated it so much, I can't remember the last time we shared a big laugh—like a really big belly laugh. I'm not sure we ever did, now that I think about it. How sad is that? Maybe it is a good thing we broke up. Who would want to spend her life with someone she can't laugh with?

Not that I want to spend my life with Heath. He and I are strictly friends. Also, I don't want to spend my life with anyone. I'm going ride or die with Minerva. We should get matching tattoos that say that. On our necks. Doris would shit.

My phone buzzes and I jump across the room to grab it.

Harrumph - it's Lucas.

"Hey little bro, how's it going?"

"Good, really good. Just sold this cute little cottage up on High Street this afternoon."

"Cha-ching!" I say, trying not to think about my pathetic savings account.

"I wanted to check in and see how you're doing. I know yesterday was…not your best day."

But it was sort of my best night… "I'm fine. Seriously. I mean, the whole thing still stings, but I'll survive."

"You sure? Because it seems like you're moving on a little fast. Maybe a little too fast?" Lucas says.

I flop down onto my bed. "Oh, that thing with Heath?"

"Yeah, that thing with Heath."

"That was just for show. He offered to come along because I told him Mother's been after me to get back together with Chase."

"Ah, so none of that was real…"

"You sound skeptical."

"It looked pretty convincing, especially when you had him pinned against the kitchen counter," Lucas says, adding, "And when you were groping his butt in front of Great Uncle Dennis."

"Not at all real, I promise."

"All right then. I believe you, but just be careful if you're going to keep playing the fake relationship game. It usually ends in someone falling in love and getting crushed."

"According to 90's romcoms?" I ask.

"Um, yeah, but there must be some truth to it," Lucas says. "Have you talked to our mother today?"

"No, did she say anything after I told everyone she knows that I'm going to sleep with anything that moves, then made my exit?" I get up and walk to the fridge to hunt around for some salsa to go with the tortillas I hope I have.

"She laughed awkwardly, told everyone not to take that seriously and that you were thinking of changing careers—"

"—To what? A prostitute?" I ask.

"Uh, no, she went with comedian," he says.

"Wow, she totally could have had a career in PR because that's some brilliant spin-doctoring." I finally locate a jar of salsa (medium spice level), but when I open the jar, it's only got a few slightly crusty-looking spoonfuls at the bottom. Hmm, I wonder if it's okay to eat...

"You might want to call her," Lucas suggests.

"Why? So she can tell me what a disappointment I am?"

"Good point. Maybe giving it a few days wouldn't be the worst idea."

"Agreed," I say, scrounging through my cupboard for tortillas.

Nope. Nothing. There goes my evening...

"Okay, well, since you're not jumping into a relationship, I guess I can ring off and tell Serena that's not what you're doing. She was worried."

"Tell her that's very sweet of her."

"I will. Take care, Hads."

"You too, Goofus."

After we hang up, I put the salsa back in the fridge in case I want crusty salsa some other day, and stand next to my counter, tapping my fingernails on it and trying to decide if I should call Heath. I could be bold like Serena and make the first move. After all, he sort of made a move by showing up poolside today…Maybe it's my turn.

A knock on the door stops that train of thought before it can leave the station (which may be a blessing, really). I rush over to answer it, obviously hoping it's Heath. Putting on my best smile, I swing open the door, only to see Chase standing there.

The smile drops. Instant rage turns everything scarlet. "What are you doing here?" I ask, trying to decide whether or not to slam the door in his face.

"I came to get my guitar," he says, covering his man parts with both hands.

I grin inwardly at the fact that he's clearly scared of me, then dial up my snark setting to maximum. "You mean the guitar you bought when you swore you were going to learn to play, only to change your mind and abandon it like you do humans?"

"Yup, that's the one," he says, stepping inside but leaving the door open.

I roll my eyes, then walk over to get it from where it's been sitting for the last two years—in the corner next to the couch. When I bring it back to him, I set it down on the floor, then back away from it so we don't accidentally come into contact with each other.

"Okay, well, I'll just go then," he says, picking up the

guitar. He starts, then turns back around again. "For what it's worth, I feel really bad that I didn't tell you sooner."

"It's worth less than nothing for me to know that."

"I figured as much," he says. "I wish there was some way we could be—"

"—friends?" I shake my head. "Not a prayer."

"If it makes you feel any better, Taylor and I broke up."

I let a tiny grin of satisfaction escape my lips. "Well, that actually does help a little."

"I'm sure it does. She just couldn't get past what I did," he tells me, shifting from one foot to the other. "I don't blame her though."

"Nor should you."

We stare at each other for a second and suddenly I realize he's not some evil mastermind duping women wherever he goes. He's an idiot. And a coward. I think about what Minerva said to me about why men cheat. "Can I ask you one question before you go?"

He runs his hand through his blond hair, with his well-practiced gorgeously uncomfortable look. "Sure."

"When you first realized you didn't want to be with me, why didn't you just tell me the truth?"

"I don't know."

"Sure you do."

"Okay, I do, but I have a feeling it'll come out wrong and you'll only be more upset with me than you already are."

"Not possible."

"Let me start by saying I'm not trying to blame you because *none* of what happened was your fault."

"Okaaayyyy…"

"The thing is, you were just so perfect all the time that there was never a reason I could put my finger on to end things. You were so agreeable and giving and I felt like a total shit when I realized I wasn't in love with you."

"As in, fell out of love with me or never were in the first place?" I ask, then immediately reprimand myself for the torture I'm bringing on myself.

"I...can I not answer that one?"

"You just did," I say, feeling tears burn behind my eyeballs.

"The thing is, Hads, I don't think I ever really knew you."

"What is that supposed to mean? We were together for twelve years. How could you *not* know me?"

He glances at the floor for a second, clearly trying to find an answer that won't get him tapped in his berries. Finally, he looks up at me. "It's like with Taylor, I knew every little thing about her — like her favourite part of her favourite movie, and her top five froyo flavours. But with you, I didn't know anything. You always said you liked what I liked. Does that make any sense at all?"

And then it hits me. It *was* a bad relationship. "Oh my God, I'm that woman from the first *Coming to America* that Eddie Murphy got to bark like a dog, aren't I?"

"No, come on," he says, shaking his head. "You're not *that* bad. But kind of, maybe."

I let out a long sigh, then chew my lip trying to take this all in. "I think I was following the Doris Jones guide to keeping a man. Try not to get in the way, try not to be too demanding, like what he likes..."

Chase's eyes light up. "Yeah, that's exactly it. At the beginning, I used to try to ask you what you wanted to do, but you were just so good at always bringing it right back to me that I gave up after a while."

"So I needed to be more demanding and pushy," I say, slightly shocked at this revelation.

"I don't think you needed to be either of those things. But maybe if you had just been yourself."

The truth is a cold slap of water from an unexpected wave. "Well, the thing is, I don't think you would've liked the real me."

"We'll never know, will we?" Chase picks up the guitar, then says, "Take care, Hadley. I hope you meet the right guy, and that he's much better to you than I was."

I nod, then shut the door behind him, and stand staring at it as a crazy thought pops into my head. *Maybe I already have.*

25

Fish Tacos and Unfortunately Decent Proposals

HADLEY

Not wanting to be alone with my new revelation, I pick up my phone. My heart pounds in my chest as I type: *What are you up to?* Then I delete it and write: *Whatcha doing this evening?* Nope, awful. *How'd it go at the hospital?*

Yes. That's the one. Send.

A minute later, my phone buzzes. Sweet! It's him.

Heath: Just leaving now. I'm starving. Have you eaten supper?

Me: Technically, yes, but I was just about to start my evening grazing so I could always do that with a friend. Also, I have something I want to talk to you about.

Heath: …

Damn. Now, he's probably worried that I'm going to tell him I'm in love with him.

. . .

Me: About that dance school idea.
    Heath: Really? Are you up for it?
    Me: I might be.
    Heath: Excellent. Let's meet and talk business. Is Franco's Fish Taco Truck still a thing?
    Me: Franco Jr. took over. Same location.
    Heath: Meet me there in twenty?
    Me: I'll be there.

Let the rushing around to get ready for another non-date date begin!

———

Franco's Fish Taco Truck is a staple in San Felipe. The same truck has been parking along the same stretch of highway leading to the nature preserve as long as I can remember. It sits high on a hilltop with an incredible view of the lush valley below. It's so popular that when the island transport authority was repaving the road, they added a parking lot for Franco at the same time.

I hop on my moped and zip through traffic, then out to the highway, singing offkey to The Bee Gees the entire way. When I arrive, Heath is already there, leaning against his car in his dress clothes (sans the tie) and sunglasses. I park next to him, then, in my excitement, attempt to pull off my helmet and do a sexy hair shake at the same time as I get off. Only that's a lot for a girl to do all at once and I don't manage to lift my leg high enough which causes me to slam my foot against the bumper. I lose my balance, and land on my side, helmet still in place on my head.

"Oh wow!" Heath says, rushing over to me as I scramble to get up.

"I'm good!" I shout, hopping to my feet. Then I lift my helmet off and do the sexy hair shake, only this time, I over-exaggerate it to make him laugh. Which he does. He has the best laugh.

Oh, and now he's brushing off my shirt and my pant leg with his hand. That's sweet. Like take-me-now sweet.

"There. That's better," he says, grinning at me. "You ready?"

"I am," I say in a tone that's way too breathy for a food truck with a friend scenario.

He gestures for me to go first, then walks slightly behind me as we get into the line-up. So this is what it's like to hang around a true gentleman. Minerva taught him well...

When it's our turn to order, Heath tells Franco Jr. we'd like six tacos and two Cokes, then he glances at me, "You still like an extra side of limes?"

I nod, a teensy bit thrilled he remembered.

"And a few extra slices of limes for the dancing queen."

I roll my eyes and tell Franco that I'm not really royalty, but secretly, my heart is doing a double pirouette. When our food is ready, we wander over to a picnic table that's set back from the road and settle ourselves across from each other. The evening air still holds the day's heat, even though the sun has been down for an hour already. "I bet they have great food trucks in New York," I say, then chastise myself for saying anything positive about places that aren't here.

"Oh yeah, but you can't get fish tacos like these. Also, it's already really chilly there so standing on the sidewalk eating a hot dog isn't exactly something you linger on."

"Good point. That's why the Benaventes are far superior to New York. The weather, the fresh seafood…the beaches…" I say, hoping to remind him of last night's kissing without sounding like I'm trying to remind him of last night's kissing…

"Yes, it's very nice here too."

Nuts. He totally didn't pick up what I was putting down. Probably for the best though…

"So, your text implied you haven't been here in a while," Heath says.

"Chase hates seafood," I tell him.

"But you love it."

"Pathetic, right?" I ask. "Don't answer that."

"Okay, I won't so long as from now on, you speak up and get what you want in life."

I want you. Scratch that. No, I don't. "Sure, *Dad*," I say.

"I'm serious. I don't know what's been going on for the last ten years, but it doesn't sound like you've had any fun at all."

"And no fish tacos either," I say, avoiding the truth of his statement. "You never answered my text question."

He swallows, then says, "What question?"

"About how it went at the hospital."

He nods, wipes his mouth, then says, "It was sort of the equivalent of having to go to the principal's office, only instead of being called because my kid is skipping class, I had to go in because my mum has been upsetting the staff. And you won't believe this, but someone got her drunk a few nights ago. Caused a real disturbance with a lot of loud laughing and carrying on."

"Oh wow, who would do that?" I ask, feigning disapproval.

"Who indeed?" Heath says with a wry smile. "They threatened to cut off her pain meds if she does it again."

"Whoops. Because of the whole mixing booze and pain meds thing?"

Nodding, he says, "Who knew senior citizens would be this much trouble?"

"Well, in your mum's case, it was probably somewhat predictable," I answer, then finally have a bite of the world's greatest fish taco. The whitefish is deep-fried to perfection with just the right amount of batter. The red cabbage is crisp, the sauce is the perfect blend of tanginess and heat, and the tortilla shell is warm and soft. I make a moaning sound while I chew, then after I swallow, I say, "Okay, so clearly I still love it. How about you? Is it still as good as you remember?"

"Even better." Hmm, is it me, or does that meaningful expression in his eyes seem to be about more than simple food truck food?

"I'm glad you're here," I tell him suddenly, then feeling silly, I add, "For your mum's sake, I mean. It's really wonderful for her, I'm sure."

He shrugs, then says, "It's the least I could do for the woman who raised me. I'm actually going to be here until close to Christmas, maybe into the new year. The doctor said she's got a long road yet."

"Well, he doesn't know Minerva."

Offering me a small smile, he says, "Normally, I'd agree, but not this time. I'm going to be here for months." He does not look thrilled about that idea, which is like a thousand needles to my heart.

"Yikes. This is probably the last place you want to be."

He stares at me for a moment before answering. "Well, it does have some benefits."

Ooh! Like friends with benefits? Because I'd be down for that.

Before I can think of some flirty way to answer that without seeming too forward, he keeps talking. "But, eventually I have to go back. I mean, it's not like I can land my dream job here."

"Right, no, and you definitely need to get back in the old investment broker game or you're never going to be wildly rich."

"Exactly," he tells me, wiping a bit of sauce off his bottom lip. "Speaking of being wildly rich, I want to hear about the dance school. You said you changed your mind?"

My heart speeds up a bit and I sit up straight on the bench. "I've been thinking a lot about what you said, and somehow, after talking to you, it doesn't sound quite so impossible."

"It's not even a little impossible," he says.

"Difficult, but…exciting," I answer. "And today, I got a teeny sample of what it would be like to work with little kids instead of tipsy adults."

"And?"

"It's about the same, but the kids are way cuter." I have a sip of my Coke, then continue. "I spent the afternoon with Clara, Libby and Harrison's little girl. She's hilarious, by the way. But also, she was just so darn proud of herself when she got the moves right—we started with the mambo, then moved into some basic ballet moves. She absorbed it like a sponge."

I talk for a few more minutes about the afternoon, then move onto the topic of starting my own studio. Soon, Heath and I are deep in one of the most thrilling conversations of my life. Here's a brilliant accountant who knows a thing or two about business, *and* who believes I have what it takes to have a thriving dance studio. And he's really interested in helping me. Like, genuinely interested. Almost like he cares.

"So, if I did go ahead with it, how much would you charge for consulting fees?" I ask, hoping he says something like, 'fish tacos once a week' or 'sex slave.' I wouldn't object to that.

He glances up at the sky for a second as though considering it. "How about you help me fix up my mum's place in exchange? It's really in rough shape."

"Oh sure," I tell him, slightly disappointed he didn't go with sex slave, but also glad he didn't just say ten thousand dollars an hour or something. "I'd love to help."

"Excellent. I want to give the yard a total overhaul, repaint the exterior and most of the rooms...as much as possible before she gets home."

"You really are one of the good ones."

Waving off my compliment, he says, "Making up for lost time."

"No, you're a giver. It's true." I smile at him, a cozy feeling growing inside at the knowledge we've just given ourselves two great reasons to spend lots of time together. "You've got yourself a deal." I hold out my right hand to shake and when he does, a delicious feeling of warmth flows through me. Mmm...friendship warmth...

26

A Taste of Domestic Bliss...

HEATH

It's been two weeks of being together almost all the time without so much as laying one fingertip on each other. We have lunch together at the resort every day while we go work on Hadley's business proposal, and when we have time off (and in between visits to the hospital), Hadley meets me at Minerva's to tackle the next project on the 'Create a Lovely Home so Minerva Will Want to Stay There Instead of Getting Herself in Trouble' list. It's a long title, but it also serves as a bit of a mission statement, so we're sticking with it.

We've given the inside a deep cleaning, tidying and rearranging the furniture so there'll be more space for my mum to use her walker wherever she needs to go. We've also managed to tame the wild lawn, did a reasonable job trimming and shaping the hedges, pulled all the weeds, and bought some lovely flowers for the bed against the front of the house that Hadley assures me are 'no fuss' perennials.

(They'll get planted after we paint.) We also pulled up all the old, cracked sidewalk blocks and replaced them with new ones.

This morning (since it's Saturday), we'll tackle repainting the old faded beige clapboard siding. Hadley picked out a nice medium grey colour with a creamy white for the trim. The door will be a deep red to make sure the house has some 'personality.' We spent the last two evenings scraping and sanding down the siding and today we can finally start to paint. I have to say, all this fixer upper stuff is a lot more fun than I ever thought it would be, but I have a horrible feeling that's solely due to who I'm working with and not the tasks themselves.

One might think that should be a good feeling, but it's not. It's awful because all the old feelings are back. I cannot deny it any longer. She's all I think about, round the clock. She's the last person I want to talk to at night (and usually is) and the first person I want to see when I wake up. I'm right back to being in love with Hadley Jones, and since she's *never* going to have those feelings for me (a guy can tell—she shows no signs of being all googly-eyed over me, doesn't make excuses to touch me, and she doesn't stare too long), I'm going to be stuck getting over her yet again when I leave. But this time, it'll be much harder to do because of that damn kiss (which totally doesn't count because of the circumstances—fresh out of a break-up and pretty tipsy. She would have kissed an eel if it showed interest at that moment). That fact is a hard pill to swallow because for me, it proved what I assumed would be the case way back in high school—that the passion we'd share would be incredible. It was the kiss of a lifetime—the one all other kisses will be judged against. Oh wow, I'm getting way too dramatic. *Dial it down, Heath.*

Hadley arrives just as the sun's coming up, with two

enormous coffees and a six-pack of donuts. We agreed to start as early as possible in hopes of finishing the entire front before it gets too hot. God, she looks cute for someone who couldn't have had more than four hours of sleep. We were working on her business plan until after one in the morning, and I badly wanted to invite her to stay under the guise of getting more sleep, but managed to stop myself. The truth is, I wouldn't have gotten a wink if she was in the house. It would have been a night of tossing and turning.

The gentle cool breeze has that feeling of promise to it that only early mornings have—a new day just for us. We sit on the cement front step next to each other and dig into the donuts. "I made sure they added two old fashioneds to the box," she says.

"You know me so well," I tell her, having a sip of coffee. "Mm, thanks for this. It's exactly what I needed. How'd you sleep?"

"Barely at all. My mind was racing all night thinking about the cost of leasing and the number of students I'll need just to break even," she says with a sigh.

"Same here. It's a real gut-churner, isn't it?" I ask, taking a bite of my first donut of the day, letting the fluffy sweet goodness melt on my tongue for a second.

"Yup. Around three a.m., I had a crazy idea," she tells me. "Well, maybe not all that crazy. I don't know. What if I ask Harrison and Libby if I can rent out the yoga studio on an hourly basis? It's tucked away from the rest of the resort and there's a direct path to the parking lot so the students shouldn't disturb guests. Also, it's just sitting empty most of the time so they could make a tiny bit of revenue from letting it to me."

I stop chewing and look at her. "That's brilliant."

"It is?"

Swallowing, I say, "Yes, definitely. I mean, they could say no, but why would they? They're all about community, and the parents would probably spend money buying food and drinks while they wait."

"Oh! Or using the spa services," she adds, her face lighting up. "Drop little Janie off at class and go get a pedicure. It would be like a wellness break for the mums."

"And dads, sexist," I say, bumping her shoulder with mine.

She grins up at me, then says, "Yes, them too. What do you think? Should I pitch the idea?" she asks, then she holds up one hand. "Wait, I don't want you to answer that. I already know it's a great idea. I don't need anyone's approval."

"Good for you," I tell her. Then, putting on a fatherly tone, I add, "You're really becoming your own woman, Hadley. I'm so proud of you."

We both burst out laughing, then she smacks me on the leg. "Wanker."

"Oh, you love me," I tease, then, realizing what I said, I swallow hard and have a sip of my coffee.

"I do," she says softly.

When I dare to look down at her, she's got a serious expression on her face. It quickly morphs into something goofy and she says, "I mean, as much as you can love a total wanker, that is…"

I laugh, even though my soul has just soared to the sky with hope, then been slammed against the new sidewalk. "Obviously. Should we get to it?"

"Yes, sir. Let's get our paint on."

We work until just after lunch time, managing to get a first coat done on the entire front of the house, including the trim and the door. The sun is now positioned over our heads, telling us we have to stop now and get into the shade. Standing together on the front sidewalk that runs along the street, we survey our handiwork. "Not bad," I say.

"Not bad at all," Hadley agrees. "Especially the parts I did. Very professional."

I laugh. "Oh yes, far superior. In fact, I'm thinking maybe you do the entire second coat yourself tomorrow so we'll know it's done right."

"Well, you're not *that* bad," Hadley says, trying to hide a grin. "What do you say, should we go hit the beach and cool down?"

"No way," I tell her. "We've got something much more exciting to do."

"Really?"

"We need to write up your proposal for Harrison and Libby."

27

Spine Straight, Head Held High...Just Like a Ballerina (But an Effing Tough One)

HADLEY - ONE WEEK Later

Text from me to Mum: I won't be able to make it to brunch tomorrow. Tell Lucas he can have my share of the bacon.

My phone rings almost as soon as I press send, and I sigh when I see who's calling. "Hey, Mum."

"What do you mean you're not coming? This is been our one family tradition for fifteen years. What could you possibly have to do that is more important?"

"Minerva is getting released from the hospital and I told Heath I'd help get her settled at their place."

"Oh, Hadley, don't tell me you're getting involved with those two again." She lets out a dramatic sigh, then adds, "That woman is insane."

"She's not insane. She's…eccentric."

"Same thing, and you can't afford to be getting involved with them. You got extremely lucky that Chase was willing to overlook your unusual friendship with Heath, but I can assure you, it won't happen a second time."

Rubbing my temples, I say, "You're not seriously going to keep beating the dead relationship horse, are you, Mum? Because if so, I'm going to hang up now."

"I'm not talking about Chase," she says, then adds, "Although if he did come crawling back, you'd be wise to forgive and forget. But in the event that that doesn't happen, you need to be careful about who you count as friends. These things matter to people."

"To who?"

"To the *right* people."

"Oh my God, how did you get to be your age and not have the first clue who the right type of people are? They're not the shallow judgy ones you seem to love so much. They're the ones who accept you the way you are, warts and all—"

"Dear lord in heaven, do you have warts now, too?"

"No, I do not have warts. It's an expression describing unconditional love and friendship."

"If by unconditional, you mean they support you in your efforts to avoid any form of self-improvement, then I suppose they are exactly the right type of people."

I pause, pursing my lips together while I tell myself to calm down. You know what? Forget it. Being calm is overrated. I'm going to give honesty a try for once. "Here's a novel idea for you, Mum: what if you just accepted me the way I am? What if you and Dad sat down and made a list of...say...three good things about your daughter and tried to appreciate them instead of always pointing out everything that's wrong with me."

"Of course I know you have lots of good points," my mother says, raising her voice. "I brought you into this world. I raised you. No one knows you as well as I do. But I'm not the type of mother who's going to sit around singing my children's praises when they're screwing up their life. That's of no use to you. What you need is guidance until you can figure it out for yourself."

"No, Mum, what I need is acceptance and a little faith that I can figure it out for myself."

The first participant in my two p.m. Hatha yoga class walks in and I give her a quick wave. "I have to go; my class is about to begin."

"Fine. I guess we'll see you when we see you."

"Yep. Bye."

"Goodbye."

I tap the red circle on my screen much harder than I need to, then put my phone on silent, and drop it into my bag. Taking a deep breath, I let it out slowly, knowing I need to become a Zen master in the next few seconds.

———

"I heard you told Mum you're not coming to brunch on Sunday," Lucas says as soon as we meet up on the sidewalk.

I came straight from work to meet him at Eldon's Fine Jewels so I can help him pick out an engagement ring for his bride-to-be.

"She's totally pissed and yet, I regret nothing. You should try it sometime," I tell him as we walk through the door into the climate-controlled lobby. A well-dressed woman at a reception desk smiles at us, and I can't help but feel under-dressed in my post-work-out gear.

"Here to pick out wedding rings?" she asks.

"Engagement," he tells her.

"Wonderful, that way she'll get exactly what she wants," she says, winking at me.

"No, not for me," I tell her.

"Ew, yuck, no," Lucas says, pulling a face. "She's my sister."

Her face falls but she quickly recovers her smooth smile. "Oh, okay, getting a little female advice. Always a smart plan. I'll just get you both to sign in here."

We do as she says, then she buzzes us in, and what I now realize is a bullet-proof glass door slowly opens, allowing the gentle sound of classical music to enter the foyer. The showroom is perfectly lit to make every gem sparkle and the floor is draped in a plush dark grey carpet to absorb the sounds of clients murmuring to each other (probably while suffering from sticker-shock). Once we're inside, I lean in and whisper, "Are you sure you can afford this place?"

Lucas shrugs. "It's been a good year."

We spend the next twenty minutes perusing the selection, narrowing it down to three choices: a massive emerald cut diamond with a band of tiny diamonds, an obscenely big solitaire with a platinum band, and a square-cut rock which will require her to do daily free weights so she can even out the strength in her right hand. The salesman has taken all three to the back to get the 'good guy' pricing for Lucas, leaving us alone to gawk at some of the gaudier necklaces in one of the display cases.

The entire time we're in here, I have to work very hard not to let the little green monster out, but the truth is, I am a little envious. After how hard I worked to keep a long-distance relationship going with Chases Women, I should be on the receiving end of a massive diamond.

"You're quiet," Lucas says.

"I'm just tired. It's been a long day," I tell him.

"You sure? Because when I told Serena I asked you to meet me, she said it was not the most sensitive thing I've ever done."

I sigh, not wanting to tell him I sort of agree with her. "Listen, I'm your big sister. I want to be here for you no matter what." Then, putting on my best Doris Jones guilt trip voice, I add, "Including to help you pick out diamonds for your fiancée after I've just had my heart broken."

He laughs, then says, "You are eerily good at that. Like, way too good at it."

"Years of careful observation of the Queen of Passive Aggressivia."

"Still impressive," Lucas says. "So, we're cool then?"

"Yeah, we're cool. I'm getting over what happened. In fact, I'm almost past the 'wishing he'd die in a fiery car crash' phase, so that's got to be a good sign." I grin at Lucas, then point to a rather delicate chain with a pearl drop in the center. "Get that for Serena someday. That's totally her."

"Good call," he says, snapping a picture of it. "And just so you know, I'm not sure I'll ever get over the 'hoping to meet Chase in a dark alley so I can murder him with my bare hands' phase."

"You're a good brother," I tell him. "Want to hear something crazy?"

"Always."

"Numb nuts and I had a surprisingly honest conversation about why he did what he did, and it's not all one-sided."

"What?! No way. Do *not* go taking any blame for that jackass's bad behaviour," Lucas says far too loud for the setting. A woman looking at watches looks over, then shakes her head and continues on.

"I'm definitely not taking the blame, but he said something that actually hit home. He told me he never felt like he really knew who I was."

Lucas blinks a couple of times, then says, "That's because he didn't bother to even try to get to know the incredible woman who is my big sister."

"Aww, thanks, buddy," I say. "But to be fair, he did try. A million years ago when we were first together, but I was so busy trying to be whoever I thought he wanted me to be that he gave up." I lower my head in an effort to see the price on a gold necklace with a chain so thick, it looks like it could double as a weapon. "Huh, they really don't want you to see the prices here. Why is that?"

"I think this is one of those places where if money's an object, they don't want you to come in."

"Ah, gotcha."

"Now, back to the matter at hand, because it sounds very much to me like you're taking the blame for him sticking his dong in some dental assistant for the last year."

I shudder at the image, then say, "Gross, never say that again. I know he's a liar and a cheater and a coward. But I was also dishonest the entire time. I never told him I love seafood or that I hate superhero movies…"

"What? You watched superhero movies with him?"

"All the time," I tell him.

"But you would never watch them with me, no matter how much I begged."

"That's because they're godawful."

"So, why…?" he asks, then his eyes light up. "Because of Mum."

Nodding, I say, "The entire time, I thought to be 'wife material' meant being super agreeable all the time. I was more chameleon than woman," I say. "Maybe if I had actually let him get to know me, it would have worked out.

Or even better, he would have realized we weren't compatible and dumped me like…eleven years earlier."

Lucas stares down at me for a second. "Our parents didn't exactly set a good example of how to have a healthy marriage, did they?"

"Not really. They're like two strangers who really don't like each other that much, but continue their awkward dance every day as though everything's fine."

"Yup. You just described them perfectly. Why do you think I chose Serena?" Lucas asks. "She's the polar opposite of our mother. She knows what she wants and she's direct about it. No games, no passive aggressive martyr crap. Just honesty. Sometimes I don't like what she has to say, but I respect her for saying it, and I love knowing where I stand with her. It's a huge relief, actually."

"None of that walking on eggshells stuff," I say. "Sounds wonderful."

"It is. I mean, once in a while, it can be a little much," he says, lowering his voice. "To be honest, I wasn't quite as excited as I let on about her proposing to me, but only because I was looking forward to surprising her. But in the end, it doesn't matter because the result will be the same. We're going to start our life together, and it's going to be nothing like that farce our parents call a marriage."

The salesman comes back with a fancy purple folder and hands it to Lucas. "I think you'll find the good guy pricing quite pleasing."

He opens it and I peer over his shoulder. "Holy shit!" I shout, then quickly cover my mouth. "Sorry. Sorry. I wasn't expecting that. Such good prices for such a good guy," I add, trying to smooth things out.

Does anyone have a paper bag to breathe into? Because none of those rings are worth less than a car with all the options…

————

"Good luck!" Nora whispers to me as I walk past her desk.

"Thanks," I say, wincing as all the nervous energy zaps around inside my body so hard, I'm sure my hair is about to straighten. "I'll need it."

"No, you won't," she says, catching up with me and giving me a huge hug. "You've got this."

Nodding, I say, "I sure as hell hope so."

A moment later, I'm standing at Harrison's open door, waiting for him to get off a call. "Honey, don't listen to your gran. The last time she had a baby to look after was in the sixties, and look how she turned out."

Oh boy, that really makes me want to meet Libby's mum.

"I know. Yes," he says, noticing me and waving me in. "You are a wonderful mother." Pause. "Absolutely wonderful. It's a fact, not an opinion. Little Will is a challenge at the moment, but remember what the pediatrician said. Some of the most well-adjusted, successful patients he's had were fussy babies." Pause. "Okay, see you in a couple of hours." Pause. "Love you too."

He hangs up and shakes his head at the phone before looking up. "My poor wife. I'm just hoping any day Will's going to figure out he can trust me too. And the rest of the family."

I offer him a sympathetic smile. "I can't even imagine how tough that would be."

"It's okay. We'll get through this," Harrison says, grabbing a yellow pad of paper from his top desk drawer. "Now, Heath told me you have a great business proposition for me, so let's have it. I'm all ears."

"Thanks," I say, my skin suddenly feeling clammy. "I've been working here for a long time—"

"What's it been? Like ten years?"

"Uh-huh. And I love it here. I really do. You and Libby are amazing people to work for. I couldn't ask for better bosses actually. It's more like a family than a job," I tell him, hoping he knows I mean it.

"Well, thank you. We're lucky to have you, Hadley. You've always brought a very positive energy to the resort."

Okay, maybe this won't be so hard. "But, as someone who's reached a certain age and place in my life…"—i.e., suddenly single and closing in on thirty—"I'd like to be my own boss."

I hand him a copy of the proposal, spending the next ten minutes (or ten hours, it's hard to say because I'm so nervous) going through it with him. He seems to be nodding a lot and say things like, "Smart, yeah."

We turn to the final page, which includes the projections for future non-dance-related profits for the resort, and I start in about mums wanting mani-pedis, massages, maybe even use of the hot tubs or the pools. I end my presentation the way Heath and I practiced, "So you see, Harrison, it's really a win-win-win. The children of Santa Valentina get a more positive dance school that will encourage personal growth instead of following the 'break 'em down to build 'em up' model, I get the opportunity to be that person they've been waiting for and use my passion for dance and my love for children for the greater good, and you get a steady stream of local clientèle who will help fill in some of the low season dips in revenue. Also, as they get used to driving out here, they'll think of the resort for special events, family celebrations, weddings, etc. Paradise Bay could become *the* beloved hotel for the people of the island who need their own getaways as well."

"This is incredibly well-thought out," he says, flipping the pages.

"I can't take all the credit," I say. "Heath was instrumental in helping me put all this together."

"Really?" he asks, giving me a knowing look.

"Yup," I squeak, wondering why I'm suddenly so hot.

Harrison looks back at the package. "He's a great guy, that Heath."

"He really is."

"Someone you can really count on."

"Definitely."

"And I'm pretty sure he still has feelings for you, after all these years," he says, then glances up just in time to catch my reaction.

My mouth drops open, my heart starts to pound even harder than it has been since I got here, and I'm filled with a total sense of joy. *After all these years.* "What do you mean? Heath and I have always only been friends."

Sitting back in his chair, Harrison says, "But he never saw you as just a friend. You know that, right?"

"No…I didn't."

"Oh, I just assumed he would have told you at some point," he says. "He had it bad for you in high school. And he still gets that moony look when your name comes up— which happens a lot, I might add."

I stare at him with my mouth hanging open. This news is a total game-changer.

When I don't say anything within the appropriate amount of time, Harrison says, "I'm sorry, the lack of sleep is getting to me. That was very unprofessional and you are here on business."

"That's okay," I say, chewing on my lip. Can that be true? No. He's Heath. Good old buddy Heath.

"Anyway, I love your proposal."

"Really?" I ask, snapping back to the matter at hand.

"Really," he tells me. "I want to run it by Libby and

Rosy first, see if they have any concerns, but I'd be surprised if they did."

"Seriously?" I ask as he gets up from his desk and holds his hand out.

"Yup."

I jump to my feet and shake his hand with both of mine, tears filling my eyes. "Sorry," I tell him. "I didn't mean to…stupid unprofessional tears. I'm just so happy."

Chuckling, Harrison says, "There's absolutely no need to apologize. This is a big deal. It's the start of a whole new life for you."

———

"They said yes?" Heath asks as soon he answers the front door.

I hold up the bottle of sparkling wine I picked up on the way over. "Yes! I'm going to own a dance studio!" I screech, jumping up and down on the newly-painted front stoop.

I hand him the bottle, then throw my arms around him. "Can you believe it?"

He gives me the greatest celebratory hug of all time, squeezing me tight and managing to lift me off the step and into the house with one arm. Oh wow. That was, well…wow. Just nice. We're still hugging, and now I'm inhaling the scent of his neck—delectable man smell. When he pulls back, we stare at each other, our lips only an inch apart and the emotional charge grows so thick, it's hard for me to see reason.

Harrison's words come back to me and for one delicious second, I think maybe we could have a future together.

But just as the thought pops into my head, he lets go of

me and gives me a little punch on the arm. "Congratulations, Hads. You deserve amazing things."

Like you? "Thanks," I manage. "It never would have happened without you."

"Oh, I don't know," he tells me, letting go of me before I'm ready. "I think you would have found a way."

Shaking my head, I say, "No, I wouldn't have known where to start."

"You don't give yourself enough credit," Heath says, walking to the kitchen. "You're so much smarter than you think."

I follow him (or more accurately, I follow his taut buttocks, feeling barely smart enough to keep my tongue in my mouth). As soon as I get into the kitchen, I smell something delicious and see all the signs that he's been making a special dinner—complete with flowers on the table and a homemade sign taped to the wall that reads *Congratulations!* in big bubble letters. He turns and notices me looking around. "I was so confident that you'd get it, I decided a celebration was in order."

I cover my mouth and laugh with excitement, happy tears filling my eyes. "Thank you," I whisper.

"That's what friends do. We help each other," he says. "Besides, you more than paid me back by turning this dilapidated place into something really terrific."

I watch as he gets a couple of wine glasses out of the cupboard. "Minerva doesn't have champagne flutes so these'll have to do."

"They're perfect," I tell him, but what I really mean is *he's* perfect.

He pops the cork causing some of the liquid to spill over onto his hand. We both laugh while I hurry to grab the glasses and he fills them up. "To new beginnings," Heath says, holding up his glass.

"To new beginnings," I repeat, my mind wandering back to Harrison's words. *I'm pretty sure he still has feelings for you…*

We each have a sip, then something on the stove starts to boil over and Heath rushes over to turn the flames under the pot down. "I'm making spaghetti. The sauce has a Ragu base," he tells me, pointing at the empty jar on the counter. "…To which I've added heavy cream, peas, and ham."

"Whoa, fancy."

"I like to think so," he says, putting on an air of false pride. "Oh, and there's garlic bread in the oven."

"Mm! Will you marry me?" I'm joking, but deep down, I really want him to say yes.

"Is that all it would take to find a bride?" he asks.

"Oh yeah. The cooking thing? Totally bride bait."

"Good to know in case I'm ever in the market for a horrible lifelong commitment," he tells me.

I scoff, like it's the last thing I'd ever want either. "Stupid married people," I say. "Spending their lives with another human. Having to share everything and wake up next to someone with morning breath every day. No, thank you."

"Exactly," he says. "Ridiculous." Holding up his glass, he says, "To good friends."

I hold mine up too. "Friends forever," I tell him in a goofy voice before sucking back the rest of my drink.

28

Let's Party Like it's 1979...

HEATH

"For someone who's been begging to get out of here for the last two months, you certainly took your sweet time saying goodbye to everyone." I came by the hospital over an hour ago to collect Minerva, and somehow she's managed to wish a long and heartfelt farewell to everyone from the lady who brings her lunch every day to a lab tech who drew her blood once a few weeks ago.

I finally wheel her out the front door, where my new rental — a white minivan — is waiting.

"What the hell is that thing?" she asks, pointing to my ride.

"It's a very practical, easy to get in and out of mini-van," I say, pushing the button on my key fob so that the back door slides open.

"I'm not. Getting into. A minivan."

"You are, if you want to leave this hospital," I say,

wheeling her closer while she leans her torso as far away from the offending vehicle as possible.

"I'd sooner get hit by another bread truck than ride in that thing," she says, her voice raised loud enough to get the attention of the staff huddled over by the side door smoking.

"Well, I guess we're at an impasse then because this is the vehicle I have for you to get around in, but if you don't want to, that's fine. I can leave you here and hopefully someone with a Harley will show up soon. Do you want me to leave your walker so it can be strapped to the back of their hog?"

Scowling, she says, "Hardball, hey?"

"I'm afraid it's the only game you'll play." I set the brake on the wheelchair, then walk around to face my mother and hold my hands out to her to help her stand and get in. "Don't worry, I got one with tinted windows so none of the cool kids will know it's you in here."

When we reach the house, I see the party has already started. Our street is lined with mopeds, motorcycles, and the odd car belonging to friends of Minerva's. Luckily, Hadley blocked off a space in front of the house for me to park. As soon as I pull in, the front door of the house bursts open and a gaggle of blue-haired gangsters comes spilling out onto the front porch.

"Oh great," Mum mutters. "You said no one would see me in this thing."

"If they're your real friends, they won't care what kind of vehicle you're in," I say, reminding myself of a dad dealing with an insecure teenager.

"Whose house is this?" my mum asks. "And what the hell happened to all my weeds?"

"Yours, only an upgraded version, and as to the weeds, they left when they found out you were going to be in the hospital for so long," I say, before getting out. I push the button to slide the door open so my mum can make her grand entrance. Then, I hurry around to the back to get her walker, set it up, and wait for her to refuse to use it. Lucky for me, her friends manage to distract her so she willingly grabs hold of it and starts toward the house.

Hadley's in the kitchen, already mixing cocktails. She hurries to my mum with a tea towel slung over her shoulder, looking very much like she belongs here. "Minerva, wonderful to see you. Can I get you a drink?"

"You bet your sweet buns you can," she says.

"Anything in particular?"

"Make it wet and keep 'em coming." My mum points to her armchair, then says, "Park me over there, Junior, and go fire up the barbecue. I'm in the mood for an enormous juicy steak."

"I figured as much," I tell her.

A few minutes later, I find Hadley at the counter putting the finishing touches on the tray of drinks. "Those look fancy."

"They're mojitos. The perfect drink for a hot afternoon of celebrating."

"One thing you learned from your mum is how to be a perfect hostess," I say, smiling at her.

"I hope that's the only thing," Hadley says.

"It is," I tell her. "Now, I've been ordered to fire up the barbecue."

My mum's voice finds us all the way from the living room. "Quit flirting and get cooking! I'm hungry!"

So nice to have her home.

———

Hadley joins me in the yard just as I'm flipping the steaks. She's carrying a tray of raw hamburger patties in one hand and a couple of beers in the other. "Harriet doesn't like steaks so she brought these for you to whip up."

"Perfect," I say. "Just what I want to do. Spend more time in the hot sun standing in front of a flaming grill."

"Are you wishing you were back in the Big Apple, hurrying down a crowded sidewalk as your skin risks freezing solid because of an icy wind?"

Laughing, I say, "That almost sounds refreshing at the moment, but right now I'd rather be here."

"Rather be here?" Hadley asks. "Does that mean you've moved out of the 'I hate island life' mode of thinking?"

Tilting my head, I say, "I don't hate it. There are some good things about it. It's just not exactly the centre of the business universe, you know?"

"Right. I keep forgetting you're a mover and a shaker."

The back door opens and Nance comes out carrying a bottle of wine with a straw in it and a plate of wieners. "Oh, sorry to interrupt the two love birds, but I picked up the best wieners money can buy and I was hoping you could grill them up for me?"

"We're not love birds," Hadley tells her, taking the plate. "Just friends."

"Well, that's stupid," Nance says.

Bea comes walking out at that exact moment. "What's stupid?"

"These two idiots aren't doing it."

Wrinkling up her nose, Bea says, "Why on earth not? You're both single, good-looking, and Heath, you're too young to have erectile dysfunction issues. What's the problem?"

"Yeah," Nance says, as if the fact that we're not intimately involved is a personal affront to her. "What's the problem here?"

"Well, Hadley is a close friend and I'm not going to be sticking around." I leave it at that, even though I doubt that'll put an end to the topic.

"So, stick around, dummy!" Bea says, taking hold of the neck of Nance's bottle and sucking straight from her straw. "A girl like her isn't going to stay on the market long." She winks at Hadley who blushes. "Look at her, Heath!"

I check on the steaks instead, which are now sizzling away, almost ready. "I've seen her. She's a lovely woman and some guy will be lucky to have her."

"No, look at her," Nance says, grabbing the spatula from my hand. "Really look."

Lowering my shoulders, I turn to face Hadley, mouthing, "Sorry about this."

She gives me an 'I get it' face and then we both stare at each other. Gosh, she's pretty.

Bea walks around behind Hadley and takes hold of her waist. "Look at this little waist and her nice hips."

"Not to mention her perky breasts," Nance points out. Like, literally points to them, with her face far too close to Hadley's chest.

"Okay!" I say. "Back off ladies. She's not a piece of meat for sale."

They both grumble but do as I've asked.

"You know, you're being rather sexist," I tell them. "Hadley is a complex human being with opinions and thoughts and dreams. She's not just a gorgeous woman with a slammin' body."

As soon as I say the words, I regret them. Hadley bursts out laughing while Bea and Nance exchange meaningful looks.

"A slammin' body?" Nance asks, raising her eyebrows at me.

"That's not...I didn't mean...I just meant you should stop objectifying her."

"Thanks, Heath," Hadley says, with more than a little sarcasm. "You're my hero."

"Oh for..." I turn my attention back to the grill, removing the steaks.

The back door opens, allowing Minerva and Harriet, as well as the rest of the gang, to pour out onto the deck. "What's going on out here?" Harriet asks.

"We were just trying to help poor Heath here to 'get some.'" Bea says.

"You're not tapping that?" Harriet asks, pointing to Hadley.

"Well, I never said he was smart," my mum tells her friends, causing them all to laugh so hard, I'm guessing at least two of them are glad they're wearing Depends.

"Ladies, please!" I put on an authoritative tone. "Let's just change the subject."

"Why?" Bea asks. "Oh wait...is *she* not into *you*? Is that the problem?"

"Is it because he's so boring?" Nance asks. "I get it. My second husband was boring, but in a lot of ways, he was also the best of the bunch. Very reliable."

"Reliable's good," Harriet tells Hadley.

I roll my eyes, then let out a frustrated sigh. "Thanks, ladies. While I appreciate your misguided attempts at 'gettin' me some,' I'll ask you to stop now. I'm fully capable of handling my own love life."

"Are you really?" Minerva asks, wrinkling up her nose. "Because it doesn't seem like it."

"I should have left you at the hospital," I tell her.

"I could say the same thing about you," she answers.

———

An hour later, Hadley and I stand at the kitchen window together watching my mum and her friends, who are sitting around the large patio table picking at the nearly-empty serving platters and killing themselves laughing. We've gone inside to get drink refills for them and to get the welcome home cake that Hadley picked up.

"Sorry about them," I tell her, glancing down at her for a second.

"It's all right," she says. "At least they were very flattering of me, but their comments about you? Ouch."

"It's no wonder I was never a ladies' man with them around crushing my ego at every turn."

Hadley looks up at me. "Is your ego crushed?"

"No," I tell her. "I just felt like being dramatic."

"Good," she says, looking out the window again. "You know…you could totally be a ladies' man if you wanted to."

I hide a grin and do my best to look exasperated. "Not you too…"

Chuckling, Hadley puts on an old lady voice and says, "What? Is it so wrong to want to see you happy?"

I burst out laughing, then shake my head at her, wishing I could pull her into my arms and just lay one on her instead.

———

It's nearly midnight by the time the last of my mum's friends finally vacates the premises. Hadley left a couple of hours ago so she can get some sleep and be back here in time for me to go to work tomorrow morning. I'm waiting outside the bathroom door while my mum gets ready for bed. She opens the door, looking irritated. "You don't need to follow me around everywhere. I haven't lost my mind."

"I know, but it's been a long day and I wanted to be able to hear you in case you needed anything."

Gripping her walker, she takes a couple of steps toward me, then pats me on the cheek. "You're a good boy."

"It's about time you noticed," I say with a little grin.

She turns and starts down the hall, bumping into me with her walker — most likely on purpose. "And I know I didn't say it earlier, but I like what you did with the place. It looks a lot better."

"Ah, it's the least I could do," I tell her.

"No, seriously," my mum says, stopping and turning to face me. "Thank you. I love it. It's like a real home, and I didn't know how much I needed that."

"You're welcome, Mum."

"I love you, you know," she says, her voice cracking a little.

"I love you back. And I'm really grateful you're alive."

"Me too." She makes the left into her bedroom and manages to maneuver the walker around the tight space between the wall and her bed. She pulls back the covers and smiles. "Ahh, it'll feel nice to be in my own bed again."

I wait while she struggles a little to get herself settled, knowing she won't accept help unless she's in real trouble. When she's finally tucked in, I say, "Have a good sleep, Minerva. I'll be just down the hall if you need me."

"I won't, but I'll be glad you're there."

29

Redemption via Email

HEATH - TWO WEEKS LATER...

I'm sitting in my tiny home office answering a few emails. In a few minutes, I have to take Minerva back to the hospital for a follow-up with her surgeon. Outside, in the shade of the Caribbean pine tree, Hadley and my mum are playing cards and sharing a laugh about something. It's a simple, quiet moment that doesn't carry the thrill of takeovers, mergers, or deals with nine zeros. But somehow, it's satisfying in a way work never could be, and the truth is, it warms my heart more than it should. It makes me wonder if maybe I'm meant to be here instead of in a tower in the Financial District. I don't want to stay at the resort, but maybe I could find something of interest to do here on the island.

If I were a person who believed in signs, I'd be looking for one right now because I'm so conflicted about my future, I find myself wanting someone else to figure it out for me. But unfortunately, I'm an adult, and that means figuring out your own shit and being responsible. Turning back to my laptop, I see a notification that makes my heart stall for half a second.

Email from: Charles.Dubanowsky@DubanowskyInvestmentBrokers.com
To: Heath.Robinson@jmail.com

Subject: RE: Big Mistake

Hey Heath,

There's an old song by some band that I forget the name of, but the lyrics have something to do with not knowing what you've got till it's gone. That's certainly the case when it comes to letting you go. I think you probably can guess by the subject line where this is going. I definitely acted rashly and have been living in a pit of regret since.

You are one hundred percent my go-to guy, and even though it will be too late for you to be part of the Kurrell-Bao merger (which incidentally does not look like it's going to go through due to a neglected step three of the due diligence bible you wrote up), I definitely want to have you ready to roll for the next one. I'll call you in one hour to beg, but I wanted to preface it with an email so you'll be more inclined to answer when you see my name pop up on your phone.

Humbly yours,
Charles

Before I can even begin to digest the email, my phone rings and I see his name. "Charles, hi."

"Thanks for picking up," he says. "I owe you a huge, *huge* apology. You were right. I was wrong. You were definitely the reason things have been going so well over the last several years. I see that now. And I see how firing you was a rash, stupid decision which may or may not have been fueled by an overdose of creatine. I've been working out really hard for weeks now and...anyway...you don't want to hear about all of that."

"Not really, no," I say.

He sighs. "Okay, right. So back to you. What do I have to do to get you back here? Switch over to a zoom call so you can see me on my knees begging? Fly there? Give up my corner office for you? What? I'll do anything. Just say you'll come back."

"My mum still needs me," I tell him, giving myself time to process what he's saying.

"Absolutely. You stay there—full salary, of course—until she's ready. Or I can hire round-the-clock nursing staff so you can come back. No pressure though, but I'll totally do it if that's what it takes. And to sweeten the pot, I'm going to make you CFO."

"You already have a CFO."

"Say the word and I'll get rid of him. Or, if you don't like that idea, I cut you in as a full partner. That's what you're really after, isn't it?"

Yup. It is.

And just like that, the one thing I've wanted for the last six years has been offered to me. I glance out the window again in time to see Hadley laughing and touching my mum's hand. "Can I take some time to think about it?" I ask him.

"Wow, you really do intend to make me pay. Okay, that's fair. That's fair, buddy. Tell you what? I'll get the MOU drawn up while you think about how badly you want to hurt me," he says. "I won't fight back. I'll just sit here and take it, okay?"

My instinct is to let him off the hook, but then I remember how shitty he was when he fired me and I let the devil in me out. "Sounds good, but know I do plan to make you pay, *if* I come back."

When I hang up, I realize it's just about time to leave for the appointment. I hurry outside to get my mum, and the second I step outside, she and Hadley see me. They both narrow their eyes, and in time with each other, they say, "What's wrong?"

"Nothing," I lie. "Except that I don't want to be late for the appointment."

"Do you believe him?" my mum says to Hadley.

"Nope."

Rolling my eyes, I say, "Believe me, don't believe me, either way, we have to get going."

Hadley stands and tries to help Minerva get up, but she waves her off. "I've got this, young chicky."

She stands, looking less shaky than she did even a couple of days ago, and Hadley and I share a quick smile. Hadley walks us out to the front, then gets her helmet off her moped. "Good luck. Let's hope the doctor has great news."

When Minerva gets into the minivan, she says, "Oh, Hadley, I need you to do me a favor and get this one out of the house tonight. I'd like to have some friends over and he's a bit of a square." She gives her a wink and says, "Unless it'll ruin your street cred if you took him out. I would totally understand if you don't want to be seen with him in public."

"I don't have any plans," she tells my mum. Then, looking at me, Hadley says, "You can come by my place if you want. We could have a *Clash of Crowns* marathon."

I think about watching those steamy scenes with her and how badly that would make me want more. "How about *Scott Pilgrim Saves the World?* We never did get around to watching it when we were kids."

Before Hadley can answer, my mum says, "Perfect. She'd love that." Turning to Hadley, she adds, "He'll be there at seven. That way I can get him out of the house before there's any crossover."

Hadley laughs. "See you at seven, then."

Throwing my hands up in the air, I say, "Yup, I guess so."

As soon as we get on the road, my mum says, "So, what happened? And don't say nothing because I already know."

"Charles called."

"What? Is he begging you to take your old job back?"

"Even better. He's offering full partnership." I keep my eyes on the road to avoid looking at her.

"Let me guess, you're not sure you want it now."

"Of course I want it. I spent my entire adult life building towards this exact thing."

"And now you have to choose between love and money," she says, making little clicking sound. "That's a real bitch of a decision for a nice guy like you."

"Not really," I say. "Hadley's doing much better. She won't fall apart just because I'm gone."

"She won't, but you will."

"What are you talking about?" I say, feeling beyond annoyed. "I left her—I mean here, I left *here*—once, I can sure as hell leave again."

"Freudian slip if ever there was one."

215

30

If You Love Someone, Cling to His Ankle and Beg Him Never to Leave...

HADLEY

"Welcome to spaghetti and movie night at Casa de Hadley," I say, holding the door open for Heath. "Should we eat in front of the TV, or at the table like civilized humans and *then* watch the movie?"

"Hello to you too," Heath says with a smile that melts my heart (and by heart, I mean knickers).

Gosh, he's cute. Should I tell him? I should. I should just tell him I think I'm falling for him. He's here, I'm here. We're both single, and according to Harrison, he's always had a thing for me. Why not just lay one on him right freaking now, then say, 'I think we might have something special here big boy, and we should see where it goes.' Except without the big boy part...

Rubbing the back of his neck, he says, "Let's eat first. I kind of have something to talk to you about."

Ooh! Wouldn't it be amazing if he's about to confess

his love feelings for me? Squee! He looks so nervous, that must be it. "Sure. Come on in."

I busy myself filling a large pot with water and setting it on the stove while Heath gets some greens out of the fridge. "I got a call," he says. "Well, *and* an email actually, from my boss back in New York."

Shit, shit, shit. That doesn't sound like a confession of love. Not even a bit. It sounds like an 'I'm leaving again' conversation. I take out a cutting board and paring knife to slice some cucumbers. Doing my best to sound breezy, I say, "Did he finally come to his senses?"

"Yeah, I guess you could say that. He was full of apologies and said he's willing to beg to get me to come back. He even offered to bring me in as a full partner."

I force myself to put on a bright smile. "Wow, full partner? That's huge!"

Don't cry, don't cry. Do not cry. He may not even take it, and if he does, be happy for him because it's what he wants.

"Yeah, it's beyond what I ever thought would happen, actually," Heath says, with — oh, no, a really huge smile. "I never thought he'd ever in a million years offer me partnership. A VP position, sure, but equal partners? It's basically the biggest way possible to show he recognizes all my hard work."

"Well, you deserve it. You really do. He never should have let you go in the first place," I say, chopping the cucumber with more force than necessary. "Stupid move if ever there was one."

"I agree," Heath says, sneaking a slice off the cutting board.

"Well, that's just wonderful. Congratulations, really. Good for you," I say, slicing the tip of my pointer finger. "Ouch, shit!"

Heath quickly takes my hand and holds it up. "Well, it

doesn't look like it needs stitches. Here, run it under some water and I'll go get you a Band-Aid."

"I'll go get it," I say, needing to get away from him for a minute. "I have them so tucked away, you'd never be able to find them."

I hurry to the bathroom and shut the door, then lock it and lean against it with my eyes shut. *Come on, Hadley. You knew this was coming the whole time. This isn't a relationship. It feels like one, maybe, in a way, but you're just clinging to a raft in the stormy sea of singledom. No promises have been made. No kisses have been shared. Well, except that one amazing time at the beach. But that was weeks ago. Since then, he's made it very clear that we're just buddies.*

I open the top drawer and grab the box of Band-Aids that's sitting neatly at the front, then take my time washing my hands and dressing my tiny wound while reminding myself to suck it up and be happy for him. I stare at myself in the mirror for a minute and whisper, "Be the cool girl. If Heath loves you, set him free. If he comes back...you won't spend the rest of your life pining for him."

There's a knock on the door and he says, "Are you all right in there?"

Putting on my most cheerful tone, I say, "Yup, great. Almost cleaned up."

I take a deep breath, give myself a firm nod, and go back out there. "Is the water boiling?" I ask.

"Yeah," he says, giving me a concerned look. "I already added the spaghetti. Are you sure you're okay?"

"Pfft! This little thing?" I ask, waving my hand in the air like I just don't care. "It would take a lot more than that to bring me down."

I hurry past him and dig around in the cupboard for some jarred pesto sauce. "So, where were we? Oh, right. You were just telling me how all your dreams are about to come true. That is totally amazing and I am *so* happy for you. So happy. It sounds like it's the exact opportunity you've been waiting for, like … years. We should celebrate. Let me see if I have a bottle of wine."

I can feel him watching me while I rush over to the fridge, but I keep going, not wanting to face him in case he can read in my eyes that I don't want him to go. "Good for you," I say again. "I just love it when nice guys finish first."

"Yeah, thanks," he says, his tone devoid of excitement. "Listen, it's okay to say it if you're not thrilled about this."

Turning to him, I put on my best confused face. "Why wouldn't I be thrilled? This is good news. You're my friend and I want good things for you. And this is a good thing, isn't it? Buckets of money, the excitement of the work you love…"

"Yeah," he says, narrowing his eyes at me. "It's just that we've been spending so much time together, I thought…"

"Thought what? That I'd get all clingy and beg you to give up everything that will make you happy just to hang out and watch movies with me?" I give him a 'that would be crazy' face.

"No, of course not," he says, his eyes searching for the truth.

"Good, because that would be a little insulting, frankly," I tell him in a teasing tone. "I mean, how could I ever expect you to give up your dream for me, especially not after you helped me get started on mine? I couldn't, that's how." And now, I'm laughing like an idiot and, oh God, this hurts.

"Actually, Hadley, I haven't given Charles an answer, and even if I do take it, I wouldn't be going anywhere until my mum is ready."

I grab a wooden spoon out of the cupboard and stir the pasta. "Oh, right, well, she'll appreciate that, *for sure*."

To be quirky, I drop the r's in for and sure so it sounds like fo sho. *Okay, bad idea. You seem like you're trying too hard to be happy which is a total tip-off that you're devastated.* "Oh, hey, I forgot to ask what the surgeon said today."

"He said she's healing remarkably well and that he thinks that in another two weeks, she won't really need her walker very much of the time. Only if she wants to go for a long walk, but she shouldn't need it around the house anymore."

"Great, that is *such great* news. Minerva must be thrilled. I can't wait to see her tomorrow to celebrate her great news."

Argh! Why do I keep saying great? Do I not know any other adjectives in the English language? And how can he be standing there so casually telling me he's most likely leaving forever.

Oh, wait, it's because I'm an idiot who doesn't tell anyone what I want. And I want him, but I'm too afraid to say it because I'm almost positive he doesn't want to marry me and have beautiful little Heaths and Hadleys. Gah! There's no way I can even hint at that. It's way too risky. I need to protect my already-injured heart. Besides, Heath has been entirely clear with me the entire time that this isn't going anywhere but friendship, forever. We're BFFs with an emphasis on the first 'F.' Harrison's intel was just old news. Old shitty news that messed me up and almost caused me to ruin a perfectly wonderful friendship.

"Are you sure you're okay?" he asks.

"Perfect!" I pop my 'p' and spit a little in his direction. Oh nice. "Whoops. Sorry about that. Yuck, right?" I ask, laughing awkwardly while wiping his shirt off.

"Hadley, are you—"

"Seriously, dude, you don't have to worry. I'm fine. In fact, I'm supa fine." Supa fine? This is disastrous.

"Really?" he asks, narrowing his eyes at me. "So, you want me to go?"

"Go, stay, it's all the same to me," I lie. "Please don't make me part of your decision. This has been really fun and you're a good, good friend, but to be honest, with us spending so much time together, I'm not exactly going to find love, am I?"

Am I? I'm actually asking because if I could find love with you, I'd never want another thing in my life. Not even a puppy.

Nodding, he says. "Yeah, no, you're right. I'm definitely cramping your style by being here. I wouldn't want to get in the way of you finding love."

I suddenly remember I've sworn off men, so I change gears (you know, so I can sound extra insane). "Not now of course. Most likely never. I am Thelma after all. Or Louise. Your mum and I haven't quite sorted that out yet."

"You know what?" Heath says, in a tone loud enough to match mine. "I think I'm going to take it."

I freeze in place, everything stopping, including my breath, my blood, and my stupid heart. "You should."

He stares me down for a second. "I'm going to."

"Brilliant. Glad that's settled," I shout. "Let's eat!"

———

The rest of the evening did not get *any* better. We ate in near-silence, then sat as far from each other as possible while we watched Scott Pilgrim. Super fun film, but I could barely bring myself to laugh. Instead, I just stayed curled up, sort of numb as my mind replayed the horror show that occurred earlier. He must know I love him after that. I made an absolute fool of myself—like a Shakespearean comedy character protesting too much. It was so glaringly obvious that he must know. And the fact that he knows and decided to go anyway is like coarse sandpaper to my soul. It hurts. So. Much.

He left as soon as the end credits started to roll under the guise of 'making sure the party doesn't get out of control.' As soon as the door closed behind him, I burst into tears, like big, huge, gasp-inducing ones. I manage to get it together enough to text Nora.

Me: You still up?

Nora: Yup. Everything okay?

I call her and as soon as she picks up, I say, "Something weird and kind of bad happened," my throat tightening.

"Oh God, you're pregnant."

What? How even? "No, I'm not pregnant."

"Phew! Thank goodness, because you are *not* ready to be a parent."

"I feel like I should be offended, and yet, I'm just going to go ahead and agree with you. It's about Heath. His boss asked him to come back to New York forever and I told him I think he should go," I say in a big rush of words.

There's a pause, then Nora says, "So you *do* love him."

I nod, then let out a shaky breath as tears start to form in my eyes. I'm glad we're on the phone so Nora can see me, but apparently she knows well enough to know I'm super upset.

"Sweetie," she says, putting on her motherly tone. "You flew too close to the sun."

I chuckle, then sniffle. "I really did and it's too late because there's no going back now. I'm in love with him."

"Are you sure it's not a rebound? They can be pretty intense since they're the best way to avoid the pain of the original break-up."

Chewing my bottom lip, I say, "I don't think so. This whole thing with Heath feels completely different than what I had with Chase—even when it was semi-decent way back in high school."

"Well, maybe it's the real thing then. You do seem surprisingly happy for someone who just got dumped after twelve years."

I groan. "It can't be real. It's probably just a rebound," I say, shutting my eyes. "Which is why telling him to take his job back was the right thing to do."

I wait, hoping she'll answer in the affirmative, but instead she says, "Was it?"

"Yes," I answer, hoping to convince myself. "I did the right thing for him. It's his dream job, his entire life is there, and I know he'll be really happy. I can't ask him to give that up. Not after everything he's done to help me get the dance studio idea off the ground. That would be horribly selfish of me. Not when he can go off and make tons of money and be super-accomplished and live out his dreams."

"What if his dreams have changed since he came home?" she asks.

"What if they haven't?" I say, my heart in my throat.

"Then at least you won't spend the rest of your days wondering."

I let out a long sigh, thinking about telling him the truth, which is that I want him to stay more than I want anything in this world. I go around in circles in my mind between being sure I should tell him and being terrified that I'm totally wrong about my feelings (and his) and that I'm going to be rejected. And this time, it would be so much worse, because unlike Chase, Heath would be rejecting the real me. Finally, I speak up. "Who am I to ask a guy like him to give up everything he wants?"

"What if you're the love of his life?"

31

A Moment with Minerva

HEATH

It's been two weeks since I told Charles I'm coming back to Dubanowsky. And in that time, Minerva is pretty much back to her normal self, which means she doesn't need Hadley in the mornings anymore, or really me at night. I've become more of a nuisance to her, even though she'd never come right out and say it. She will, however, imply it from time to time.

I helped Harrison find a new accountant—a young Irish woman fresh out of university who is so enamoured with the Caribbean, I swear Harrison could have asked her to pay to work there. And now I'm preparing to leave again. It's for the best. That's what I keep telling myself every time I'm tempted to tell Charles to sod off, and rush to Hadley to tell her I think we should give this a go.

But she's given me not even one tiny hint she wants me to stay. Nothing. Nada. We've both mainly managed to make excuses not to see each other, which I tell myself is the best way for me to get used to not having her in my life again. Whatever I thought was starting to happen between us, clearly was my own wishful thinking. Why wouldn't it be? After all the years I've spent wanting her to see me—like *really see me*—and love what she sees, she hasn't and she never will. I'm the same guy I've always been and she's the same girl who sees me as a friend. That night on the beach with all the kissing was purely a result of alcohol and her need to feel better, even just for a few minutes. It wasn't about me. If we were meant to be together, we already would be. There's been plenty of opportunity for it to happen, but it hasn't.

I grab my suitcase out of the closet and lay it on my bed, then unzip it. After a few minutes of packing, I hear a light knock on my door.

Minerva is standing there with a small smile. "So, this is it then?"

"Yup," I say, staving off a swell of emotions. "But I'll be back in three months, so that'll come before we know it, right?"

She nods, but I can tell she doesn't believe me.

"I will, Mum. I've worked quarterly holidays into my new contract and I promise you, I will be spending them here. Or wherever else in the world you want to meet me."

Giving me a skeptical look, she says, "Even Spain?"

I glance at the ceiling for a second. "For tapas and touring art museums?"

Shaking her head, she says, "Such a disappointment. I should have had a girl."

I chuckle, then walk over and surprise us both by dropping a kiss on top of her head, then giving her a big hug.

She folds her arms around me, somehow managing to make me feel small again for a second. But because that thought seems like too much for me at the moment, I say, "God, you're so tiny."

"Hey, what I lack in size, I more than make up for in gumption."

"Gumption?" I ask, pulling back a bit. "You really are old."

She slaps my arm and we both laugh even though we're sad.

"You going to be okay?" I ask her.

"I'll be fine. The question is, will *you* be okay?"

"Of course I will. I'm going back to New York where I'll be given a massive corner office and a big, fat raise. And I'll be doing what I love again. I'm not sure if you noticed, but being a nurse isn't exactly my calling."

She chuckles. "You were a hell of a lot better at it than I would have been."

"True, but let's not have a repeat, okay?"

"My moped days are behind me," Minerva says with a sigh.

"Promise?" I ask.

She nods, then gives me a wicked grin. "I'm thinking of getting a Harley trike."

Letting out a chuckle, I shake my head at her. "Of course that's what you'd choose."

"Hey, this lady likes the feeling of the wind in her hair."

Pulling her in for another hug, I say, "You're amazing. Don't ever change, Mum."

"Ah, now, let's not get all mushy here. That's not our style," she tells me, patting me on the cheek. "But I will say this. You're not so bad yourself, kid. I know I don't say it often, but I don't regret having you."

We both laugh and hug again, this time letting our

arms say what we can't voice. When we let go, I get back to packing, apprehension coming over me.

'You're sure it's worth it?" Minerva asks.

"Worth what?" I say, narrowing my eyes.

"Worth giving up Hadley for?"

Shaking my head, I say, "She was never mine to give up."

"What are you talking about? She's definitely in love with you, you big goof."

"No." I let out a sigh and turn back to my suitcase. "She'll never see me that way."

Wrinkling up her nose, Mum says, "What makes you think that?"

"I just know. But in the end, it doesn't matter anyway. I come from a long line of people who never marry because we know love doesn't really work out in the end."

My mum comes and sits on my bed. "That may be true for me, but I don't know...some people do seem meant for each other."

"Like who?" I ask, tossing a shirt in my suitcase.

"Um...well...Tom Hanks and Rita Wilson seem happy."

"They're both talented actors so who would ever know if they weren't?"

"Good point," she says, plucking the shirt out of the suitcase and refolding it, in a very un-Minerva moment. "Look, Heath, just because I'm hard to love, doesn't mean you are."

I start to protest, but she waves me off. "I am. I know it. I'm as prickly as a cactus."

"You're an acquired taste," I admit.

"But you're not. You're easy to love and I'm pretty sure if you ask, you'll discover that Miss Hadley Jones loves you."

The thought that she might actually love me overwhelms me and I shake my head, unwilling to believe it could be true. If she was ever going to love me, it would have happened by now. "No, she really doesn't. I was a good distraction. Nothing more," I say, needing to hear it as much as I need to convince my mum of that fact. "And even if she did have feelings for me—which she doesn't—it would never work. She's starting a new adventure here and I'm going back to my life. Period. The end."

"And nobody lived happily ever after..." Minerva says.

"Yes, they did. Just not in the predictable, conventional, make-you-miserable-in-the-end way."

32

What Happens at the Airport, Sometimes Ends up on YouTube...

HADLEY

The last two weeks have been tumultuous to say the least. Things are progressing quickly with my dance studio, and I've moved onto the applying for loans phase, which is likely going to be my least-favorite phase of owning my own business. I won't need much, since I'll be saving on my biggest expense—renting a space—but I'll still need an influx of cash for advertising, music rights, and various teaching aids.

In other news, I exist in this weird limbo state of completely questioning my decision to hide my feelings for Heath. We've actually done such a great job of staying carefully within the friend zone that I sometimes find myself thinking I can't possibly even have feelings for him. But then I let myself think about how I feel when I'm with him and the only answer I can give is deliriously happy. But as of today, that ends.

I finish tidying up the studio, then check my phone.

There is a text from Nora: *A little bird told me Heath is leaving for the airport in a few minutes. Last chance to tell him how you really feel.*

Me: *Nope. As far as I'm concerned, he's already gone.*

I slowly walk through the resort grounds to the staff parking lot, my heart sinking a little more with each step.

I love him.

Like, madly, truly, deeply, forever love him.

And I'm about to lose him permanently.

My brother and Serena pop into my mind and I think about how she just went for it. She knew she loved him and she dropped to one knee and ended up getting exactly what she wanted. I think about Minerva's mantra—*life is for the bold.*

She's right. And Serena was right too. You have to tell people what you want, not just sit back and hope they'll figure it out. Especially with men. And especially in a really confusing situation like what Heath and I have.

I love him and I have to make sure he knows it.

Dammit.

I'm going to end up doing that thing where I rush to the airport, aren't I?

Yes. Yes, I am.

I weave through traffic, trying to figure out how to say what I need to. It would help if I actually knew what I wanted. I guess I do in a way— I want him. Every day and every night, I want him here for the rest of my life.

About three blocks from the airport, I run a yellow light and nearly cause an accident. When I glance back behind me, I see a bread truck stopped in the middle of the intersection, the driver shaking his fist at me and shouting, "You damn women on your mopeds!"

Whoops.

When I reach the departure terminal, I park on the

sidewalk, climb off, and race inside, forgetting to take my helmet off. Luckily, I catch sight of myself in the mirror as I'm running through the airport and manage to remove it without breaking my stride. I stare around wildly at the airline counters and the lineups, looking for Heath.

By the time I spot him, I'm a total sweaty mess, and he's near the front of the security check-in. Well, this is it. I open my mouth and shout, "Heath! Heath Robinson!"

He turns slowly and sees me, then offers me an awkward wave.

Shit. I'm going to have an audience for this. Welp, this is the way it's gotta be. Sometimes a girl has to humiliate herself in the name of love...

Glancing around, I see I've already captured the attention of nearly everyone in line. "What if you stayed?" I shout. "What if you stayed and we made a really great, not-so-rich-but-crazy-happy life together?"

He seems frozen in place, staring at me with his mouth slightly ajar, so I keep right on going. "I made a huge mistake. Back in high school when I went with Chase to the movie instead of staying home to watch Scott Pilgrim with you," I yell. "If I'd been smart enough to realize what I had with you, we could've had a whole life together already — maybe with a couple of kids by now, or...or those cats we talked about. The ones we'd put in pouches on our sweatshirts."

A random lady in line pipes up with, "Oh, don't get cats. Get dogs. They're so much more loyal."

I glance at her and say, "Thanks, I'll keep that in mind," then looking back at Heath, I say, "And I screwed up when you came over for pasta and to finally watch Scott Pilgrim with me. When you asked me if you should go back to New York, I should've said no. I should have just told you the truth, which is that I am madly in love with you and I don't think I can see myself ever being happy again if you're not with me."

One of the security officers tells Heath it's his turn and he glances back and forth between him and me a couple of times before he tells the person behind him to go ahead. My heart does a quick *ciseaux* as I watch him weave his way through the lineup.

Oh wait. He's not smiling.

Why isn't he smiling?

Is it because this is too monumental a moment for something so trivial as a grin?

When he finally reaches me, he lowers his voice and says, "Look, I really care about you, Hadley. But I can't do this." He rakes one hand through his hair. "Your feelings for me aren't real. They're just a reaction to what you've been going through."

"But what if they're not? What if what we have — true friendship — is the basis of long-lasting love?"

"Okay then, answer this: Why now?" he asks.

"Well…I mean…I've been second guessing myself about how I feel because I'm so fresh out of that other thing with that idiot. But the last few days, I've been sure, *like really sure,* this isn't just some rebound. I'm in love with you."

He drops his shoulders. "No, I mean, why not when we were kids? I'm the same guy I was back then. There's nothing different about me. And you didn't have feelings for me then, and you haven't had them the entire time I've been here. I just think you're scared to be on your own so you're fooling yourself into thinking you're in love with me. But you're not."

"So, you think you know what's in my heart better than I do?" I ask, thoroughly annoyed now.

Heath stares at me for a second, then nods. "Yeah, in

this case, I do. I've been a soft place for you to fall, but that's not enough for me. I don't want a life with someone just because I happened to be there when her life fell apart."

"That's not what this is," I whisper.

"How can you know for sure, Hadley?" he asks. "Because you're asking me to make a decision about my entire life right now. Can you really guarantee it'll work out?"

I don't bother to fight back the tears. Instead, I just nod like a fool and say, "Yeah, no, I guess not. You're probably right."

The woman who wants us to get dogs clearly doesn't agree because she says, "No, he's not. He's a dumbass. Nobody ever gets a guarantee. Love is a leap of faith. You don't get to look first; you just have to jump."

"That is the least-logical thing I've ever heard," Heath tells her. "And honestly, it's really none of your business, so please butt out."

Dog lady says, "You're a coward."

Rolling his eyes, Heath says, "Yeah, sure, I'm definitely going to change my mind because some random person at the airport called me a coward."

"Look at me," Dog Lady says. "Don't bother with him, hon. You need a man with a backbone, which clearly he lacks."

Heath glares at her for a second, then turns back to me. "I'm sorry. But I really have to go. You take care of yourself, okay?"

Then he turns to walk away and I have to stop my hand from reaching out for him. I'm pretty sure my heart is about to burst into a gazillion pieces. I told him I'm in love with him and he accused me of being a confused, clingy gold-digger. Oh, wow. The pain of this is...ouch bad.

The line has thinned now so I watch as he makes his way through the maze of ropes toward the front, doing that awkward one-eighty with his suitcase dragging behind him. I stand, motionless, utterly humiliated and alone (and most likely about to become a YouTube sensation for the most pathetic admission of love ever at an airport).

Finally, I force myself to move again, starting back toward the door, only to be stopped by a lady at a news-stand. "Would you like a free candy bar?" she asks me.

"No, that's okay. Thank you, though."

"It's the least I could do. That was just humiliating."

33

The Worst Person on the Plane...

HEATH

Have you ever been late for a flight? Like, really late so the plane is waiting and they've been calling your name over the speaker for ten minutes, and by the time you board the plane, everyone is buckled in and pissed right off at the moron who's delaying their trip to Disneyland?

Yeah, take that kind of hate, multiply it by a thousand, and now you'll have a rough idea of how the people on this aircraft feel about me. My time at the gate with these people was pretty much me staring at my phone while the other passengers stared at me. And of course, I'm in the last group to board, after people needing assistance, those with small children, first class, Flight Club Gold members, Flight Club Platinum members, Smiles Elite passengers, people celebrating their birthdays this month, and anyone disgusted by the jerk who turned down that nice lady back at the security gate.

Somehow, the news about what a terrible human being

I am has already spread to the cabin crew, who, instead of greeting me with welcoming smiles, give me the pursed lips and eyebrow shrug you'd think would be reserved for Harvey Weinstein if he ever gets out of jail and, say, shows up at a movie premiere.

I manage to find an overhead bin into which to squeeze my carry-on, then settle myself in my seat, wishing I'd gone window instead of aisle. As soon as my seatbelt is buckled, the middle-aged man sitting next to me offers me a polite nod. "Hello."

'Hi," I say wearily. Not in the mood for small talk (or to find out if he's on Team Hate the Guy Who Ditched the Nice Girl at the Airport), I immediately close my eyes and pretend I'm sleeping, which I plan to do for the next five hours until I have to change planes. I stay like this, regret blanketing my entire body while the flight crew checks the cabin and prepares for departure, and as the plane backs out and heads to the runway, turning, taxiing and taking off. Why couldn't I just tell her I'm in love with her? Seriously, why? All those logical reasons I have seem so insignificant now. Like, really meaningless.

But they're not. They're real. And what may not be real are her feelings for me. It's only been a couple of months since she got out of a twelve-year relationship. That's not *nearly* enough time to get over someone. I don't think, anyway. I wouldn't know because the only person I've ever had to get over is Hadley. And I don't actually think I ever really did.

The seatbelt sign dings and I hear a few seat belts unbuckle. A moment later, I hear a woman's voice say, "Pig."

I open one eye just in time to see her walk past, confirming that I am, indeed, the farm animal to which she was referring.

"You did the right thing," my seat mate says.

Opening one eye, I say, "Excuse me?"

"That situation back there in the airport with that desperate girl. Good move. Cut 'em loose, never look back," he tells me with a firm nod.

As relieved as I am that he doesn't want to chastise me for being an awful person, I also don't like him calling Hadley desperate. "Oh, well...it's a bit of a complicated situation. She's not desperate actually. I know she seemed like it, but she's actually a wonderful person. Very special, actually."

"They all are at the beginning," he says. "See this tattoo of a wedding ring?" he asks, holding his left hand.

It would be hard to miss. It's one of those Celtic designs with a blood red heart. It's so wide, it takes up half of the space between his knuckle and the bottom of his finger.

"Third wife talked me into that." He shakes his head. "It lasted about two years. Just long enough for her to clean me out of what the first two didn't."

"Ah, I see. Bad luck," I answer, hoping he'll wrap up the divorced guy life lesson now so I can go back to pretending to sleep.

"Yeah, that could be the title of my memoir," he tells me, then holds out his hand. "I'm Paul."

"Heath," I answer, shaking his hand.

"Nice to meet you, Heath. Did you know marriage was invented by a woman?"

"No, I didn't."

"I don't have proof of that, but I'm convinced that's how it happened," he says. "They're the only ones who get anything out of it. I used to be wealthy. Like, set-for-life, you know? I drove a Ferrari back in the nineties. But between the three harpies and their legal teams, now I'm living above my son's garage. Took me three years to save up for this trip and it turns out Paradise Bay Resort isn't a place for singles and swingers." He sighs, opening a family-sized package of peanut M&Ms. Holding it out to me, he says, "Want one?"

"I'm good, thanks," I say.

He digs around in the bag noisily before selecting a green one. "Yeah, I used one of those discount travel sites. I meant to book at Paradise Island in Jamaica. That's the one for swinging singles," he says, leaning in and crunching in my ear. "Apparently, it's like Hedonism on 'roids. Nobody leaves there without getting laid multiple times."

"I'm guessing nobody leaves without at least one STI, either," I say with a wry smile.

"Ha!" he says, popping another candy in his mouth. "Maybe it's a good thing I booked in the wrong place."

"Maybe," I tell him, closing my eyes again.

He's finally quiet. Well, other than the incessant rustling and munching. Now that he's not distracting me, I'm forced to feel the weight of what I've done. I've made sure that the only woman I've ever really loved is likely going to hate me forever. There really is no coming back from this, is there? Not after breaking her heart like that. But it had to be done for both our sakes. Better that she feels a little hurt now than she gives up her dream to come live with me in New York, sitting around waiting for me to come home all day and night. She loves the island. It's in her blood, and she could never be happy anywhere but there. But she'd sure as hell try if I asked her to. Because that's who she is.

That's it. The pain is too awful. I can't just sit here thinking about what happened. *Anything* would be better than feeling the way I'm feeling now. I open my eyes and look at Paul, who, incidentally is staring at me. Okkaaayyy…

He nods. "I know, buddy. Been there, and I can tell you it's going to be a while before you feel good again." He holds the open end of the bag toward me and this time, I take one.

"It gets better, right?" I ask him.

Shaking his head, he says, "Nah, not really."

We both sigh and sit quietly chewing. And then, for no reason at all, I tell him the entire story. I tell him about my father and how he never bothered to come back to meet me, having only missed my entrance into the world by a few hours, by choice. I talk about how I felt about Hadley in high school and how she fell hard for a total douche bag and spent the last twelve years with him.

When the drink cart comes by, I buy us each a beer and pretzels, and I just keep talking. Now about my mum's accident and how terrified I was, and getting fired, and kissing Hadley at Smuggler's Cove, and working at the resort, and Charles calling me to beg me to come back. I talk about Hadley helping me get the house ready for my mum's return and how much fun we had together, and about me helping her get her business plan prepared so she can live her dream. And I talk about how I know she'll never love me the way I love her because if she were going to, it would have happened already, and that deep down, there's a part of me that believes she can only love a total asshole because she was raised by two of them and she doesn't really know what love is supposed to feel like—not that I know.

The flight crew shuts the lights off now, and Paul turns on the light above his head and gives me an encouraging smile. Finally, I'm done talking, and I ask, "Do you think I made the right call?"

"Yeah, I think so," he says.

"Yeah, I did." Nodding, I add, "I made the right call. I can't ask her to give up her life any more than I'm willing to give up mine. Not for something that isn't even close to a sure thing. And if I had said yes and then in a few weeks she realized she didn't actually love me, she would *never* have admitted it if she changed her mind. She would have made the best of it, and someday, when I'm on my deathbed, she'll say to herself, 'Thank God this is almost over. I should have just told him forty years ago but I didn't want to hurt his feelings.'"

"Wow," Paul says. "So, you've really thought this through to the very end...like all the way to your deathbed. I never think anything through past the next couple of months. Probably why I got married so many times."

"Yeah, maybe," I tell him. "I take it you'd never get married again?"

"No, I'd do it again in a heartbeat."

"Seriously?"

"It's magical while it lasts."

I let out a laugh, I'm sure too loud for the sleeping passengers around us. Then, lowering my voice, I say, "What happened to you agreeing that I made the right move?"

Shrugging, he says, "Look, Heath, you're clearly a smart guy. You made the move that's going to lead you to wealth." Yawning, he adds, "You won't have any memories, but you'll sure as shit have enough cash to make up for that."

34

Ride or Die...

HADLEY

Text from Nora: What are you doing right now? And do NOT say you're watching that stupid YouTube video again.

Me: I'm not watching the video again. That would be a horrible idea.

Nora: Dammit. You are, aren't you? I'm coming right over to save you from yourself.

I stare at my phone and let out a deep sigh. I've spent the last... oh, I don't know, three years? watching myself be rejected on repeat. It's excruciating — especially the bit when he walks away from me for the final time. You can hear the voice of the guy who was recording it saying, "Oh man, that's the exact moment when her heart breaks forever." Then, whoever was standing with him says, "Yeah, dude. She is *never* going to get over that."

As much as I hate to admit it, that guy is right because if I thought I was falling apart after I found out Chase was cheating on me, that was *nothing* compared to the empty vat that is my soul since Heath left the island. I'm just about to text a big fat lie to Nora when there's a knock at my door. Her voice follows immediately. "Open up, you dingus."

"How did you get here so fast?"

"I was parked out front texting you. Now, let me in!"

"Not by the hair on my chinny chin chin!" I yell.

"Seriously, Hads, open the door."

"What? Are you going to huff and puff and blow your way in?"

"It's blow the door in, and no, but I will go upstairs to tell your landlady that you're cooking meth down here. In five..." There's a pause, and I stare at the door from my position in bed.

"Four!"

Dammit. What is the point of having friends if they won't let you wallow in self-pity and dejection?

"Three! And I am *not kidding*, Hadley."

I let out a loud groan as I force myself to get up and stumble over to the door. Oh wow, is it possible that my muscles have atrophied that quickly? I barely have the strength to make it the ten steps to the door.

"Two!"

I glance at myself in the mirror, and my head snaps back in shock. I look rough. "Can you come back in an hour?" I ask. "I'd really rather shower before I let you in. Also, I wasn't kidding about the hairs on my chin. They need to be dealt with."

"Absolutely not. I'm about to say one..." There's a

short pause and then I hear, "Okay, Hadley. Here comes the one…"

I yank open the door and point in her face in a way I hope is somewhat menacing. "Not a word about my appearance."

Her jaw drops and she looks me up and down before she walks in. "Whoa."

I start to shut the door on her, but she squeezes past me. "Whoa is not a word."

I finish closing the door, then turn to face the absolute mess that my normally tidy little basement suite has become. "Okay, I can see it's bad with my own eyes. You don't have to tell me. But what you need to remember is that I am coming off of a serious breakup in which I was a cuckold, followed by falling madly in love with my best friend — present company excluded."

"Of course," Nora says with a little nod.

"And you also have to realize that it's extra tragic because I had no idea he used to be madly in love with me until it was too late and I had already squandered all that valuable time I had with him in which I could have told him the truth, that I was pretty sure I was falling for him. Only I waited too long and it's all too late and he rejected me hard, and according to the ever-growing comments on that video, I'm a totally pathetic idiot who should never go out in public again."

"Uh-huh. What's your point?" Nora asks, folding her arms across her chest.

"That I don't need any shit from anyone."

"What makes you think I'm here to give you shit?" she asks.

"Well, if you're not here to give me shit, then I'm going to assume you're here to give me some type of pep talk, and I don't need that either. I'm showing up for all my shifts at the resort, I haven't insulted anyone or accused any old men of being philanderers, I'm not eating myself into a food coma every night. So, other than how I have been spending my days off this week, I'd say I'm doing just fine."

"Sure, you look just fine," Nora says, raising her eyebrows sarcastically. "And if it were up to me, I would've left you well enough alone to do as you please, but your brother has been texting me incessantly because apparently you haven't been answering his calls."

"Urg, don't remind me. Every time he calls, it's about his stupid wedding. 'Hadley, we'll be at Mum and Dad's making party favors tomorrow, hope you'll be there,' 'Hey you, Serena and I wanted to ask you to play a special role in our wedding. Call us back so we can talk about it, okay?'"

"Sounds awful," Nora says, walking over to the sink and taking out the pile of dirty dishes.

"Leave those," I say, flopping down onto a kitchen chair.

Ignoring me, she plugs the sink and squirts some dish soap in, then turns on the water. She opens the cupboard under the sink and bends down. "Don't you have any dish gloves?"

"No. I hate how they make my hands smell."

She straightens up and gives me a strange look. "The smell is only temporary, whereas dishpan hands are forever."

"That's not right," I say, shaking my head.

"Google it. Dishpan hands make them age twice as fast. And hands are the new neck as far as showing signs of aging goes." She starts plunking the dishes in, then walks over to the table to gather some more. "So, I hope you know what a sacrifice I'm making for you here. This is true love."

Dropping my shoulders, I say, "Thank you, Nora."

"You're welcome. Now, I know the last thing you want to do when you're nursing a broken heart is to go to a stupid wedding, but he's your brother, so you don't have a choice here. You're going to have to buck up and go do all the pre-wedding stuff or you'll regret it forever. Set the man troubles aside for a few weeks. You can go back to moping when Lucas and Serena are off on their honeymoon."

"It's not the man trouble that's upsetting me," I say, resting my forehead on the table.

"Well, what is it?" Nora asks, shutting off the water and returning to the table. She sits down and I lift my head just enough to see the pile of mail. I point to the letter on the top. "I'm not only a romance reject, I've also been rejected by the business world as well." I put my forehead back down and listen as Nora flips through the three letters from San Felipe's banks, saying no to my request for what Heath called a modest business loan.

After a minute, she says, "Oh, sweetie," while she rubs my back. "I am so sorry. I thought you were a shoo-in for getting a loan."

"It's because I don't own anything. Other than my moped, and they don't consider that enough collateral. Oh God, Nora," I moan. "How am I supposed to face everyone at that wedding? My whole plan was that I was going to be able to tell people, 'Sure, yeah, I may have been cheated on and gotten dumped on my sorry arse, but it doesn't matter now because I am about to become a successful businesswoman.' And now I can't even say that. It's going to be an entire weekend of Jones family judgment, all *tsk*ing and shaking their heads at me in between trying to introduce me to weirdo third cousins because, according to Aunt Velma, it's legal."

Nora screws up her face. "Eww, gross."

"Right?" I whine. "Oh, screw it, I might as well marry one-eyed Eddie. He's got his own boat."

"Oh my God. Stop." Nora gets up and goes back to the sink and starts washing the dishes. "Do you even hear yourself?"

Dragging myself out of the chair, I grab a tea towel and get started on drying them. We work side-by-side for a few minutes in silence, then a thought pops into my head. "Maybe I'll go back to school. I could become a medical receptionist like Serena."

"Don't you dare," she says, using her manicured fingernail to pick at some stuck-on taco meat on one of my plates. Now that's friendship. "Look, so you had a little setback. Big deal, it happens to everyone. You just have to be creative, just like you were about renting out the yoga studio on an hourly basis. You figured that out, now figure out how to get the money because it's not impossible."

"Yeah, I guess..." I say, opening the cupboard and placing a clean dry glass in it.

"Oh, why don't you ask Lucas? He's been doing really well, and he and Serena have been sharing their bills for a long time. He's got to have some decent savings."

"No," I say. "It's too much pressure. If the business fails, I would never be able to pay him back and things would get really complicated between us." Needing to talk about something else, I say, "Anyway, enough about my sad life. What's going on with you lately?"

"Nothing much. It's just been another few weeks of singlehood with no decent prospects in mind. Plus, I've been pretty lonely since my best friend has basically fallen off the face of the earth."

"I'm sorry," I say, looking up at her. "I'm going to get my shit together."

"Yes, you are," she says, smiling as a loud vehicle comes up the street, invading the quiet.

The closer it gets, the more obnoxious it becomes until it's almost deafening. I lift myself onto my tiptoes to peer out the window above the sink. "Oh, my God," I say, watching Minerva get off a three-wheeled motorcycle. Glancing over at Nora, I say, "You didn't."

"Oh, I did," Nora says. "And I am not sorry."

Minerva unstraps her cane and starts up the sidewalk, looking pretty spry for someone who's been through what she has.

Nora dries her hands, then walks over and swings the door open. "She's in here, and it's as bad as we suspected."

I sigh and shake my head while I wait for Minerva to come in. As soon as she makes her way through the door, I give her a small smile. "Nice ride," I tell her.

"You like it?" she asks with a wide grin. "I had the guys at the shop remove the muffler."

"Oh, we know," I say.

"Come here," she commands. "Give me a hug, you big loser."

I do as she says, and my eyes fill with tears as she squeezes me tight and rubs my back. When she pulls away, she puts her hands on both of my shoulders. "Do you know what makes you a loser?"

"The awful video of your son rejecting me that's been viewed over three million times already?"

"No, that makes Heath a loser because he missed out on his chance to be with the girl he's always loved," Minerva says. "What makes *you* a loser is that you have let a man stop you like this."

"To be fair, it was two men. And getting turned down for my bank loans, so I've not only lost my dream of ever being happily married and having a family, I've also had my dream of owning my own dance studio ripped out from under me."

"Meh, don't worry about that," Minerva says, shuffling over to my fridge and opening it. "How do you not have any beer?"

"Well, I didn't exactly know you were coming over," I quip.

She shuts it and says to Nora, "Be a dear and run to the liquor store, will you? Louise here and I need to have a long talk about her future."

Nora grabs her purse and salutes Minerva, then says to me, "Anything for you?"

"Yeah, if they have those sampler boxes with the little chocolate bottles filled with booze, I'll have two of those."

Nora wrinkles up her nose, but says, "If you're sure."

Minerva's eyes light up. "Make it three."

As soon as Nora leaves, Minerva says, "Now that we're alone, I need to tell you something but you can't repeat it to anyone ever."

"Okay, I promise. It stays between us."

"Good." Letting out a big sigh, Minerva says, "I'm lonely."

Instant guilt. Instant. "I am so sorry. I've been meaning to stop by, but then the thought of showering and—"

"Yeah, yeah, I know you weren't spiriting me."

"Ghosting."

"Same thing."

"I'm not sure it is."

"Anyway," Minerva says, giving me a little glare. "I kind of got used to having someone living with me, and since Heath's not coming back and you're the only other person I wouldn't want to smother with a pillow after a few days, I thought I'd ask if you want to come live with me."

She glances around at my place and says, "You know, in a house with windows you don't need a ladder to see out of."

"Really?" I ask, trying to process what that would be like.

"Yeah, really. But only under one condition—no money changes hands." The expression on her face makes her seem almost vulnerable for the first time since I've known her. "You save up to get your dance school going and I...have someone around to watch *The Fast and the Furious* with."

I chuckle, then say, "Are you sure? I don't want you to put yourself out just because you feel sorry for me."

"Listen, kiddo," Minerva says, giving me a pointed look. "When you agree to go ride or die with Minerva Robinson, that means something. It means we've got each other's backs, no matter what. It means we don't let little things like men or bank loans get in the way of our dreams."

Feeling as though a thousand-pound block of poo has been lifted off my chest, I nod. "Okay. Let's do this."

"Yes," she says, grinning. "Thelma and Louise for life."

"Minerva, Thelma and Louise end up dead at the end. You do know that, right?"

"But they went out on their own terms. And I figure with the two of us together, we can do slightly better than that," she says with a wry smile.

35

Back in the Big Rotten Apple

HEATH

"Oh, son of a…" I stop myself before I finish that sentiment. After all, there's a family of tourists standing next to me on the crowded sidewalk. They're taking photos of the man who just got drenched from head-to-toe by a city bus (me) while the Chipmunks' Christmas song blares from the speakers of the cafe I just left. I'm drenched in dirty ice water - seriously, I have ice chunks in my hair and I'm dripping brown liquid from everywhere. I toss my to-go coffee and the accompanying breakfast bagel into the nearest bin, spin on my heel, and start the frigid walk back to my apartment.

Managing to find two tiny dry patches on my wool coat (in the armpit area, just for extra dignity), I wipe my hands as best I can. I dig around in my pocket for my cell, then text Anita: *Just got soaked by a bus. Going home to sterilize myself so I can start this day over.*

Anita: Happy Monday.

I shove my hands in my pockets and brace myself against the biting wind. A bike messenger stops short on the sidewalk in front of me, and I nearly smash into him. He climbs off without apologizing, but he does give me a quick once-over, then says, "Damn, that sucks, dude."

"You know what else sucks? Cutting someone off on the sidewalk, you wanker."

"Wanker! Ha!" he says, locking his bike to a light pole. "Good one."

By the time I get to my building, I'm shivering, pissed off, and have fielded an irritating phone call from Charles, who, although he is clearly trying to pretend he can be reasonable, is still wondering how soon I can be in. I open the front door to the lobby, only to be assaulted by "Grandma Got Run Over by a Reindeer." How has this made the lobby playlist? Cracking my neck, I stalk to the elevator, wishing I'd never traded in the warmth of the Benaventes for this loud, awful place.

It's been a month since I came back and I can honestly say I have yet to find anything redeeming about the city I once loved. While I was gone, my favorite donair place shut down and is now a nail salon, my elderly, super-quiet upstairs neighbor moved into a nursing home, only to be replaced by some asshat who must weigh three hundred pounds and wear wooden clogs, and Charles has been clingy to the point of being co-dependent.

I turn on the water and wait for it to heat up while I strip down. Oh look, he's calling again. Wonderful. Decline.

I hate it here. I really, really hate it here.

Okay, Heath, don't catastrophize this. You're just having a bad day. No, bad hour. Just get in the shower and start over.

I test the water again but it's still cold. "Are you kidding me?"

After another minute, I realize the hot water must be out again, so I'll just have to get in and get this over with. At least I'll be clean. "Fuck me! That's cold," I yell, reflexively arching my back to avoid the pain.

Two minutes later, I'm as clean as I'm going to get (which may not be all that clean, to be honest, since I could barely stand to keep my head under the cold spray for more than a couple of seconds at a time). I dry off vigorously to get the circulation back in my skin, then stand next to the radiator in my underwear.

Ah, that's nice. It's almost warming my fingertips. If only there was a way to climb in there.

———

"There you are!" Charles says as soon as the elevator doors open.

"Yup, I finally made it," I tell him.

He glances down at my outfit—I've had to pair my suit paints with a ski jacket since my only dress coat is going to have to go to the cleaners. "I know," I tell him. "You don't have to say anything. I realize how ridiculous I look."

"No, I wasn't going to comment," he answers with a little grin. "I was just thinking how you would literally never get laid again if you went out like that all the time."

I start walking to my office. "Right, yeah," I say.

Charles follows me. "Speaking of getting laid, I need to tell you about my weekend and the chick I banged."

I close my eyes for a second, wishing he would disappear into thin air.

"Met her on a Christmas pub crawl that some of the guys from my squash club went on…"

I tune out his words at this point, not wanting to lose any more respect for him than I already have. He shuts the

door and helps himself to a chair by the window,
yammering on about his weekend while I settle myself at
my desk (leaving my ski jacket on) and turn on my
computer.

"…takes me back to her place…"

Yuck. No. On what planet would anyone want to hear
about his fifty-eight-year-old boss's sexual exploits?

My mind wanders back to Hadley as it has for the
millionth time since I got here. I torture myself with the
memory of her face when I turned down her offer to
spend the rest of my life with her. Or at the very least, give
it a shot. Whenever I think about it, I absolutely hate
myself. There she was, nakedly offering her heart to me,
and I said, *'Nah, no thanks. I'm gonna go with a lonely life in New
York where no one gives a shit about me.'*

Why? Because I'm a coward who can think of a dozen
logical reasons that we shouldn't risk a relationship. Well,
two or three anyway, like bad timing and not wanting to
risk our friendship, and being more than a little concerned
that I'll uproot my entire life and she'll change her mind.
So, decent reasons, really…but *are they?*

"…legs wrapped around…"

"So, Charles!" I interrupt, not wanting to hear any
more. "I heard back from Mrs. Bao. She's willing to take
my meeting."

He stops, looking slightly putout that I'm not riveted by
the fascinating tale of his latest one-night-stand. "Great.
Set it up."

"I should do that right now," I tell him, picking up the
receiver on my desk phone. "Strike while the iron's hot and
all that."

"Absolutely." He nods, then remains seated while I
stare at him. Finally, I give him a 'please leave now' look
and he seems to get it.

253

Standing up, he says, "I'll let you get to it. Try to be on time from now on, okay?"

And just like that, it all becomes crystal clear. I stand up and say, "Yeah, I don't think so, Charles."

"What?"

"I don't think I'm going to be on time for work ever again. Well, not here, anyway," I tell him, grabbing a box out of my credenza. A sense of calm comes over me and I start to whistle to myself while I load my personal items in it.

"What are you doing?" he asks, watching me intently.

"Oh, I'm quitting," I say. "I'm done. I never should have come back here. I've been trying to convince myself it was the right move, but it wasn't."

"You can't quit," Charles says in a raised voice. "Not after I let you come back."

"Begged is more like it," I tell him, pausing what I'm doing to give him a pointed look.

"Are you kidding me? You're going to turn down the greatest opportunity that's ever been handed to you? To do what? Go back to some poor island in the middle of nowhere so you can be a loser for the rest of your life?"

"No, I'm going back home to paradise, where my family, my true friends, and the woman I love are waiting," I tell him, dropping my stress-ball into the garbage. "I won't be needing that anymore."

"You're leaving all this for a woman?" he spits out.

I glance at the ceiling for a second as though trying to decide, then nod. "Pretty much. If she'll have me, that is."

I look around my office one last time, then pick up my box and walk to the door. Turning to Charles, who is frozen in place with his mouth hanging open, I say, "Good luck, Charles. I hope you stop being such a douche some-day. People genuinely don't like you."

With that, I turn and walk down the hall to the elevator, for the first time in my life, utterly positive that I'm about to do the right thing for the right reasons. Now, all I have to do is get back home to Hadley, and hope she'll give me another chance.

36

Sometimes a Girl's Gotta Take a Stand...

Hadley

"Minerva, have you seen my phone?" I ask, rushing around the kitchen.

Today is the big wedding, and Minerva and I were up far too late playing gin rummy last night, so I overslept. I've been living with Minerva for almost 3 weeks now, and I have to say, I wish I had done it sooner. Everybody in this world needs somebody who's got their back. So what if mine isn't a tall, smart, and handsome man? Instead, I've got a short, sassy, and slightly wild 72-year-old woman. Big deal. The main thing is to have someone. Between her and Nora, I'm covered.

"I think I saw it on the bathroom counter earlier," Minerva says. She's still in her bathrobe and is getting ready to make herself some eggs, like she does every morning. How that woman hasn't had a heart attack, what with her love of all things meat and alcohol-related, is beyond me. She stops in her tracks with the carton of eggs in her hand. "Well, don't you look beautiful."

I give her a grin accompanied by a little curtsy, then zip down the hall in search of my phone. "Yep! That's where it was." I swipe it off the counter and shove it unceremoniously into my small beaded white clutch, then rush to my room to grab my wedge sandals out of my closet and carry them to the kitchen.

"Did you eat anything today?" Minerva asks from her position in front of the stove. "I can pop a couple of extra eggs in the pan for you."

"No time," I say. "My parents will be here to pick me up in five minutes."

They didn't want me to ride in on my moped and for once, I agree with them on account of the lovely flowy long dress I'm in and the hair that took me over an hour to get just right.

"Well, at least have one of those disgusting yogurts you like so much," Minerva says with a little shudder. "Going to a wedding on an empty stomach is a recipe for winding up with your head in the toilet."

I laugh, then rush over to the fridge and take her suggestion, grabbing an individual-sized container of raspberry yogurt.

Minerva gets a spoon out for me and holds it out, only when I try to take it, she pulls it away. "Don't take any shit from anyone today."

Giving her a confident nod, I say, "I won't. I'm going to go full Minerva sass through the entire event."

"Well, don't go *that far*," she says, relinquishing the spoon. "If you go full Minerva, you'll wind up alienating your entire family. But somewhere between channeling your inner me and agreeing to marry your one-eyed third cousin Eddie."

Chuckling, I say, "I'll aim for somewhere in the middle."

Minerva grins at me. "Good stuff. Now eat up. We can't have you wasting away."

Remembering I'm in a hurry, I wolf down the yogurt in six completely unladylike bites, then I toss the container in the garbage and my spoon into the sink. As much as I've been dreading this day, I am happy for Lucas and Serena. They deserve a wonderful day.

"You gonna be okay, kiddo?" Minerva asks, walking me toward the front door.

"I am," I say. "When they start in on me about not having a man, I'm just going to change the conversation and start talking about my future dance school."

"And if that doesn't work, just start a rumor that your Aunt Velma has syphilis."

I burst out laughing at the idea, then see my parents pulling up in their white Cadillac. "Wish me luck."

"Give 'em hell."

I hurry out into the heat of the day and rush down the sidewalk, noting that the shrubs could use some water when I get home. As soon as I get into the back seat, my mom turns to me. "You look nice today," she manages.

"Thanks, you too. Good morning, Dad," I say, buckling myself in.

"Morning, Hadley," he says, pulling out onto the road.

"Are you guys nervous?"

"I'm not," my dad says. "Lucas will be just fine. Your mother on the other hand…"

"I'm fine," she snaps. "I just don't think that the way they're doing things today is going to be what anyone is expecting."

Serena and Lucas have elected to forgo the traditional church wedding and get married at Hidden Beach. There's a lovely meadow that overlooks the ocean where the ceremony will be held and they've had a large tent brought in for the reception. "That's what's fun about it," I say. "It's different — memorable."

"Tacky," my mother says, setting her jaw. "The meal is going to be served by two food trucks, for God's sake. I still cannot believe this is what they want. The family is going to be talking about this one for years — and not in a good way."

"What's more important than Lucas and Serena having their special day exactly the way they want it?" I ask. "I mean, is it about Aunt Velma or is it about them?"

My father answers the question. "Aunt Velma, obviously."

"Oh, fine," my mother says. "Gang up on me. That's all I need today. I've got one daughter who's pushing 30 and lives with a Harley-riding tattooed senior citizen, and a son who lets his future wife do the proposing and who thinks food truck food is a good idea for a formal occasion." Her voice cracks as she continues, "I just don't know where I went wrong."

"I think you went wrong when you expected your children to turn out to be clones of you and Dad. Why can't you just be happy that we're both responsible, kind human beings that are out in the world, charting our own paths?"

"Because I can see where your path is going to take you — and I don't like it one bit," she spits out. "You're going to end up a lonely, broke spinster like that awful roommate of yours."

That's it. I'm putting my foot down. Now. "Mum, I love you. I always will, but I've really had enough of your shit. Either accept me the way I am, or don't expect to see me very often. I'm never going to be size two, I'm never going to be an amazing cook, and I'm never *ever* going to wind up married to a man who barely pays any attention to me. No offense, Dad, but it's true."

My heart jumps up to my throat as soon as I'm done. I close my mouth and wait, breathless, for her to respond. I expect her to get angry, or start crying and try to find some way to make me feel guilty about the fact that I've just set some limits with her.

But she doesn't.

She just turns her head and stares out the window for the rest of the ride to the beach. My father turns on the radio to his favorite country station, and I sit back against the plush seat and stare out to the sea, hiding a smile.

The truth is, I cannot wait to get home and tell Minerva about what just happened. Then, just like with every bit of news I've had to share in the last month, I think, 'Oh, I have to tell Heath,' before I remember he's gone for good.

I close my eyes for a brief second and tell myself that everything worked out for the best and that it's definitely getting easier the longer he's gone. I don't need a man to be fulfilled. Because I'm enough on my own — I have wonderful friends, who have become the family I chose. And as much as I think I would've loved making a life with Heath, I'm still going to do really well on my own and that's not nothing.

37

Do You Reckon He's Sexy?

HEATH

"We'd now like to welcome the rest of our passengers on Flight 835 to San Felipe. Please step forward now."

The gate agent, who I've been standing directly in front of for the last five minutes, finally looks at me and takes my ticket and passport. I'm literally the only person left who hasn't been called, so why she felt it necessary to make that final announcement is beyond me.

Giving me a cursory smile, she hands back my things. "Enjoy your flight, sir."

I thank her, then start down the ramp only to hear her mutter, "Try not to publicly humiliate any poor women this time."

I stiffen slightly, although by now I should be used to it. I've been recognized in the strangest of places over the last couple of months for that damning video that provides proof to the world that I'm a world-class asshole. I suppose I should've expected I'd be more likely to be recognized as

I get closer to the scene of the crime. Any yet, it still chaps my arse.

But, no matter, only a quick three-hour leg, then I can rush to Hadley and beg her to forgive me. (Well, technically a three-hour flight, followed by roughly thirty minutes of deplaning, then lining up to go through customs, then renting a car, then zipping over to my mum's place where Hadley's been living for a few weeks now, *then* the begging.)

I find my row and can't help but notice two young women staring at me from the seats directly behind mine. One is smiling and the other one is not. I climb over my two seat mates to get to the window seat (where I can hide from haters), and settle myself in just in time to hear the women behind me.

"That's that guy from that video where he broke that woman's heart. Remember at the airport?" one of them says in an Australian accent.

Oh, God, that horrific video made it all the way around the globe?

"*That's* where I know him from. For a minute there, I thought maybe he was a weatherman or something."

"Nope. He's internet famous for being a dick."

"I don't know. There are always two sides to every story," one of them says.

I nod to myself, feeling a tiny sense of redemption. That is, of course, until she says, "Do you reckon he's sexy?" and the other one says, "No, not a bit."

Ouch.

"Me neither, but obviously that poor woman did."

"I read in the *Weekly World News* that she killed herself as soon as she left the airport. Drove right off a cliff into the ocean."

What? Seriously? I'm tempted to turn around and correct her, but luckily the other woman does it for me. "No, that's not right."

Thank you.

She continues with, "I heard that too, but when I looked it up, it turns out she didn't kill herself. But she did check herself into a mental hospital and no one's heard from her since."

"I bet she is dead."

"The world's hardly fair, is it?" one of them asks.

"Not at all," her friend agrees. "He should be the one who is dead. Not her."

Nice.

———

Five Hours Later

"Heath, what the hell are you doing here?" Minerva says, looking none too pleased to see me.

"I miss you too, Mum," I say, lifting my two giant suitcases and walking inside.

"Did you get fired again?" she asks, shaking her head a little.

"No, you'll be happy to know that your very dull accountant son has finally done something wildly reckless in his life."

Lifting one eyebrow, she gives me what is quite possibly the most skeptical look I've ever seen. "What? Did you mix patterns on an outfit recently?"

"Hardy har har," I say. Lowering my voice so Hadley won't overhear me, I say, "I quit my job, gave up my apartment, and I am moving back home to see if I can get Hadley to give us another try."

"What?" Mum shouts at me. "Why are you whispering?"

"Shh! I don't want her to overhear what I'm saying. It won't be nearly as romantic that way."

"Oh, don't worry about that. She's not here," Minerva says, turning from me and walking to the kitchen with the energy of a teenager.

"Really? I saw her moped out front."

"Her parents picked her up earlier. It's her brother's wedding today."

"Oh, that's today?" I ask, trying to decide if I should just go for it and show up at the wedding.

Minerva sits at the table and starts shelling some peas. I think about my options for a minute, then it simply occurs to me that my own mother has had absolutely *no reaction* to the news that I'm moving home for good. "Wait. Are you not happy that I'm moving back?"

Shrugging, she says, "I'm not *unhappy*, but Hadley and I have a really good thing going here and I'm afraid you're going to screw it up," Minerva says. "No offense. It's nothing personal, it's just more of a *Thelma and Louise* vibe in the house, and as you may or may not know, whenever men were added to the mix, things went way off the rails for them."

"Again, I haven't seen that movie, but I'm familiar with the premise, and I feel fairly confident that you shouldn't base your actual life on it."

"We're not robbing people, if that's what you mean. We're doing things like walking around the house with no bras on, men bashing, watching *Grey's Anatomy* and arguing over who's better—McDreamy or McSteamy. We can't do *any* of those things with you around here." The way she says 'you' is almost like she's a nun and it's a dirty word.

"But no offense, right?" I ask, for the first time wondering if coming home might've been a terrible idea.

"Eh, some offense."

"Nice homecoming for your only child," I tell her, walking over to the cupboard and getting myself a glass. I pour some cold water in and drink the whole thing in one go, then say, "I thought you wanted me to end up with Hadley."

Tossing another empty pea pod into the pile, she says, "Yeah, well, that was before she moved in here. I've gotten kind of used to having her around. She doesn't nitpick or nag me like you do, and she's an awful lot of fun."

"I see, so you're worried that by me moving back to the island, I'm going to spoil your fun," I say.

"When you say it like that, it sounds almost like I'm being selfish."

"You think?" I ask.

"Don't get cheeky, young man. I'm still your mother." She sighs, then says, "Of course you can stay here," she says. "Although, it might be a little awkward, especially if Hadley decides she doesn't want you back."

Oh God, maybe I should have called first before I quit. My stomach drops to my knees and I suddenly feel the need for a paper bag to breathe into.

"Put your bags in the spare room for now and we'll see how things go," Minerva says, popping a couple of peas in her mouth. "But I don't want any guff from you about my new mode of transportation. It's loud, yes, but it's totally me."

"You got yourself the Harley, didn't you?" I ask.

Minerva fixes me with a satisfied smile in lieu of an answer.

"Thought so. Now, are you going to tell me where this wedding is so I can crash it or am I going to have to figure it out for myself?"

"Huh, maybe you have changed a little," she says, looking at me with what could be construed as respect, if I didn't know better, that is. "You might have some potential at becoming interesting after all."

I chuckle and shake my head. "It's good to see you, Minerva."

"You too, Junior. The shindig is at Hidden Beach."

"Hidden Beach? Doris must be beside herself."

Breaking into an evil laugh, Minerva says, "And the best part is, the wedding supper will be provided by two food trucks. One of them is fish tacos."

My eyes grow wide and I can't help but laugh. "Fish tacos? I have got to see this."

But first to shower and get all the airplane off me so I can look and smell my best while making my grand gesture...

38

Sometimes a Girl's Gotta Make
an Awkward Speech...

HADLEY

"What an interesting wedding," Aunt Velma says, sidling up next to me.

I'm in line for Juan Jr.'s fish tacos and I could not be more pleased. The only thing I've had to eat today is just that one little yogurt and I am starving. (Read: about to eat five fish tacos without caring who sees it. Yup. I'm a total badass now.)

"Wasn't it a lovely service?" I ask. "The vows were so heartfelt and I just love that they both had bare feet. So much better than a stuffy church wedding," I add, just to get a rise out of my aunt.

"I see you didn't bring a date. It's very brave of you to show up alone. Back in my day, a woman wouldn't *dream* of attending an event without a man on her arm."

"And that is just one of the many reasons I am so glad I was born fifty years after you."

She narrows her eyes at me. "I was thirty-two when you were born."

"Close enough," I say, just as my order is up.

Juan Jr. calls my name, and I give Velma a phony smile. "Don't need a man now, never did, never will," I say with a lot more swagger than I'm feeling.

Taking my plate of fish tacos, I make my way back toward the tent where I intend to eat every bite of this and wash it down with some ice-cold beer. The expansive tent has been set directly on the grass with two dozen wooden picnic tables under it. On each table is a simple arrangement of pink and orange Gerber daisies tied off with purple ribbons for a pop of color and set in large mason jars. There's a dance floor just outside with strings of lights attached to poles above the floor. Because there isn't an official wedding party, Serena and Lucas are seated at a small table at the front next to the podium. I carry my plate and drink to a picnic table reserved for immediate family and sit down to enjoy my meal. Yes, I may be alone today, and I may have even felt lonely at certain moments here and there (like now), and I also do feel a little envious of my little brother, well, and slightly embarrassed that he's getting married and I'm not, but hey, it's all good because I'm rising above things like worrying what others think of me.

Whoa. Five fish tacos is a lot of fish tacos. I am full to the brim. All that foamy beer in there probably doesn't help matters. Honestly, I would pay a thousand dollars just to get out of these tummy control knickers and just go lay in the shade somewhere. But the speeches just started so it would be excessively rude for me to duck out now.

As the matriarch of the family, Aunt Velma has been

selected to welcome Serena's family to ours. She's been at
the mic droning on and on about tradition, love, and all
the things that make for a happy family for about five
minutes now. I glance around to see that I don't need to
worry too much about her offending people with her veiled
judgment of anyone who doesn't think exactly like her
because most of the people appear to have tuned her out
by now. In fact, I haven't heard a word she's said pretty
much since she got started. That is, until I hear my name.

"Hadley, Lucas's big sister, would love to say a few
words herself," Velma says, giving me a decidedly nasty
smile. "Everyone, please welcome Hadley Jones. And for
those of you single fellas out there, Hadley here is back on
the market after over a ten-year absence."

My entire head heats up with embarrassment and I
glance over at Lucas, who winces at me. He shakes his
head and whispers, "You don't have to get up, if you don't
want to."

Having enough liquid courage in me not to care, I
remind myself I'm channeling my inner Minerva and I
stand up, giving Lucas a firm nod. "It's okay, I've got this."

Stepping up to the podium, I say, "Thanks, Aunt
Velma." Then, with a slightly evil grin, I add, "And
nobody worry because Aunt Velma does not have syphilis."

Gasps can be heard around the tent along with some
laughter.

"Hadley!" my mother barks.

Giving her an innocent look, I say, "What? I said she
doesn't have syphilis." Then, glancing out over the crowd, I
decide to enjoy this. "As you've all heard, Lucas comes
from a long line of people who have lived very traditional,
predictable lives. Good people who take out the trash
before it overflows onto their kitchen floor and keep their
lawns trimmed neatly. People who show up for work on

time and volunteer on the parent teacher advisory board and are generally good little citizens. Lucas and I, however, are going to shake things up a little bit I'm afraid. My dear brother here, by finding a bride with a big set of ovaries — the kind of girl who will get down on one knee and propose to the man she loves without caring what anybody thinks."

I give Serena a thumbs up, then say, "Good on you, sister. I'm also taking my own path, and I can tell you honestly that is not one that is necessarily appreciated by everyone here. Yes, I was a domestic wannabe for most of my life — always doing and saying the right thing for the man I loved. But it turned out he didn't love me."

I hear one of the guests on Serena's side of the tent asking if I'm talking about the guy from the airport video.

I stop mid-speech, and squint my eyes, trying to see who said it. "I imagine you've all seen the horrific airport video that the young gentleman over at table number five is talking about. It's okay. We can talk about it." I nod reassuringly. "That was my one shot at love. And it didn't work out, but there's no reason for you to feel sorry for me. None whatsoever. Just set that whole emotion aside when you think of me because I. Am. Doing. So well. In fact, I have never been happier. I live with a seventy-two-year-old gangster who rides that super loud Harley trike all over the island." I pause and see people nodding. "Some of you are nodding yes, so you know her. That's my dear friend Minerva, and believe me, we are living the good life. Terrific actually. I wouldn't want it any other way. Although I'm very happy for Serena and Lucas because they're doing their thing their way — yay, food truck weddings rock! Am I right?"

There's some scattered applause, so I decide to wrap it up. "Anyway, well done you two lovebirds." I give them the snapping finger guns, then turn back to the crowd. "But there are lots of ways to be happy, and I wanted to take the opportunity to mention that in case anybody who's sitting here today is feeling like a loser because they are not married or in a serious relationship. You don't have to feel that way. I don't feel that way. And I never will. I don't need a man, and the truth is, I never did."

A voice at the back of the tent interrupts me loudly, saying, "Well, that's a shame because I've come all this way to ask you if you might consider spending the rest of your life with me, but having heard your opinion on the matter, maybe I should just go."

My heart makes a full stop, then, just as suddenly, starts to thump in my chest. I scan the tent until we lock eyes, and I whisper right into the microphone, "Fuck me. It's Heath."

And that's the moment when I completely forget that there is anybody else here because I'm too busy staring at him, waiting for him to say more.

He takes a few steps toward the front and says, "Hadley. Hadley Jones, what if I stayed? What if I stayed, and we got married? Or didn't — it's really whatever you want—but what if we made a life together with a couple of kids or dogs or I don't know, budgies, even. I've been thinking about the whole cat thing and I'm not sure I really want to wear a cat in a pouch on a sweatshirt, but if it would make you happy, I'll do it."

I stand, slack-jawed like a complete yokel. "Is this really happening?"

He nods and takes a few more steps toward me.

"Yes."

"Are you sure this isn't just a hallucination brought on by too many fish tacos?"

He chuckles and shakes his head. "No, this is happening all right. Wait, how many did you eat?"

I hold up my hand with all five fingers outstretched.

"Wow. Impressive," he says, then he sighs and gets back to looking intensely worried. "I came back, Hadley. Because the truth is, I can't have a full life if it's not with you."

Well, that's sort of sweet. I have a sudden urge to run to him and throw myself into his arms a la Jennifer Grey in Dirty Dancing. But then I remember the airport and I stay rooted to the spot. "But what about your dreams of taking over corporate America one merger at a time and the thrill of the deal and all that..." I ask, too afraid to think this could really be real.

"Turns out it's all malarkey. And it's lonely, and I just hate New York now."

"But you love New York."

"Not if you're not there. The thing is, Hadley, I'd much rather have the not-so-rich but wildly crazy in love life with you than another life any place else. That's if the offer is still on the table."

Serena stands and nudges me out from behind the podium.

I look at her and whisper, "But I can't really say yes, can I? Not after I just made such a big show about the fact that I'm planning to spend the rest of my life alone."

Shaking her head, Serena says, "There is not one person here who believed any of that. Not even you."

"Really? Because I thought it was rather convincing."

"Not in the slightest," Lucas says. "Now, are you going to say yes or do I have to put you in a headlock and give you a noogie until you admit you love Heath?"

"What are you? Twelve?" I ask him.

Standing, Lucas points to Heath. "Go already before he changes his mind."

There's a thought that didn't occur to me. He might change his mind. I look at him and he seems to read my mind because he shakes his head. "Won't happen. I promise."

Narrowing my eyes at him, I say, "Are you one hundred percent sure? Because I can't risk my heart on anything else."

"A thousand percent."

"Okay, then," I tell him. "Let's fall in love."

Heath laughs and we rush into each other's arms. He lifts me up (not like Patrick Swayze over his head, but still, it's pretty damn good). And now we're kissing in a way that is not in any way appropriate for public viewing. But, again, damn good, so who really cares?

There's a smattering of applause, then when it dies out, there's the odd 'ah-hum' that I'm relatively sure is meant to make us stop. But I don't want to stop because, after a lifetime of friendship and love, I'm finally falling in love. For the first time.

"Okay, Hadley, wrap it up, dear," my dad says, tapping me on the shoulder. "It's Lucas's big day, remember?"

I pull back from Heath and say, "Right."

Grabbing a glass from my distant cousin, One-eyed Eddie, who's sitting nearby, I hold it up and say, "I almost forgot to finish my speech. As I was saying, to Lucas and Serena, and to true love."

I tip back his wine, have a big swig, then put it back down in front of Eddie. For a guy with one eye, he's really managing to make it do double the work on looking disgusted. "Don't worry about it. We're all family here," I tell him.

Heath laughs and shakes his head at me. "You've been spending far too much time with Minerva."

"Oh, I'm just getting started," I say with a crazed grin.

"I'm going to regret this aren't I?"

"Some days, I imagine so." Wrapping my arms around his neck again, I plant a kiss on his lips, thrilled right down to my bones that I get to do that.

"Totally worth it."

Epilogue

One Year Later...

Heath

"Are you trying to seduce me, Mrs. Robinson?" I ask Hadley, who clearly isn't trying to seduce me at all. Instead, she's rushing around the bedroom trying to find her other sandal before she has to rush out the door.

She rolls her eyes at me, then says, "When are you going to stop asking me that?"

"When it stops being funny," I tell her, crouching down and finding her shoe under the bed. "Is this it?" I ask, holding it up.

"Yes! Thank you," she says, hurrying over to grab it.

I hold it up and say, "Trade?"

She gives me a quick kiss, then says, "Now give me my shoe, you arse."

"What's the hold up in there?" Minerva yells through

275

the door to my old bedroom (which I now share with my wife).

"I couldn't find my sandal!" Hadley calls to her.

"We really need to get our own place," I say.

"And leave Minerva on her own? No way," Hadley tells me.

"But what if we get a bigger place? Maybe with a garden suite for her?" I ask, pulling on my tie.

"Not until I pay off my loan for the dance school," she says, rushing over to the closet and grabbing a flimsy shawl. Wrapping her shoulders with it, she says, "There, do I look like a dance studio owner-slash-instructor about to put on her inaugural Christmas show?"

"You look hot. Are dance studio owner-slash-instructors supposed to be this hot?"

"I'll take that as a yes," she answers, practically sprinting to the door.

A few minutes later, we're in my new Jeep (with Minerva in front of us on her three-legged hog) on our way to the resort where the First Annual Paradise Bay Dance Academy Christmas Show is going to start in a couple of hours. It's going to be a wildly hectic but amazing day, but all I can think about is when we will get home again because Hadley looks amazing in her dress. "You're beautiful, you know that, right?"

She's flipping through a bunch of pages, making a few last-minute changes to the emcee's lines. "Thanks, babe. You're the best."

"I love you," I say as we pull off the freeway and onto the road that leads to the resort.

"I love you, too," she answers, looking completely distracted.

"No, I really, really love you, and you're going to be wonderful today like you are every other day, and the show is going to be an absolute hit, and come January, you're going to have a bunch of new people signing their kids up."

She stops and looks over at me, her eyes shining. "How do you know exactly what I need to hear?"

"It's a gift," I say in a cocky tone.

Laughing, Hadley says, "It certainly is."

We pull into the stall next to my mum, get out of the Jeep, and I watch as the chaos begins. Some of the kids are already here and they swarm Hadley like adorable chubby bees as soon as they see her. She greets each one and slowly starts to herd them through the resort grounds toward the large outdoor auditorium.

The first official day of classes was September ninth, and over the last four months, word has spread fast that there's a new dance school on the island, and that mums can get spa treatments at a discount while they wait. Hadley already has enough students to run twelve classes a week, which I keep telling her seems pretty darn impressive.

I've opened my own accounting office right next door to the Turtle's Head Pub. Robinson & Associates. So far, my only associate is Alexa, but that's okay. Eventually, I'll have enough clients to hire an assistant. And then, as time goes on, more accountants. But for now, just being back home and being in love is enough excitement for me.

We got married on a beautiful Monday afternoon in May on the Banks family yacht. As a sea captain (and person who got certified online), Harrison officiated our wedding, and we had a wonderful time partying the night away on the open water. Minerva and her crew were in fine form, insisting there were no laws since we were in 'international waters.' Doris and Glen were there too, and that's all I'm going to say about my in-laws.

The show goes exactly as planned—other than one of the students getting so nervous, she peed on the stage. Well, and another little girl pulling the hair of the dancer next to her who was 'Too close!' and the couple of times the kids were all lined up ready to go when the wrong music started, or no music at all. That happened too. But nobody minded, and the parents loaded Hadley's arms with bouquets of flowers and thank you cards when it was all over. Harrison and Libby took all the flowers in a golf cart and are delivering them to the Jeep for me on their way home with Clara and baby Will, who is no longer a mama's boy, but is firmly attached to his dad, running after him wherever he goes. Smiling little thing, too, and quite the daredevil, just like his namesake.

It's evening now as Hadley, Minerva and I wind our way slowly back through the resort, the scent of flowers in the air and a full moon to help light our way.

Minerva lets out a contented sigh. "So, kiddo, what do you think?"

"I think I'm happy, Mum. I have an amazing wife, a wonderful life, and we're just getting started."

"Good stuff. I'm glad to hear it."

"I've been thinking, maybe it's time you and your wife found your own place."

"As much as *I'd* love to, Hadley will never leave you."

Hadley smiles up at me, and I take that to mean I'm right.

"Well, I'm afraid it's going to get a little too crowded in my place," Minerva says.

"How so?" I ask, narrowing my eyes at her.

"Babies take up an absolute ton of space."

I stop walking and let my mouth hang down. Hadley stops too and grins, tears in her eyes.

"Baby?" I ask.

Nodding, she says, "Yup."

I pick her up and swing her around in my arms, then we give each other a huge kiss. When I set her down, I feel a lump in my throat. "When? How? Well, I know how, but when?"

Laughing, Hadley says, "Middle of August, if all goes well."

Turning to my mum, I say, "You knew about this?"

"I'm the one who told her," she says. "I realized her PMS wasn't going away and it had already been almost two weeks of her crying at commercials for animal shelters."

I give Minerva a big hug, picking her up too.

"Put me down, you big ninny," she tells me. "You'll break my new hip."

Wrapping my arm around Hadley's shoulder, I plant a kiss on her forehead. "I love you so much."

"I love you too."

My mind starts reeling. "We're going to need to child-proof everything and we have to trade in the Jeep for a minivan. And no more moped for you, at least not until the baby's born."

"Told you he'd go straight to the minivan thing," Minerva says. "I could tell he secretly loved it."

"Yup. you were right," Hadley answers.

Letting go of Hadley, I jump up in the air, suddenly overcome by the biggest thrill of my life. Bigger than the biggest merger in the history of the world. Because, in a way, *this* is the biggest merger of my life. "A baby. A real baby. Wow."

"A real baby. The crying, pooping, peeing, spitting up kind," Minerva says. "And don't think I'm going to be staying home every Saturday night to babysit so you two can go out."

"Of course not," Hadley says.

"I'm only available Sunday through Friday. And I'm sorry, but I'm not budging on that."

"Well, a woman's got to have boundaries," Hadley tells her.

"She sure does."

We continue on along the path, toward the future, toward all the celebrating and laughing and crying and heartache that make up a life worth living. Me with my two favourite ladies. And if I'm really lucky, three.

Or a boy would be good too. Even out the playing field around the house…

"Say, do you think they make little Thelma and Louise onesies?" my mum asks.

Hadley lets out a little squeal. "Wouldn't that be adorable?"

"No," I tell them. "No Thelma and Louise baby anything."

"You're no fun," Minerva says.

"Someone's got to be the voice of reason here," I answer.

"Really?" Hadley asks, wrinkling up her nose.

"Yes."

"Better him than us, am I right, Louise?"

"You are, Thelma."

"Oh, you know what I bet you can buy?" Hadley says. "Ride or Die onesies."

"Perfect!" Minerva says.

And it is perfect. Everything about this life is absolutely perfect.

Even when it's not.

Afterword
MANY THANKS FROM MELANIE

I hope you enjoyed Hadley and Heath's story. I hope you laughed out loud, and the story left you feeling good. If so, please leave a review.

Reviews are a true gift to writers. They are the best way for other readers to find our work and for writers to figure out if we're on the right track, so thank you if you are one of those kind folks out there to take time out of your day to leave a review!

If you'd like a fab, fun, FREE novella, please sign up for my newsletter. GET YOUR NOVELLA HERE.

All the very best to you and yours,

Melanie

About the Author

Melanie Summers lives on Vancouver Island in Canada, with her husband, three kiddos, and two cuddly dogs. When she's not writing, she loves reading (obviously), snuggling up on the couch with her family for movie night (which would not be complete without lots of popcorn and milkshakes), and long walks in the woods near her house. Melanie also spends a lot more time thinking about doing yoga than actually doing yoga, which is why most of her photos are taken 'from above'. She also loves shutting down restaurants with her girlfriends. Well, not literally shutting them down, like calling the health inspector or something. More like just staying until they turn the lights off.

She's written twenty one novels (and counting), and has won one silver and two bronze medals in the Reader's Favourite Awards.

If you'd like to find out about her upcoming releases, sign up for her newsletter on www.melaniesummers-books.com.

Made in the USA
Las Vegas, NV
13 September 2021